PIRATA

HARPER ● PERENNIAL

NEW YORK • LONDON • TORONTO • SYDNEY • NEW DELHI • AUCKLAND

PIRATA

A NOVEL

PATRICK HASBURGH

HARPER ● PERENNIAL

PIRATA. Copyright © 2018 by Patrick Hasburgh. All rights reserved. Printed in the United States of America. No part of this book may be used or reproduced in any manner whatsoever without written permission except in the case of brief quotations embodied in critical articles and reviews. For information address HarperCollins Publishers, 195 Broadway, New York, NY 10007.

HarperCollins books may be purchased for educational, business, or sales promotional use. For information please email the Special Markets Department at SPsales@harpercollins.com.

FIRST EDITION

Designed by Jamie Kerner

Title page photograph by iFerol / Shutterstock

Library of Congress Cataloging-in-Publication Data

Names: Hasburgh, Patrick, author.
Title: Pirata : a novel / Patrick Hasburgh.
Description: First edition. | New York, NY : HarperCollins Publishers, 2018.
  | "HarperPerennial."
Identifiers: LCCN 2017047890 (print) | LCCN 2017049782 (ebook) |
  ISBN 9780062742780 (E-book) | ISBN 9780062742773 (pbk.)
Subjects: LCSH: Americans—Mexico—Fiction. | Surfers—Fiction. |
  Murder—Fiction. | Witnesses—Fiction. | GSAFD: Mystery fiction. |
  Suspense fiction.
Classification: LCC PS3608.A7897 (ebook) | LCC PS3608.A7897 P57
  2018 (print) | DDC 813/.6—dc23
LC record available at https://lccn.loc.gov/2017047890

ISBN 978-0-06-274277-3

18 19 20 21 22 LSC 10 9 8 7 6 5 4 3 2 1

For Cheri, Jensen, and Wheeler . . .

Never leave good waves for better waves . . .

PIRATA

1

was watching the waves at a left point break we call Palmitos while soaking my foot in a tide pool. I'd just kicked the
ficus root that's humped up like an armadillo in the middle
of the path that cuts down from my casa to the beach. It's a
big chunk of black bark and harder than marriage, and I've
probably smacked my toes into that fat bastard a hundred
times—back when I first tried to surf this wave, and back
when that first time nearly killed me.

I should know better than to walk around in the jungle
before sunrise. But that's a lesson I just can't seem to learn.

The tide pool was unexpectedly cool, considering that
last night was a dry night. The only thing that can break a
big heat is a heavy rain, but it hadn't rained for days. Maybe
it was because of the wind, which was coming steady onshore and opposite to where it should be blowing this early

in the morning. But when I turned my face to it, it felt right—and like it was time to go.

I was leaving Mexico, probably for good. Today was my last day.

I picked up my surfboard and hobbled a few steps before belly flopping over the shore break and then gliding down the back of a wave and into the current that loops out to sea. I surf a Red Fin, an old-school California longboard still considered a big deal by people who care about such things. The board is dinged up and waterlogged, but it still paddles straight and true, even if it rides a little lower in the water than I'd like it to—like we all do.

I wasn't going to try to make my last day at Palmitos heroic. I just wanted to get in and out with a few decent waves and a good feeling. Nothing epic. No magic. I'm not one of these kooks who croon about how surfing can save lives or cure cancer. I'm just grateful for the energy that somehow hooks up to give me a one-of-a-kind wave that I can ride for a few special seconds, and how it feels like I'm getting a little bit of a peek into this mystery while I'm doing it.

I caught my first wave of the morning. It was a head-high peeler with enough pulse to make me forget about my foot. I had three or four more just like it, fat and clean backhands, nothing scary, not too big, and everything I needed to say good-bye.

By the time I made it back to my casa, the dump trucks were already lined up. I had tried to sign the place over to a local couple—something that was more about reparation than generosity—but they wanted no part of it. "The future here has too many gringos," they said, and moved to Compostela to start a farm. So I decided to just tear it down and put the lot up for sale.

A couple of cholos covered in LA gang tats and wearing backward baseball caps were pitching and catching adobe *tejas* from the roof and stacking them like cords of wood in what was left of the garden. A backhoe was dragging my Suburban down the muddy ruts of the driveway. It was paint-balled with blasts of scat from the bats that dive-bomb for figs when the *higuera* blooms, but the dependable old beast had survived a million miles of memories.

Someone was unhinging the casita's front door. My little piece of paradise was being torn down.

"Are those surfboards for sale?" someone asked.

"Everything is," I said, and then turned around.

An albino gringo wearing a camouflage bush hat had his hand on the shoulder of a very pale boy. Or maybe it was the zinc sunblock. They were both covered in it. For the last three days I had been having a yard sale, and it looked as if these guys might be my first paying customers. They were searching through a stack of old surfboards I'd dragged out of the bodega.

"I want my kid to learn to surf," the gringo said.

"Lucky kid," I said. "There's a Wavestorm in that pile."

"But not on a foamy," he said. "He's going to need a *real* board."

I tried not to shake my head and just smiled instead.

"What about this one?" his kid asked.

The pale boy had already dug his way to the bottom of

the pile, and he was holding a surfboard that I had inherited from an ex–pro surfer I used to know. It was the board my son had learned to surf on.

"Is that a Town and Country?" the dad asked.

I nodded. Town & Country Surfboards was a big-deal Hawaiian brand, and the board of choice for a lot of guys who rip the North Shore.

"It's a Glenn Pang," I said. "He's a shaper."

"I know who Glenn Pang is," the dad said—not with any attitude, exactly, but it was clear that he wanted to let me know that he knew. "That guy made incredible boards."

"He still does," I said.

"How much do you want for it?"

"It's not for sale."

"I thought you said everything was for sale," the boy said.

He looked like he was about to cry, and his dad took the board from him. It was missing a fin, but I could see by the way this guy was holding the board that he appreciated it.

"That board's for free," I said.

"You're giving away a TC Pang?" the dad said. He was pretty astonished.

"Yeah, I am," I said. "How do you like that?"

"I do," he said.

I could see that he thought there might be more to this story—and he was right.

IT WAS MID-AUGUST AND A COUPLE OF YEARS BEFORE THE GOLF-course designers and condominium contractors devoured the peninsula, back when the future didn't feel so close and corn tortillas still counted as a health food.

We were walking through the jungle after an early session at Gagger's. I had my Red Fin under my arm, all twenty-four pounds of it, and Winsor was balancing the six-foot-two TC Pang on his head. Our feet were covered in mud to the ankles. The narrow trail was slick. It was hard to walk.

"C'mon, Pirata, let the boys get ahead of us," Winsor said. "They'll attract the mosquitoes."

"Jesus Christ, Winsor," I said. "They're your kids."

"They're *Meagan's* kids," he said and shrugged, as if he barely knew his current girlfriend. "The gook mix is, anyway. That other one she inherited from an ex. But no way that makes them my kids. Even if the ex *is* dead."

"Did you kill him?"

"Nah," Winsor said. "I can't even remember if I ever met him."

You could see what was left of Winsor's big-wave conditioning rituals. He still had those epic shoulder caps and a chest about two feet thick, but most of it had been covered up with an inch of fat because of all the street tacos and beer. Lots of beer. Even now, he had a can of Tecate jammed into the back pocket of his board shorts, and he was swigging from another one in his left hand. I had never seen Winsor without a beer or some kind of a buzz.

"But I'm not saying it's impossible," he said. "It's in me to kill a guy like that."

Gagger's is a right-hand point break that used to be called Sewer Pipe before the *locals* had the pipe stopped up with concrete, which caused it to rupture and permanently saturate the sand with raw sewage. No matter how many times that pipe got flushed out or a hurricane swell reshaped the beach, it still stank like hell. It was an unbearable, gag-making kind of stink, the kind you'd get at a rendering yard. But if the waves were good enough, it got to be that you didn't mind. The shit smell was worth it because it kept the lineups thin.

Surfers will paddle into waves just offshore from a nuclear power plant if they think the radioactive waste will keep the tourists and kooks away. If someone could bottle the stench at Gagger's, they could sell it as crowd control, cash in, and kick back.

But an effort like that would take the kind of focus and energy I haven't had in years, and one that Winsor probably never had—except maybe when he trained for the Pipeline Masters and actually made it into the quarterfinals before getting knocked out by Kelly Slater, back when Slater was just a kid. A long time ago.

Gagger's is about a ten-minute drive from Sabanita, once a small fishing village that's since morphed into a surf town on Mexico's south-central west coast. I had been lucky enough to stagger into the "little blanket"—which is what *sabanita* means—about six years ago, and it was exactly what I needed to wrap myself up in at the time.

The break at Gagger's was always kind of a petri dish, but during *tormenta*, which is what the Mexicans call monsoon season, it became a full-on bug hatchery. Despite Winsor's using his girlfriend's kids as decoys, I could see that the fatback on his fat back was feeding a swarm of mosquitoes, and a squadron of them was buzzing around the black patch that covered up the hole where my left eye is supposed to be.

So every once in a while, I had to slap myself in the face—which is something I should probably do more often.

When we finally made it back to my Suburban, the boys were already inside, with the windows rolled up and the dual-side AC on. They each had an earbud from the same iPod jammed into one ear and were singing along with something that sounded like Spanish rap.

"Did you guys have fun?" I asked.

Even though they weren't blood brothers, these two thirteen-year-olds were homies from the same hood—the messed-up parenthood. They had matching headfuls of bleached-out dreadlocks and the kind of tropical tan you only get from growing up outside without ever having to wear long pants or a shirt with sleeves.

Obsidian had pale-blue eyes. Jade's were deep brown and almond shaped. Both of them needed braces and a better attitude. The duo had it worked out that they would act like everybody was always talking to the other one, so neither of them ever had to respond. It was a calculated kind of unavailability that approached performance art. But I had picked up on the scam.

"Hey, assholes," Winsor said as he pushed our surfboards up between the seats. "This man is talking to you." He half closed a fist and knocked Obsidian hard on the collarbone. "Did you have any fun?"

"Up until now, loser," Obsidian said. He was the braver of the two, and Winsor's favorite target. "Why'd you hit me?"

Winsor climbed in on the passenger side. He cracked open the beer from his back pocket and tossed a small bag of marijuana into the glove compartment.

"I'm in the mood," Winsor said. "You don't like it—kill me in my sleep."

"We talk about that," Jade said in a way that was soft but not gentle. He usually let his stepbrother do their talking. "It'd be an honor to put you out of your misery."

"Have at it." Winsor grinned.

"C'mon, Winsor," I said. "They're just kids."

"*Meagan's* kids," he said again.

I closed my door and started the Suburban. It was a '97 GMC with an overhead console package and power door locks. The tinted windshield was cracked and there were 373,000 miles on the odometer, but it was long enough to lock my nine-foot Red Fin inside, and in a pinch I could live in it.

"Was your dad a surfer, Obsidian?" I asked, illegally U-turning over the muddy potholes of Calle Punta Mirador and trying to change the subject.

"I don't know," he said. Obsidian never talked about his dad. "He just fixed guitars for this band."

"Cool," I said. "Would I know it?"

"Dave Matthews?" Obsidian said, and squirmed a little.

"Bullshit." Winsor snorted and spit out some beer. "More like a Dave Matthews *tribute* band—the Lip-Syncing Dicks."

It was the kind of malignant pimping the surfer-burnout routinely taunted the boys with, but it looked like this little tumor hit Obsidian particularly hard.

"My dad surfed," Jade said as he slipped his stepbrother a hard chunk of surf wax. "In Vietnam. My aunt is the Napalm Girl."

"Like Miki Dora was my dad," Winsor said, as if the groms had a clue about the Malibu surf star and *Beach Party* stuntman. "You guys are idiots if you think the world is that small."

"And you make it even smaller," Jade said.

Winsor ignored him, lit the joint that was stashed behind his ear, and took a hit. He offered it to me, but I shook my head. I was feeling a little too out-of-body already.

"If people invent shit around me, they're going to pay the price, and that's right," Winsor said, apparently to himself. He exhaled a long stream of smoke, and I cracked my window.

"Look out!" Obsidian yelled, and then winged the chunk of wax just as Winsor turned. The lump of Sticky Bumps smacked him on the left side of the head.

"You little prick," Winsor said, and started swinging—but both boys scrambled for cover behind the Suburban's third seat.

Winsor rubbed his ear.

"This is what I get for putting mac and cheese on the table," he said, and then looked over at me. "Think about that if you ever want to have kids."

I made the turn into the village of Sabanita from the Punta de Mirador side. The dirt road turned to cobblestone and a stray dog barked, announcing our arrival.

2

The growling between the groms and Winsor was the only bump in a pretty sweet morning. Gagger's wasn't that stinky until the wave you were riding closed out, and before that, it could even be barreling a little. The snarly surf dog even got a little coaching in, which was part of the deal he had with Meagan.

Winsor told Jade to focus on the wave instead of his board, and Obsidian to worry more about carving top to bottom instead of always trying to throw airs. He didn't give me any tips, though—my surfing was way too old-school SoCali. But everyone was basically aloha. No *agua mala*. Nobody got his backpack ripped off. No one even brought a backpack. Anybody who lives down here travels pretty light. Anything of value that we used to bring to the beach had already been stolen.

Winsor had told me that once Meagan became the boys' sole caregiver, she renamed them Obsidian and Jade. The names on their passports are something like Wayne Stangle and Kim Phuc.

Meagan wasn't exactly a trained jeweler, but every day she tried like hell to sell her shiny baubles from under this old golf umbrella that she put up in the plaza. I think she thought that having two handsome sons named after semi-precious stones would be a clever marketing campaign, and that the hippie silversmiths would be easy to beat. But the business was insanely competitive, as if every ponytailed ring-maker and painted-rock salesman from Argentina to Tijuana had decided that twelve square feet in Sabanita Plaza was the place to open up shop.

The big sellers were hash pipes and roach clips, not obsidian earrings and jade peace pendants. But despite her predilection for puffing bud, Meagan tried to be a role model for her kids, and she drew the line at selling dope gear.

So a while back, it started to seem up to me to front the boys some taco money just about every other day. And then all of a sudden I was lending them surf wax and buying them flip-flops and repairing dings in their boards.

The thing was, though, I didn't mind it that much—even if I hardly knew them. I could see that they were really good surfers. And if one of them ever ended up on the cover of *Surfer* magazine, he just might remember that sap back in Sabanita who took a thorn out of his paw.

My Social Security Disability Insurance isn't a lot of money, but if I'm not bingeing, I can usually afford a little generosity—which I had rigged up in my head to justify my bingeing, something I used to talk about at AA meetings back before I figured out that AA made about as much sense as Scientology.

I'd started drinking more than I knew I should right after I was shot in the face during a carjacking.

Actually, I was shot in the eye—which is why I wear the pirate patch—while demonstrating a new Impala to a customer at Jacobs Chevrolet in Encinitas, California. I was the new-car manager at the time. I had been selling cars on and off since I got out of high school.

I was pretty good at it. At least, good enough to use it as a reason to drop out of UCSD with a year to go—a decision that broke everyone's heart but mine. I had made enough money selling cars during the three months of summer to pay for an entire year of college—but there was nothing that I really wanted to be, and I was suddenly positive I didn't want to be an English major. So I quit. For the next decade, slinging it in car lots made me about 200K a year, which wasn't bad for a college dropout.

Not bad until this one particular customer turned out to be a car thief.

I can remember changing seats with him at a stop sign. I got out of the driver's side and walked around the front of the car.

As I passed him, I handed him the keys—and he pressed a .22-caliber pistol against my left eye and pulled the trigger. I can't remember what the carjacker looked like, but the Impala was an ashen-gray metallic LTZ with a power sunroof and eighteen-inch aluminum wheels.

Getting permanently disabled is good for a monthly SSDI payment of $2,350—for life. That's not a lot of dough up in San Diego County, but down here in Sabanita it's enough to make the fishermen jealous. But losing an eye isn't great. And I really miss being able to sling it like I used to. "Dude, you could sell dry stems to a Maui dope dealer," my surf buds used to tell me.

It's hard out there for a bullshitter when that silver tongue gets all tied up. I also have this pretty jagged bald spot on the back of my head from the exit wound. It's about the size of a quarter. And I don't like that I can't remember what happened in junior high, or anybody's phone number—or if there was ever anything good about being married.

I stopped the Suburban in front of Alberto's Tequila Bar, and Winsor got out. He grabbed his board and slammed the tailgate closed, and then stomped off without saying a word or even grunting thank you. Obsidian threw him the finger.

"Adios, fart breath."

His stepbrother laughed.

"You guys want me to drop you at the plaza?" I asked.

"Sure," Jade said for both of them.

I pulled up across from the plaza, and I could see Meagan dozing in one of those red plastic Coca-Cola chairs that probably outnumber all the asses in Mexico. I honked, and Meagan jerked awake. The boys jumped out and grabbed their boards. They didn't say thank you, but Obsidian sort of waved.

"Are you having a good day?" I called out.

"Any day I can feed my kids is a good day, Nick." She half smiled back.

I wasn't crazy about Meagan's always playing the survivor card, but for some reason I really liked this lady.

Not that it mattered.

Meagan was living with Winsor, who wasn't exactly a best pal, but he was someone I surfed with. If pushed, I could shove him off the list—I had known him for only four years—but for now I had his back, which, when applying the buddy rule at its most basic, meant that I shouldn't try to bang his girl.

The summer before last, Winsor had brought Meagan back from San Blas, a little city a few hundred miles north that's famous for boat builders and drug smugglers and for its access to Bahía de Matanchén—home of the longest wave in North America. The name literally means "kill Chinese."

No shit.

Matanchén is a wave that only works on a south swell, and its tactless designation comes from back when *local* laborers were striking for higher wages at the silver mines in Guanajuato. Management tried to break the strike with scabs from China, but the Mexican miners stormed the junks moored in the bay, killed the Chinese interlopers, and dumped their bodies into the home of what has become one of the world's tastiest rights—which is a fun fact you won't find in a surf guide.

I'd been planning to make the trip to San Blas with Winsor, but we had waves here in Sabanita, so I passed.

"Never leave good waves for better waves," I told him—
my go-to mantra about appreciating the good that I've got.

The waves in Sabanita were awesome that weekend,
but what went off at Matanchén Bay will be remembered
as all-time. Winsor said he'd had a career weekend. "The
longest waves of my life." And some of the best sex he'd
ever had.

"Thanks for being so nice to my boys, Nick," Meagan
said, snapping me out of it. She never called me Pirata. She
probably figured my eye patch was a prop.

Jade and Obsidian had just crossed the plaza and huddled under the golf umbrella. They were drinking fresh
orange juice out of a single plastic bag with a couple of
straws. Meagan grabbed two handfuls of dreads and took
a deep whiff of the saltwatered locks. She made a face, and
Jade stuck his tongue out at her as his stepbrother tried to
juke out of reach. It was the fun kind of messing around
that was hard for me to watch.

"No worries," I said. "They're good kids."

"With lice," she said, flicking off the *bicho* that was
hiding out on Jade's head. "But I'll take 'em any way they
come."

My throat tightened.

"Don't miss this, Nick," she said. "Don't miss having
kids."

I tried to swallow, but I couldn't. I nodded and drove off.

3

I didn't make it back to my casa until about seven o'clock the next evening, which was about a day and a half later than I had planned. Not that I ever really had a plan in Mexico. And even if I did, they're pretty hard to stick to down here. You can plan to have the plumber come on Tuesday, but don't plan on being shocked if he doesn't show up to fix your toilet until after dinner on Sunday. One time, I got a refrigerator delivered to my door at two in the morning.

After I'd dropped off the boys, I turned toward the beach—instead of making a left on the street behind the plaza and driving the three short blocks home.

I had made this mistake before. This time, I told myself it was because I wanted to watch the sunset session here in town at Sabanita's right break. But I was lying. What I really wanted to do was drink to get a buzz going—and then score some dope.

I yanked the Suburban between the ruts of the dirt road that gets you to the beach by the panga boats, and then parked on the sand. I could see that both the right and left breaks were firing. But the left was on the side of town closer to my casa, and I didn't want reason or responsibility to tempt me to head home.

Nothing makes me feel guiltier than not surfing when the waves are good. It hounds me in an ugly way, like I'm wasting daylight on my last day on earth. So I grabbed my Red Fin and paddled out. I figured I had about a half hour before the sun dunked below the horizon and then maybe another twenty minutes of dusk—there'd still be plenty of time left for self-medication.

Not many guys were out. Mid-August is heavy *tormenta* and really hot, so only the cheapest of tourists visit Sabanita then, and they're generally not surfers. They're generally Canadians. When I reached the lineup, I could see Adan and Ticho. Sergio was paddling in, and I waved to him. There were a couple of other guys I didn't know. And Lola and Resa were on longboards, as elegant as always.

A set came through, and I watched Adan effortlessly make the first wave. He stalled at the top of the drop but then let gravity take over, arcing into the bowl and leaning against its hollow blue face as the wave walled up.

It was a nothing-special wave but a very special surfer, and no matter how many times I see the good guys up close, I'm always stunned at how fast they can rip. By the time Adan cranked off a finishing three-sixty, he must have been going thirty miles per hour.

"Pirata! Out the back!" Ticho yelled, in English in deference to my Spanglish, and pointed to some sweet lines hulking up farther offshore.

I paddled hard to make the set wave and then pivoted just under its peak—my board began to rise and I charged down the face to make my get-up—and then, like it was nothing, I carved a lazy bottom turn and claimed the wave with a nod.

"¡Animo!" Ticho cheered, flattering me more than he needed to.

"Gracias," I said.

I trimmed the board and settled her down the line. The Red Fin was as stable as a picnic table. I didn't have to move much. I occasionally raised an arm or tilted my head. Old-school.

I paddled in after making only two more waves, but I still felt privileged in the way that I do when I get to surf my home break—like I'd just shared a favorite sandwich with a good friend.

4

I put my Red Fin in the surfboard rack in front of El Gecko and took the corner seat on the far side, just behind a concrete half wall that was all chipped and cracked. I put my feet up on it and watched Ticho make his last wave of the day—a head-high nugget that he killed and then belly-rode to shore. I threw him a casual shaka, as if he was my protégé, for the benefit of these two loos sitting behind me, but I don't think they were impressed.

"Is surfing hard?" one of them asked.

Or maybe they were.

"For some people," I said, paying tribute to the kook in me.

"Are you a local?"

"No. I just live here."

"Is it expensive?"

"Only for the very poor," I said.

The two loos paid their check and left, and then this vintage gringa wrapped in a slightly too-tight beach sarong sashayed over and sneezed on me. Her name was Sarah. I'd met her my first day in Sabanita, six years ago this coming Christmas morning.

"It's just allergies," Sarah said, wiping her nose on the end of a red bandanna she had tied around one wrist. "I'm not healthy enough for the flu. I'm a bad viral host."

Sarah waited tables for tips, and she dealt a little, but her real specialty was over-sharing.

"You're the hostess with the mostest," I said. "It's okay."

"Who's been on her feet all day," Sarah said. "I need to get better shoes."

She was wearing beautifully embroidered sandals, but the leather soles were worn down and lopsided.

"I saw you make a few waves out there," Sarah said, sticking her tongue through the space where a front tooth should have been. "Step back on your board and you'll be able to wheel it into a better cutback."

Sarah claimed she had been the ISP longboard champ back in the seventies, and she couldn't resist giving surfing advice—whether it made sense or not.

"That's how Hynson designed the Red Fin," Sarah continued.

"Thanks," I said. "I'll work on it."

No one believed her, but most of us were polite. Part of the deal with expats in Mexico is that we get to be whoever we want to be—as long as we don't cause too much trouble.

"But you're not bad for a middle-ager." Sarah smiled.

"I'm not *middle-aged*."

"Are you fifty yet?"

"How can you ask me that?"

"Because in a few days it's sixty for me," Sarah said, suddenly a little sad. "Which means middle age is over, unless I live to be a hundred and twenty."

"Anything is possible," I said. "I'll be forty in March."

Sarah's eyes began to fill up.

"And unless I get lucky and come across a blind man who digs zaftig women, I'll have gone my whole fifties without having had sex once. An entire decade. Not once."

"Where's *Zaftig*?"

"Nowhere," Sarah said. "It's a polite word for *fat*."

"You're not fat," I said.

"We're all fat," she said.

It was easy to miss how smart Sarah was. She had the *mujer excéntrica* thing working, and her flaws were obvious. But under that dealer pushback and exaggeration, there was a sensitive and self-aware woman.

"And I'm all about someone who set records up into my forties," she carried on. "I love men. I loved being touched. There's nothing wrong with that."

"There isn't," I said.

I wasn't up for hearing about how Sarah was wounded in action during the sexual revolution. I was on my own mission at the moment.

"I'd like a Pacífico and a shot . . . Please?"

But she gave me this weird look, because she knew I didn't booze that much anymore.

"The ceviche is fresh," she said, meaning that she didn't think I should drink on an empty stomach.

"I'm not going to eat, actually," I said. "And I'm going to want some blow, too."

Sarah stared at me. "No, you don't."

"I do."

"It's off-season."

"This is year-round, Sarah," I said, pointing to my eye patch. "And it's medicinal. In the States, I even had a prescription."

Sarah smirked at me. "For coke?"

"A synthetic version," I said.

"That's how people can get into trouble," Sarah said. "My products are for recreational purposes only."

Way back on our first day together, Santa's little helper had stuffed a couple of eight balls into our stockings, not to mention our noses. I could see that Sarah hadn't forgotten what one particularly ugly Ghost of Christmas Past looked like. I think it was the day she lost her tooth.

"Does it ever feel like you're looking out from way too far back in your head?" I asked.

Tunnel vision was a classic TBI pre-fit phenomenon, but I wasn't sure she was getting it.

"Not exactly," Sarah said. "But it sounds interesting."

"It's terrifying," I said.

It's hard to explain exactly what Post–Traumatic Brain Injury Syndrome feels like, except to another TBI victim, and even then it's almost impossible to find the words, not to mention keep their attention. It's like this growing out-of-body buzz where everything feels like it's out of proportion—like when Alice shrinks and the Mad Hatter gets supersized.

The feeling starts coming from far away, and it can take days to get here. Like today at Gagger's, I could feel it getting closer. I knew that it was out there—not in any real place, exactly, but in my future. I know that doesn't make much sense, and that's part of it, too. But I did know I had to try to knock it back. I hated the feeling. I lived in fear of it. And that's what I was doing here.

"It's extradimensional," I said, in the exact way I used to say it to my TBI counselor at Sharp Rehab up in San Diego. "Like a real-life Wonderland."

"Maybe you should meditate more," Sarah said.

"Just get me the bindle," I said.

Like a lot of survivors of penetrating head trauma, I suffer epileptic seizures—those big guys they call tonic-clonics, the grand mals—and there's some leftover aphasia, too. These are the commissions I still collect from my car salesman days, and the main reason I left the US.

California revoked my driver's license a few months after I got out of Sharp because I had a major fit behind the wheel of my company demonstrator and ran into a tree. My seven-year-old son was sitting in the passenger seat.

My caseworker at Sharp said I'd lost control because I'd gone off my seizure meds. I really didn't have a better excuse. But it wouldn't have mattered. Marshall broke his neck and spent the next year strapped to a Stryker frame.

My wife split. I lost my house. I lost my job. How the

hell can you sell cars if you're not allowed to drive one? Which was the question I had preoccupied myself with as I begged for sympathy and forgiveness—a one-eyed kook riding the bus to Nicky Lutz's used-car lot.

But nothing is worse than knowing you'll probably never see your son again.

So I left the Golden State. I didn't leave a note. I didn't say good-bye.

Down here in Mexico, *anyone* can drive. Nobody needs a license, and it doesn't matter if you have TBI and PTSD or whichever PC word soup is being used to mean "brain damaged."

The first thing they do after you start having fits is to load you up on drugs like Dilantin that make your body feel like it's filled with cement—like in those dreams where your legs are so heavy, you can't run.

But when they stop working, you get moved up to what are called the *psychotropics*. Which sounds like where you'd send your brain for a vacation. And that's exactly what those drugs do—until they made me start to twitch, which was as bad as the fits.

So I just stopped taking them altogether—except for the *recreationals*.

It's not an exact science, but the occasional binge with a little bit of blow turns down my recurring crazies better than what the head doctors had me on.

did a couple of bumps and then had two more shots and three more beers—and it finally began to feel like the size and shape of things to come were going to stay more normally sized. This was what I called the *window moments*—those fleeting moments of being high when you are at exactly the right height. They never last, but they are sweet. I never have a hole in my head up there, and I can see for miles and miles.

But the trouble with doing blow in Mexico during off-season is that there's no one to coke-talk to. And you can't just call up Norman Fackler from the second grade—*Hey, Norman, remember when we got into a fight over that lightsaber*—because that's going to eat up too many of your Telcel minutes.

So if it's a weeknight in August and you don't speak

a lot of Spanish, you can find yourself high as shit with nowhere to go. For about an hour, I cruised Sabanita Plaza and tried to corner some of the cabdrivers into a conversation. But none of them was into American politics, and if a gringo starts talking about Mexican pussy, it's a great way for him to get his ass kicked. These guys are all married with children, and they only get loaded on Sundays.

Which might explain why I headed up toward Puerto Vallarta instead of just moonwalking back to my casa.

PV is an hour's drive north on Mexico 200, which winds along the coast just like Highway 101 up in the States. But down here, it's mostly two lanes of potholed blacktop—fifteen hundred miles of acquired taste sluicing through cartel country and the poverty-stricken pueblos of old Mexico.

I figured I'd go to a strip bar. A lap dance sounded like the perfect nightcap—even if I wasn't exactly dressed for professional-level debauchery. I still had on my board shorts, and I was wearing a Rip Curl T-shirt.

But then it started to rain in sheets. Big, wet squares of peso-sized drops ricocheting off the pavement. I slowed way down. It was nearly impossible to see, and I had only one working windshield wiper to go with my one working eye.

I was just a mile or two out of Sabanita when I saw Sarah, soaking wet and standing at the bus stop on Highway 200. She was trying to hitchhike. I turned around and drove back to her.

"What are you doing?" I asked, rolling down the Suburban's window and pulling up next to her.

"I was waiting for the bus," Sarah said. "But it's late."

"It's a monsoon. They'll all be late," I said. "Where are you going?"

The raindrops drumming down on the Suburban's hood made it hard to hear.

"Tepic."

"The *capital* of Nayarit?" I shouted over the noise.

"I didn't know there was another one."

"That's a long ride."

"I was hoping to sleep on the bus."

"Get in," I said.

"It's dangerous to pick up hitchhikers in Mexico, Nick."

"I'll take my chances," I said, and unlocked the passenger door.

6

You should put this on the roof rack," Sarah said, immediately starting in with the surf advice.

When Sarah dove into the Suburban from the downpour, she had hit her head on my Red Fin, which I had slid up between the seats.

"I wasn't expecting company," I said.

"That's how they get dinged. Surfboards are instruments. You need to take care of them."

"I will," I said, hoping to dodge the lecture on the care and feeding of a Red Fin from the former champ. "What's in Tepic?"

"Great health care," Sarah said.

"Better than in Puerto Vallarta?"

My Suburban hummed along at about eight miles to a gallon. A run up to Tepic and back would cost fifteen hundred pesos.

"Vallarta's for medical tourists looking for overnight face-lifts," she said. "I've got endometriosis."

I tried to appear sympathetic as I braced myself for the horror story that was probably heading my way.

"It's a female issue," she continued.

"I've had them," I said.

"This quack in the States told me I got it from having too many abortions. But I've never had an abortion. Ectopic pregnancies aren't abortions—they're miscarriages. I didn't even get a real chance."

I was trying to calculate how much over-sharing Sarah could do during the next hundred miles.

"It's like having tumors. But benign."

"Thank god," I said. I was trying to keep it short.

"I'm seeing a specialist," Sarah continued. "World-renowned. I was lucky to get an appointment. He's usually booked a year out, but one of his patients died."

"That's not a good sign, is it?"

"It was a heart attack," Sarah said. "You can't really die of endometriosis. Unless your husband murders you for bitching about it too much."

Sarah laughed, but she was mostly sad.

"I'm sorry I'm always telling you my life story," Sarah said. "I know it can be creepy when someone tells you personal stuff—I know I do it too much. But I'm lonely."

"It's okay," I said. "I know what lonely is."

"And not getting laid sucks."

But I only nodded—there was no way I was going to pull the pin out of that grenade.

"I was lucky to get an appointment," she said again. "I'm grateful. The guy is world-renowned."

"Do you need surgery?"

Sarah shook her head. "Surgery is for doctors and butchers," Sarah said. "This treatment is noninvasive."

"This world-renowned guy isn't a doctor?"

"A Huichol priest," Sarah said.

"A priest?"

"A high priest," she said. "Like the heaviest shaman they've got."

And I readied myself to hear about the awesome effectiveness of chanting cures.

"He's perfected the peyote douche."

But I had underestimated her.

"It's like tea, but you have to take it differently," Sarah continued.

"I would imagine," I said.

The Huichol are native Mexicans known for worshipping deer while high on mescaline. Their magical kind of thinking has been hijacked by new age gringos and less sympathetic *locals* who exploit this primitive beauty by hawking wax Bambis covered in plastic beads and absurd cures for anxiety and menopause.

"And it has to be done during a full moon—which is why I need to get up there," she said. "The moon raises our healing energy, just like it does high tides."

I was trying to sort through all the questions I wanted to ask about this undoubtedly ancient yet suddenly revolutionary cure, but I settled for just one.

"How much does a peyote douche cost?" I asked.

"I'm not sure," Sarah said. "He was supposed to give me an estimate, but his cell phone battery ran out."

Sarah closed her eyes and fell asleep in about two minutes. I turned on the AM radio and searched through the white noise for something worth listening to.

7

filled up at the Pemex just outside of La Peñita. I figured I could make Tepic in a few hours if we didn't run into any roadblocks or get stuck at a checkpoint. I don't like to drive too far north in Mexico. And I never like to drive north at night. It can get a little sharky. Not sharky in the great white way but in the surf-speak way, like sketchy.

The drug wars and cartel violence are pretty overrated if the only information you get is from the US press. A lot of those stories are all about trying to make Mexicans look like bloodthirsty lunatics so Americans don't feel guilty about paying immigrants shit wages to cut their lawns and make their beds.

But still. Nobody's head looks good on a stake.

There are about forty-five minutes of stomach-turning switchbacks on the way to Tepic that you have to share with all the bus and truck traffic on its way to Guadalajara, a boomtown of six million people and a symbol of where Mexico is going. Tepic is just a couple of hours away from the big city but much poorer, stranded in the old economy. One hundred pesos a day is the average wage—which is about six dollars.

There aren't any BMW dealerships in Tepic. It's hard to find good sushi.

Every few miles of this switchbacked section of Highway 200 is memorialized with homemade crosses that mark fatal accidents. By the really sharp turns with cliffs or at the bottom of steep hills, the number of crosses stuck in on the roadside increases because of accidents with higher body counts. They're like hazard signs—CAUTION: THREE-CROSS TURN AHEAD. So I snuck in another bump to stay extra-alert.

We arrived at the outskirts of Tepic, and I nudged Sarah awake. It took me a while. Her sleep apnea must have shut off some oxygen, and she was sleeping like she was in a coma. I nudged her again, this time a little harder.

"Hey," she said, and then surfaced. She blinked. "Did I sleep?"

"Three hours," I said.

Sarah smiled into a yawn. "*Nice*," she said, and then slid her hand down the rail of the Red Fin.

"I have a Red Fin," she said.

"You do?" I was a little disappointed. I thought I had the only Red Fin in the area. Maybe even in Mexico.

"Mike Hynson is a friend of mine," she said. "He gave it to me for doing him a favor."

"It must have been a big favor," I said.

"It was," Sarah said. "I told him how to invent the down rail."

I let out a breath. This was gold-medal bullshit. Hynson was the star of *The Endless Summer*, a classic surf documentary filmed in the '60s. He's also credited with perfecting the down rail, which is the soft slope shaped into a hard edge at the back half of a surfboard.

The harder rail helps the board carve into steeper and hollower waves, like down in Puerto Escondido or over at Pipeline on the North Shore. Before Hynson figured out down rails, pulling into a barrel was more about big balls and dumb luck than skill.

"You don't believe me?"

"That's a lot to believe." I shrugged. I felt sorry for her, and she knew it.

"Well, it doesn't matter what you believe, Nick," Sarah said, and then scraped a little wax off the Red Fin with her fingernail. She tasted it.

"There's a gringo over at Litibu beach who makes biodegradable surf wax," Sarah said, spitting wax out the window. "This shit is poison."

"I'll check him out," I said. "Where to?"

"It's called Litigoo," she continued, ignoring me. "Made from beeswax so it doesn't wreck the ocean."

"Okay."

"Or stick to the reefs," Sarah said.

"I get it," I said.

I was ready for another toot, but I'd have to offer one to

my hitchhiker, and she was already chatty enough. Sarah pointed out her window.

"Turn right, up there," she said.

There was a blinking yellow light at an intersection with a dirt road that crisscrossed about half an acre of stacked Detroit iron. Dozens of old, rusted cars and trucks.

"You can drop me off."

"*Here?*" I said.

"It's the Huichol Reserve," she said. "Sacred ground."

"It's a junkyard."

"I'm an optimist," Sarah said. "Honk your horn."

I pulled over and honked, and after a moment a tall man in traditional Huichol dress stepped into the head-lights. He was wearing pure white, top to bottom, with a beaded belt pouch, a straw derby, and embroidered sandals exactly like Sarah's. On the cuffs of both his sleeves was a rainbow weave of dancing deer.

"Is that the high priest?"

"One of them," Sarah said.

"He's pretty tall," I said. Huicholes were among the shortest people on earth, second only to Guatemalans. This guy was six three, easy.

"He's a convert."

"You can do that?"

"He had to," Sarah said. "He's from San Francisco."

"So there's a California branch."

"Don't be a smart-ass. I'm in pain."

Sarah got out of the Suburban and walked to the sha-man. They bowed at the waist, and I could see that he had a blond ponytail. He looked about thirty. Seemed kind of young for a high priest, if you ask me.

He gently lifted Sarah's chin so she could see the moon, and then he placed a hand across her stomach. The clouds had cleared, and for some reason I was relieved.

Sarah walked back to my side of the Suburban. I had already rolled down the window.

"This is going to cost more than I thought," she said. "But what's relief worth, right?"

"Depends how long it lasts."

"I need five thousand pesos," Sarah said.

"Did you tell him you're a frequent flyer?"

"Shut up—and it's only two hundred and fifty dollars, moneybags," Sarah said.

"That's all I got."

"It's a loan."

I took ten five-hundred-peso bills out of my wallet and handed them to her. "Good," I said. "I've got kids to feed."

"You want an eight ball for collateral?"

"I'd rather trust you than me, thanks."

"Smart," Sarah said, and then she leaned down and pecked me on the cheek.

"Are you okay to drive home?"

"I drove you up here, didn't I?"

"You're precious cargo, lovey," she said and threw me a shaka. "Don't forget that."

I threw one back.

Sarah walked over to the knockoff Huichol in the straw derby. He handed her a candle and they disappeared into the night. She was braver than I was.

8

It was about an hour before sunup, and I had already made it down through the switchbacks. The "prevent" defense seemed to have worked—my pre-seizure sense of lunacy had been degaussed. I was feeling good. My epileptic curse had been pushed back to the future.

And I was proud of myself for going out of my way—by *two hundred* miles—to give Sarah a ride. Despite her claims to fame, there was still a sad mystery to her, and I could relate. Very few foreigners move to Mexico to escape success.

I tapped my fingers on the nose of my Red Fin and made an instant decision to drive due west and surf Bichos for an hour or two. I had to take the highway a little farther north to get there, which meant that the drive wasn't going to be as safe. But if Bichos was still getting the scraps of that southwest swell we had snagged at Gagger's, it could be a great morning.

I looked out at the palm trees. Not a frond was stirring. It was going to be a windless morning at a mysto break. I felt blessed, and still a little buzzed.

Until a small group of men stopped me at a roadblock— they were wearing black ski masks and carrying machine guns. But their camouflage pants gave me hope, and I could see that some of these guys were wearing combat boots. There was a chance they were military and not with the cartels.

Or they could be the Mexican *seguridad policía secreta*, the Grupo Marte—a very badass undercover outfit that was originally organized to target left-wing Americans and Mexican socialists. But the *locals* will tell you that today, the SPS is just in charge of disappearing people.

I wasn't sure enough to make the call about who these guys were, so my immediate strategy was to play dumb.

I rolled down my window.

"*Bono days*," I said, intentionally overmangling my typically mangled Spanish. "*Me, surfino. El gordo olas at Bitchens. Yes?*"

I smiled, proud as hell of my ability to play Doofus Kook from SoCal on his first surf trip to Mexico. If there were such a thing as a Mexican Academy Award, I would have just won one.

The man closest to me pulled off his ski mask and shouldered his machine gun. He looked at me with a little disgust. He was about thirty years old, with black eyes and a shaved head. There was a tiny hangman's noose tattooed under his left eye. I couldn't tell if he had any rank, but it was clear that he was *el jefe*.

"Don't bullshit me. I speak English," he said with an accent so crisp it sounded nearly British.

"Sorry," I said. "I didn't mean to insult you."

"You just figured I'd go easy on an idiot tourist."

Okay. So the boss had me dead cold. I decided to let him lead. I nodded.

"I'm going to ask you a couple of questions."

I nodded again.

"But first I need to tell you that it is very important that you tell me the truth."

"I will," I said.

"Don't answer so fast. I want you to think about that. I want you to understand how important they are."

"The questions?"

"The answers."

I didn't nod this time. I just stared back at him.

"What's your name?"

"Nick Lutz," I said, but then I couldn't hold this guy's gaze. "Nicholas. Sometimes they call me Pirata."

"Who does?"

"My amigos," I said.

"Because of the patch?"

"I hope that's why."

I looked down at my hands. They were gripping the steering wheel as if it were a trapeze.

"What happened?" he asked, pointing to the patch.

"I got hurt at work," I said.

He turned my head so he could see the round scar on the back of it. If he knew what an exit wound looked like, he didn't show it.

"Do you have a passport?"

"Not on me."

"Are you a US citizen?"

"I have an FM3," I said, and nodded. "Yes."

I could see that about half the guys wearing camo were also barefoot. I'd never heard of barefoot soldiers. And the secret police probably all wear shoes. So maybe this was a cartel kidnapping, after all.

"Do you have it with you?"

I nodded and reached for the glove compartment. When I opened it, Winsor's bag of dope fell out. I grabbed at it.

"Don't touch that," he said. "Just get me the FM3."

I got the FM3 and handed it to him.

"It's expired," he said.

"No way," I said, faking surprise. "Really?"

But the performance wasn't very believable. I might have to return my Oscar.

"Yes, really," he said.

"Is there anything I can do to fix this?" And I immediately regretted giving all my cash to Sarah.

"Are you offering me a bribe, Pirata?" El Jefe asked, and then smiled. "Remember—the answer is the important part."

"I'm not," I said.

"Correct answer."

He handed me back my FM3.

"Just two more questions," he said.

"No *problema*, señor," I said, and then grimaced an apology. "No problem, sir."

"Who is the president of México?"

"You're kidding?"

"I'm not," he said, as if he had been trained in interrogation by my ex-wife. "If you are a Mexican resident, you should know who our president is."

"I do," I said.

"So?"

And somehow I remembered.

"Peña Nieto."

God bless this cocaine. It must have been cut with Adderall.

"*¡Profe!*" El Jefe called out to one of his soldiers, and laughed. I could see that he might even have been a little impressed. Then he turned back to me.

"Are you ready for your Final Jeopardy question?" he asked.

"It's called the Final Jeopardy answer," I corrected, and then instantly regretted it. "At least up in the States, I mean."

"But we are not in the States," he deadpanned.

"I know."

He squinted slightly.

"Do you have any drugs, Mr. Lutz?" he asked.

I glanced over at Winsor's bud-filled baggy, which had landed on the passenger seat. I picked it up and handed it to him.

"Just this," I said. "It belongs to a guy I surf with."

He sniffed Winsor's pot and put it in his pocket. "So, no drugs?"

"No."

"You're sure?"

"I'm sure," I said. "Positive." And for the first time, I was able to hold his gaze.

"Okay."

I started up the Suburban, but El Jefe reached through the window and shut it off.

"Not yet," he said as he removed the keys.

Then he clapped his hands, and a very large and very white German shepherd appeared from the back of a canvas-topped truck that I hadn't seen parked in the shadows. As I squinted, I could see that it was a 1979 Dodge Power Wagon, jerry-rigged into a troop transport.

"Who's that?" I asked him, faking a grin at the dog.

"He's our drug-sniffing dog," he said. "We got him from our friends at the border. But every time he sniffed somebody out up there, a customs agent got beheaded, so they said we could have him."

He opened the door, and I stepped out. The dog sniffed over every inch of the Suburban. El Jefe even had the dog sniff through it twice. But the Suburban was clean.

"It's not the drugs, you know," he said. "The drugs don't matter. The problem is the lying."

"It is?" I asked.

"Countries whose people no longer know that the truth matters can't survive. It's very simple."

They must not watch much cable news down here, I thought.

"Lies are the bricks of corruption," he said. "We have to teach *la paisa* that truth is power."

"*La* who?"

"*Los mexicanos.*"

"But I'm an American," I said, bobbing to take myself out of a fight that wasn't mine.

"So you should understand this more than anyone."

"It does makes sense," I said as I crossed the finish line.

And then, like one of the biggest idiots in the history of mankind, I reached down to pet the dog.

"I love dogs," I said.

The German shepherd began wagging its tail like crazy.

"And he must love you, too," El Jefe said.

I tried to snuggle this beauty, but the dog started barking at me.

El Jefe smiled. Then he reached to the side pocket of my surf shorts, unzipped its zipper, and removed the bindle.

"You lied."

I could barely nod. "I'm sorry," I whispered.

"Lying matters," he said.

He snapped open the bindle of coke and deftly tapped a small pile onto a knuckle. He snorted it.

"Is this stuff any good?" he asked.

"I thought so."

"But all good things come to an end, don't they?"

El Jefe tapped out another tiny dune of cocaine and held his knuckle under my nose. He smiled—and I snorted.

"Thank you," I said.

"Don't confuse generosity with weakness," he said.

If it weren't for the coke, I probably would have fainted.

"I don't have any money left." I was begging. "I gave it to a friend who was having a medical emergency."

"You're a saint. Every gringo is."

"I'm not—but it was a good deed."

"And one that won't go unpunished."

This guy must have memorized the Big Book of American Clichés.

"What happens now?" I asked.

"We're going to send a message to your friends," he said.

I imagined my body hanging from a bridge. I gulped for air. There is a big debate going on in Mexico over which side is committing more atrocities in the drug wars—the military or the cartels. But it didn't matter, because it appeared that I had both covered. Unless this guy was *policia secreta* and then it mattered even less because I would probably be disappeared.

"Then don't shoot the messenger," I said, flashing my cliché-club membership. I forced a smile.

"Good one," he said.

El Jefe nodded to two of his soldiers, and they instantly pinned me over the hood of the Suburban and ripped the back of my shirt wide open.

"In Singapore, this is known as a caning," he said. "But down here in México, we just call it *el vapuleo*."

"I don't speak much Spanish," I said.

"You won't need to."

Another soldier handed El Jefe a four-foot switch of bamboo about half an inch in diameter.

"Are you kidding?" I said.

"You'll see," he said.

El Jefe flicked his wrist, and the bamboo whistled. He spread his feet and whipped the thin reed behind him as if it were a fly rod, slowly winding up—and finally releasing its vicious hollowness expertly between my shoulder blades. I screamed.

"*¡Primero de veinte!*" El Jefe counted out.

He wound up again, and then deliberately crisscrossed his first wicked slash. I saw a flash of light. My ears rang, and I could feel a warm stream of blood begin to trickle down my spine. Seven casts later, I blacked out—until a bucket of stagnant water choked me awake for the back nine.

I looked back at El Jefe. He was smiling, and pressed the bamboo reed against his lips.

At that moment, I was certain I would never lie to him again—and El Jefe was certain, too.

9

Mi casa was a tiny *ejido* design—a casita, really—barely a thousand square feet. Two small bedrooms and a *baño* separated by ten feet of open porch. A *cocinita* was at one end, and at the other, two steps led down to three banana trees. An *higuera* overshadowed everything. I parked my Suburban on a dirt driveway out front.

The casita sat on a little hill two hundred yards up from the beach and surrounded by what's left of the jungle. When I stood on my porch, I could see whether the waves were good. It was the kind of place that surfers dream about when they're working nine-to-five *el norte*. I'd bought it six years ago for 58,000 US dollars—furnished. I hadn't changed a thing except for adding Internet and replacing the fridge.

I don't usually get attached to things. I've never had

a favorite watch, or a car that I loved to polish. I might fe-
tishize my Red Fin in the way surfers do, and I'll admit I'm
enamored with the board's sweet pickup and steady flow—
but I love my casita. When I had to heal, this was where I
hid out. I have paced its floors and wept in its bedrooms
and felt whole and content just sitting on the front steps.
Which is why when I finally pulled into my driveway, I felt
safe.

It had taken me five hours to drive the last sixty miles
back to Sabanita. Whenever I leaned against the driver's
seat, it felt as if it was stuffed with hot coals. My hands were
spastic, and I kept losing my grip on the steering wheel.
Every mile or two, I had to stop to vomit. I'd already pissed
my shorts. I hadn't felt this bad since I was shot in the head.

I didn't leave the casa for five days. I couldn't dress myself for the first three. I was also humiliated. I kept flashing
on the sadistic tempo of El Jefe's whipping—those psychot-
ically long moments between the bamboo's attack, and my
babbling and begging.

When I finally found the courage to bend around and
look at my back in the mirror, the bruising was the color of a
baboon's ass—neon purple and leaking into various shades
of red and blue that the jungle hadn't even invented yet.

I had e-mailed Winsor a couple of times since making
it back from Tepic and El Jefe's roadside torture. I wanted
to fill him in on the adventure, and, despite my shame, he'd
get a kick out of the brutal details—Winsor was like that.
But I hadn't heard back from him.

Maybe he had hopped a bus up to the States, which

he often did unannounced. That would explain Winsor's e-mail unavailability. Mexican buses didn't have Wi-Fi, but you can pretty much count on overflowing toilets and busted air conditioners.

There was some mystery in Winsor's life that I just couldn't put my finger on. For one thing, he owned this joint that he wanted to be the hot hangout, but it was never open during off-season and only rarely in high season. And every year, he got the bright idea to change the name—so it would be Sabanita's "next big thing."

For the season coming up, he was calling his joint the Wave of the Day, and he went a little agro when I told him the name sounded like kook bait. Last year it was the Close-out, which was also pretty cringeworthy, and, even worse, it confused everybody about when the place was supposed to be open.

Winsor always seemed to have a little bit of money—not a lot, but enough. Who knew where it came from. He was too young for Social Security and too uncouth to be a trustafarian.

I'd never seen him work, except for tending bar at his own joint, and he never talked about what he'd done for a living before he came down to Mexico. I asked him one time, and all he told me was that he produced some kind of mixed media.

"It's sorta freelance," Winsor had said over tacos and shots one night. "I produce bits and pieces of shit you never heard of."

I hadn't seen the boys, either. They usually came around

to borrow something or other every few days—or at least ransack my fridge and con me out of some pesos. But they were MIA.

So I started to wonder if maybe Meagan and the kids had split town—which would have bummed me out more than I wanted to admit. Especially if they'd left with Winsor. The guy was a good surfer, for sure—but he was a kook when it came to being a dad. Which was something I knew a little bit about.

10

When I first slipped into the saltwater, I screamed. The stinging was unbearable, but I knew I had to get back in the ocean. The contusions on my back had bled out and scabbed over, but I hadn't taken a shower in a week.

I also needed to get over feeling like a coward. It's not like I could've taken on El Jefe, or whoever the fuck he works for. Everyone has a breaking point—even if everything inside has already been broken. After you run away from your kid, what's left is a footnote.

I paddled toward the point on Sabanita's right. It was still pretty dark. I could barely see. But as I got farther out, I realized that someone had beaten me into the water this morning, which was unusual.

"Winsor?" I called out.

Whoever it was didn't answer. As I paddled closer, I could see that it was Obsidian.

"Hey, dude," I said. "You're up early."

Predictably, Obsidian looked away, faking that he didn't know I was talking to him, even though Jade was nowhere around.

"Where's your brother?" I asked.

"Jade's not really my brother," Obsidian said, which was true, but I'd never heard him say it out loud before.

"Being a family takes a lot more than some biological coincidence," I said, as if I had a real clue about families.

I always tried to come off as wise and measured when I talked to Obsidian and Jade. I never raised my voice. I always explained things in a calm and logical way—and it always felt like a pose, as if I was auditioning to get my old job back.

But maybe this whole idea about truth really mattering was something I could impress on the kids—although it'd be a career ender in car sales. Keeping it real could prevent those unforced errors caused by trying to dupe people into believing you're somebody different than who you are. Like, when I was a salesman I was mostly just a professional bullshitter—but maybe that's not who I am. Not anymore, at least. And maybe it takes life kicking the shit out of you a couple of times to see it that way—so maybe there was a shit-kicking or two I could help the boys avoid.

The dark lines of a set were coming in, so I spun my board around to get ready.

"Do you want the first one?"

Obsidian didn't respond. So I turned and paddled and dropped into a sweet little wave. I trimmed the Red Fin and cross-stepped to the nose. Then I paddled back out, and Obsidian was still sitting there—staring at the horizon. I started to think that things might not be so good at home.

"Is everything okay?" I asked him. "I tried getting hold of Winsor, but I don't think he's around. Has your mom been working in the plaza?"

Obsidian furiously slapped the water and then paddled away from me.

"Talk to me, Obsidian," I said.

I tried to catch his eye, but he charged off on a wave—and crushed it.

This kid was pro material, no doubt. And whatever was making him miserable this morning, he was channeling it into some insane surfing.

I sat out there and watched him make five or six more waves. But whenever I tried for one, he paddled to my inside and snaked me. That's not a cool thing for a surfer to do to a buddy in the lineup.

"Dude, are you pissed at me?" I asked. "Did I do something?"

Or maybe the problem was that I *didn't* do something? Maybe the boys thought I was going to take them surfing or somewhere and I'd stood them up. I can do that, with this memory thing I struggle with.

"Winsor," Obsidian finally said, and covered his face with both hands.

"What about him?"

"He's dead."

"Dead?"

Obsidian nodded.

"Jesus," I said.

And then he started to sob.

I have to admit, I was a little surprised. I didn't think the boys liked Winsor all that much. But this kid was really broken up.

"He fucked Jade," Obsidian said. "So Mom killed him."

11

Obsidian and I paddled in, but I couldn't get him to give me any details. He was a wreck. Every time he went to wipe his eyes, his hand was shaking so much that he had to clench it into a fist. When I moved closer to him, he tried to hit me with it.

"It's okay, Obsidian," I said. "This is the kind of awfulness you're supposed to cry about."

We left our boards on the beach. I followed him up a path that paralleled the north side of the river that runs through the heart of Sabanita. It's a seasonal Pacific tributary that stays dry most of the year and sometimes even works as an extra road into town—but in *tormenta* it becomes a torrent of trash and human turds.

The Wave of the Day was in a cinder-block building that had been Sabanita's original *policía* headquarters. It was kitty-corner to the sewage treatment plant and behind the baseball field, which worked as a kind of open range for grazing horses. It was in a part of town that didn't smell so great.

The building was windowless and covered with graffiti. Its black steel door was hung with a flip sign that currently read CERRADO.

Whenever I saw that word, it reminded me of my first day in Sabanita, back when I was looking for a place to land, back when my future felt like it was leaking out from that still-new hole in my head. I needed simple, and what could be simpler than a small town where virtually every business and restaurant was apparently owned by one of only two families—the Abierto family and the Cerrado family.

Or so said the signs on the front door of nearly every establishment.

Obsidian knocked on the black steel door.

"It's me," he said.

The door opened, and he stepped into the darkness. I was right behind him.

It was hard to see and hot as hell. I knew there was air-conditioning in here because I had helped Winsor bash a hole through the brick wall and install it. But obviously the power had been shut off. Obsidian closed the door, and I could hear him slide the bolt. It was pitch-black. I was sweating.

Obsidian lit a candle. And then two more. I could see Meagan and Jade sitting at a two-top near the bar. A bottle of tequila was open. Most of the chairs were upside down on the tables.

There were maybe five barstools tipped against a small concrete bar. Behind it hung the big-wave gun Winsor claimed he surfed in the Pipeline Masters.

Meagan looked freaked out but somehow still beautiful. She was wearing a tank top, and I could see dried blood on the backs of both hands and all the way up one arm. Jade was snuggled up next to her as if he were cold.

Obsidian had gotten hold of himself a little. He was breathing deep and slow, and I could see that he was trying to stand tall and look tough.

"Obsidian told me you've got some bad news," I said.

"He shouldn't have," she said. "It's nobody's business."

"Mom," Obsidian protested, "how else do you think—"

"You should shut up, is what I think," Meagan said.

Meagan glared at Obsidian and poured three fingers of tequila into a dirty glass. She took a gulp and then handed what was left of the tequila to Jade.

"You think that's a good idea?" I asked.

"If you got a better cure for child rape, I'd love to hear it."

"Jesus," I said.

I wanted to pull up a chair and sit down, but I was afraid that would start looking like an interrogation. So I just stood in my board shorts, shirtless and dripping wet.

"When did it happen?"

"Last night," Meagan said. "Obsidian and I took the bus into Vallarta because I promised him a 3-D movie for his birthday."

"I've never seen one," Obsidian said. "And I'm, like, almost fourteen."

"They're overrated," I said. "The glasses are dumb."

Jade tried to drink the tequila and gagged.

"But the power went out at the Liverpool mall," Meagan continued, "so we came home. Winsor was supposed to be keeping an eye on Jade and helping with his homeschooling. When they weren't at our place, we came here. The front door was locked, but I have a key. They were in the cooler."

"I would have just let him kill me," Obsidian said. "I'd rather be dead than gay."

"He wasn't going to kill me, jerkface," Jade hissed. "He was going to kill Mom."

"He just told you that," Obsidian said. "It's what they always say."

Jade lunged at Obsidian, but I was able to grab him. I held him as tightly as I could without hurting him. I held him for a couple of minutes. Everyone was quiet, and Jade just shook.

"Dude, okay, listen," I said. "First, there is some good news here."

The three of them looked at me as if I was out of my mind.

"There is," I said.

"Like what?" Obsidian finally said.

"Well, first," I said, "Winsor didn't kill Mom. Meagan's okay."

"If it woulda kept him from doing what he did," she said, "I wish he would've."

"No, you don't," I said.

And I thought about how it's easy to be glib about death

until you've brushed up against it. It's like a hero is someone who's never been hit by a car.

"Only one person deserves to die over this," I said. "And I think you already killed him."

Meagan nodded.

"Are you sure he's dead?"

"Oh," Obsidian said, "he's for sure the fuck dead, Nick."

"Don't say the f-word, honey," Meagan said, almost to herself. This was a mom in shock.

"Can I make sure?" I asked.

Meagan nodded toward the walk-in cooler at the far end of the bar.

I moved over to that side of the room. I wasn't looking forward to what I was probably going to see, but like Obsidian, I was trying to stand tall and look tough. I yanked open the cooler's heavy stainless-steel door and instantly almost puked. The smell was horrific.

I took a candle from the table and extended it with one arm into the cooler. I held my nose and tried not to breathe. I could see Winsor, slumped on the floor as if he had toppled out of a chair. He was still bent like he was sitting. His pants were down around his knees, and he had an erection.

He had also crapped himself—probably because both claws of a long-handled framing hammer were deeply embedded into the back of his skull. I recognized the hammer. It was the one he and I had used to bash the hole in the wall when we installed the air conditioner.

"Okay, Obsidian is right," I said, still holding my nose

and sounding like the guy who sings in "Yellow Submarine." "*Full speed ahead, captain*—he's for sure dead."

I closed the cooler door—and was nearly knocked over by a wave of angst-ridden nausea. Whatever the reason, my surf buddy was dead. It didn't feel good.

"Nobody else knows about this?" I asked, looking directly at Meagan.

I was pretty certain the boys wouldn't have told anybody. Jade was still in shock, and Obsidian radiated humiliation and grief.

"Just us," Meagan said.

"Okay, good," I said, forcing the *we're really fucked* out of my voice.

I opened the black steel door and motioned Jade and his mom outside. Meagan blew out the candles, and I almost said happy birthday to Obsidian but then thought better of it.

"Let's go to my place," I said.

12

It was midmorning and pouring rain, but the heavy cloud cover accompanying the revolving thunderstorms made everything look like dusk with an electric glow. Meagan had been standing out in front of the casa for the last half hour, buck naked, with her arms stretched wide and her palms open to the sky. It was pretty obvious that she was desperate to make herself feel clean.

And it appeared to be working. She was spotless.

The boys were still sound asleep in my bed. I had the ceiling fan cranked to the max, and I had left the door to my bedroom open just a crack. I even went in once or twice to check on them and make sure they were both still breathing. It was something I used to do with my son, Marshall, all the time.

Meagan came out of the rain, and I handed her a towel.

She dried herself off, completely cool with her nakedness, despite how it made me fixate on only her eyes, as if I were a hypnotist with a stiff neck. But no way was I going to let her catch me sneaking a peek at her body—as beautiful as it was.

I had made some tea, and I poured her a cup. She sipped it.

"What is this?" Meagan asked.

"Tea," I said. "I figured you'd like tea."

"But what kind is it?" she asked again.

"The kind that isn't coffee."

Meagan wrapped the towel around her waist and slipped on an old sweatshirt I had put out for her. Then she sat down and balanced the cup on her knee.

"This is going to ruin him," Meagan said.

"No, it won't," I said. "People survive stuff. We're hard-wired for it."

"Not stuff like this," she said. "Jade saw me kill someone."

"Who deserved it. In some ways, that could end up being a positive."

"He was *raped*," she said quietly.

I wasn't exactly sure how to be the strong one here, so I decided to just be real.

"We can survive ourselves, Meagan," I said. "And I think it's our job to help Jade understand that."

"Don't say shit like that to me," Meagan said. "You don't have kids."

She was really pissed and just glaring at me.

"I have a son," I said.

I said it slowly, like a confession. It backed Meagan off some.

"You do?"

"Yeah."

"Where is he?"

"I don't know."

"How can you not know where your kid is?" she asked.

I could see that Meagan wasn't particularly impressed with my commitment to fatherhood.

"Because I fucked up," I said, "and behavior has consequences."

She let out a breath and smirked.

"Clichés like that make you an expert on parenting?"

"I know what not to do," I said.

I wasn't exactly closing this deal, but at least I was keeping my customer from walking out the door.

"We have to believe that we can survive ourselves, Meagan. And that's what we need to show our kids."

"Did you ever get over getting shot in the head?"

"Not yet," I said. "But thanks to your kids I'm working on what isn't permanent."

Meagan didn't know what to say—and then she motioned for me to bend toward her. I did. And with the index finger of her right hand, she began to trace the scar on the back of my head.

"It's pretty ugly," I said.

"I've seen worse," she said.

Meagan kissed me on the scar. It was the first time anyone had ever done that. I pulled my T-shirt away from my chest and tried to let some air in. It was soaking wet and I was sweating—but somehow enjoying the salty sting dripping down my back.

I cleared my throat. "When the *policía* find out what happened, this'll just end up as a justifiable homicide. I wouldn't worry."

But I had no idea about the law down here or how it works.

"I'm not," Meagan said. "Ninety percent of Mexican crimes go unsolved."

"Where did you hear that?"

"It's common knowledge."

For someone who had just killed a guy with a hammer, she was a lot calmer than I was.

"And it was self-defense," she said. "A mother's right to defend her child, or whatever."

"But it still needs to be reported. I mean, if we don't, we'd be, like, criminals."

"Report it to who?"

"The *local policía*," I said. "At least."

"How's your Spanish?"

"I can say good morning."

Meagan laughed.

"And a few other things," I said. "How's yours?"

"Not good enough to defend myself in court," she said. "And in Mexico you have to prove your innocence. They don't have to prove you're guilty. You start out that way when you're arrested."

"Jade is a witness."

"There's no way I'm letting my son testify about what happened to him."

"Okay, so we find the best defense lawyer in Mexico," I said, ignoring the oxymoron and just sounding like a regular one.

"While I'm waiting in jail?"

"The boys and I'll visit you," I said.

Meagan shook her head. "No fucking way," she said. "We need to hide this."

"It's a small town, Meagan."

"In the off-season." She smiled. "I mean, who's going to know?"

"Look, Meagan," I said. "I'm, ah, kind of a coward, actually."

"Everyone's a coward, Nick," Meagan said. "It's why nobody ever wants to get caught."

And I suddenly had this feeling that in a lifetime of bad decisions, I was about to make one of my worst.

13

I shouldn't have waited until dark. By now, Winsor was probably in worse shape than King Tut. Still, there was no way I wanted to drag a dead guy with a framing hammer stuck in his head out of a bar and into the back of my Suburban in broad daylight.

I had my longest surfboard bag, the one I use for the tanker I ride when the waves are small. I also had a flashlight and a pair of those nostril pinchers that old guys wear in swimming pools. I was hoping to keep most of the stink out.

I let myself into Wave of the Day. I lit a candle and snapped on my nostril pinchers.

I opened the cooler door and shined my flashlight toward the floor. Winsor was there, pretty much like we had left him, except that he'd lost his erection and the poop had dried up, so the odor wasn't as bad. I'd surfed Gagger's when it smelled worse. This was barely waist-high Gagger's.

I unzipped the bag and laid it out next to Winsor. What it lacked in width, the bag made up for in length. I was pretty sure he'd fit inside, though as a lifelong shortboarder, he'd be bummed.

It was time to pull the hammer out of Winsor's head. I had been dreading this part, imagining that once the holes in his head were unplugged, there'd be a fountain of blood. But then I thought that if Winsor's blood pressure was zero, like it's supposed to be in dead people, the blood thing wouldn't be much of an issue.

I pulled on the hammer's handle, and the claws easily came out of Winsor's head. There was just a trickle of blood—unlike when I got shot. I bled buckets. But that was probably because the .22-caliber bullet was traveling at about one thousand miles per hour. Serious shooters use .22s because the slug gets trapped inside the skull and bounces around, creating a shitload of tissue damage. A fatal result is just about guaranteed—and one potential witness is taken care of.

But the bullet with my name on it had blown out the back of my head, and despite the ugliness of what it left behind, the fact that it exited rather than ricocheted probably saved my life, not to mention whatever brainpower I might have left. I lost some significant memory. I have fits, and sometimes a little trouble hooking up the right thoughts and words, but that's getting better. And I'm still paddling out, which is something Winsor can't say anymore.

It was a pretty good hammer, and tools are hard to come by in Mexico, so I decided not to bury the murder weapon with the victim. Not that this was a murder, or that Winsor was a victim. The victim was back at my casa playing *Minecraft* on my computer.

I put the hammer on the table next to the tequila.

Grabbing Winsor by both ankles, I stretched him out and flipped him onto his back, sort of the way you tip a wheelbarrow onto its side. He wasn't really that stiff yet.

It was pretty easy to roll Winsor into the bag. I started to zip it up.

Not so easy.

I had to kneel on his chest as I pulled the zipper closed. I even had to bounce up and down a little bit, and when I did, he croaked out a burp that was ghastly—Gagger's double overhead, easy.

I finally got the board bag closed, except for the last little bit. Winsor's face was framed by black canvas, and the jagged plastic tracks of the bag's big zipper dug into his fat cheeks. His eyes were closed, and there was some snot on his face. I wiped his nose.

We had been friends. I had surfed some good waves with this guy. So I figured I should probably say something. But I barely believed in luck, let alone God and heaven, so what the hell was I going to say.

"Adios," I finally said. And then, like recovering Catholics everywhere, I made a sloppy sign of the cross.

I got a good grip on each side of the board bag and yanked up hard to hoist Winsor over my shoulder like I had seen in a hundred war movies—as if Winsor were a fellow soldier I was trying to retrieve from behind enemy lines. But the dead pedophile barely budged.

There was no way I was moving this body on my own. Winsor probably weighed more than two hundred pounds. I could barely drag him—forget getting him to the curb and hoisting his carcass into the rear of my Suburban. Deadweight was everything I had heard it to be.

"This is fucked," I said, absorbing the fact that my only experience with hard-core crime was what I'd seen on television.

Real crime is hard.

And committing one that you might actually get away with is probably even harder.

I was going to need help.

14

I was aware that the chances of getting caught for pulling stupid shit increased proportionally with being even stupider and telling people about it. But you have to spill some beans to get someone to help you get rid of a body. And to get really good help, you probably had to spill a lot of beans.

When people say "partners in crime," they're not talking about a business plan. There is no honor among thieves. Just desperation.

Which was my problem.

I was missing the big cash advantage. Nobody was going to make a centavo off this gig. Winsor wasn't the chartreuse four-door with a standard transmission and no AC that earned a sales bonus if it was sold before the end of the month.

That's the problem with crimes of passion—there's no profit motive. What I really needed was a favor. A big one.

If I had a best Mexican friend in Sabanita, it was this *local* I knew named Chuy González. The González family had lived in this part of Mexico for so long that Chuy's grandparents didn't even speak Spanish. They spoke Nahuatl, the language of the Aztecs.

Chuy's mom learned Spanish from the nuns at the Catholic school, and then English from the gringo tourists who bargained her down on the price of the Chiclets she sold on the beach. She named her son Cuāuhtliquetzqué, which is Nahuatl for "eagle warrior" and is impossible to pronounce without pulling a throat muscle, so everyone in Sabanita just called him Chuy—the nickname for Jesus. It's also what I called him. Because Chuy had become my savior, too.

I made my way over the back side of Gringo Hill and then into the jungle where Chuy lived with his wife and kids, six of them, three of each. Yohana was twenty-three. Their oldest child was nine.

I had helped Chuy install a *tanque de agua* in his cinder-block house. The roof was *palapa. Casa de la familia* González was small and damp, but built with Chuy's own hands. The water tank we installed was a big deal—Chuy's only toilet flushed, and the casa also had electricity and Internet. Chuy was on Facebook.

He had learned to speak English from the tourists on the beach, just like his mom, but Chuy sold dope instead of Chiclets—or, more accurately, he sold dope to everyone but *me.* Chuy wouldn't sell to surfers. He said it was because he hated having guys in the lineup who were high. But when it came to me, I think his reasoning went a little deeper than that.

"Chuy," I called out.

It was pretty late, but there was still a light on inside. The kids were probably watching YouTube.

"Pirata!" Chuy yelled back.

He was in a loft he had propped up at the very top of his *palapa*. He swung down like Tarzan—if Tarzan had been half an inch under five feet with an exceptionally large head. Chuy wore a ponytail and had a network of homemade tattoos. I had never seen him wearing shoes or a shirt. Not flip-flops or even a tank top. Not once. Not ever.

His trademark look was a pair of black cargo shorts worn low, the huge pockets full of inventory and contraband. He had a family to take care of.

"Amigo, it's late," he said. "Are you okay?"

Anything after sundown is late during *tormenta*.

"Yeah, yeah, I'm good," I said, lying a little. "I just need a favor."

Chuy had a solar-powered smile. He beamed. I looked down at my feet.

"Sure," he said.

A lot of gringos ask too much of their Mexican friends. They smuggle down a couple of pairs of old sneakers and a few boxes of throwaway textbooks, and then they expect the Lord Jim treatment, as if the poverty-stricken paradise they've barged into owes them something for their meager generosity—like cheap labor or easy sex.

Chuy called these gringos *yo-yos* because their good deeds always came with strings attached.

"Just don't ask me to help you move," Chuy said. "You gringos have too much stuff."

"I'm not moving."

"Good."

"You know Winsor?"

"Your buddy?" Chuy asked. "That guy who rides the T and C Pang?"

At one time, Chuy had been the No. 2 longboarder in all of Mexico, and he was still one of the best surfers in town. And like every *local* in the lineup, he knew just about every surfer who had ever paddled out at Sabanita. It was uncanny.

"Well, yeah, sort of," I said. "Except that he's dead."

"No shit?"

I nodded.

"How?" Chuy asked, not really that surprised. People die down here pretty regularly.

"He got hit in the head with a hammer."

"On purpose?"

"Yeah," I said. "Self-defense."

"Like a suicide?" Chuy asked, his beach English failing him a little. "That's hard to do with a hammer. *Huevos grandes.*"

"No, someone else hit him."

"Well, that prick could drop in," Chuy said. "He cost me more waves than a job."

My amigo was already choosing sides and reminding me how often Winsor had taken waves that weren't his.

"At some point, what else can you do, right?" Chuy continued.

"It wasn't me," I said.

"Doesn't matter. He deserved it."

"It's complicated," I said.

I could hear Yohana laughing with her kids from inside the casa.

"I need to get rid of his body," I whispered. "Do you know how to do that?"

Chuy shrugged. He was pretty nonchalant.

"I'm not an expert," he said. "But it can't be that hard."

15

Chuy was a foot shorter than I was, but about twice as strong. With him, it took us less than a minute to get Winsor into the back of my Suburban. If anyone looked in the rear windows, all they would think they were seeing was a longboard bag stuffed with too many surfboards—not a board bag stuffed with too much body.

We were driving through town.

"Turn your lights on," Chuy said.

I clicked on the Suburban's lights. My one wiper was wearing out, and I could barely see. It had been raining hard all day. A system a couple hundred miles off the coast was upgrading itself into tropical-storm status. No one expected it to be a big deal—even though every surfer in west-coast Mexico was praying for a weather catastrophe that would bring big waves but spare the women and children.

Chuy hefted the hammer. "I like this hammer."

"It's a good one," I said.

"Can I have it?" Chuy asked.

"Sure."

It wasn't like the cops were going to dust it for prints.

"So, what did this guy do, anyway?" Chuy asked.

"He owned that Wave of the Day place. It used to be called the Closeout?"

"To get hit with this hammer is what I meant."

"Some mom didn't like all the attention Winsor was paying to her thirteen-year-old."

"He was a creep?"

"And the family surf coach."

I could see that Chuy considered that to be a betrayal of surfers and groms everywhere.

"She caught him and one of her kids with their pants down," I said. "The guy died with a boner."

"I have that same dream," Chuy said. "But if it was my kid, this hammer's the nicest thing that happen to him. Is the kid okay?"

"He will be, I think," I said. But I decided against getting into too many details.

"God will make sure," Chuy said, and crossed himself.

I bowed my head for a split second and then nodded at the board bag. "Do we take Winsor to the dump? Toss him into the pile that's always on fire there?"

"That's too good a board bag, Pirata. If you don't want it, I'll take it."

"It's going to stink, Chuy. I'll get you a new one."

"It's a *ridículo* waste."

Throwing things away was a luxury Mexico couldn't afford up until very recently. It's why there's so much trash around. A leather water jug would last for a couple of generations, and then when it finally wore out, its leather would be made into sandals. But what do you do with the millions of plastic water bottles that replaced the leather jugs?

Chuy was like this—anything I wanted to throw out, he took home. He was using an old HP OfficeJet printer I tried to toss in the trash as a footstool.

"And those dump dogs would just drag him back into town before he burned up."

"Okay. So let's just bury him," I said.

"The wild pigs will smell him out," Chuy said, shaking his head. "It's why they have those flat noses. We got to cut him up."

"What?"

My instinct is always to play dumb when the going gets weird.

"Into pieces," he said. "Then it's easier."

"I have to draw the line at dismemberment," I said, in a voice that sounded as if it were coming from somebody else.

"You never slaughtered a cow?"

"It's not something I learned in shop class," I said. "But—just for the sake of argument—what would we do with the pieces?"

"We throw them out the window. Cartel style—up and down *el Carretera Pacífico*."

Which was what hard-core Mexicans still called Highway 200.

"In plastic bags or just in big chunks?"

"Probably chunks," Chuy said. "That way, they don't hang around."

I looked over at Chuy, gagging like a guy who skips over the Surgery Channel.

"We need to backtrack," I said. "Maybe we should go to the police."

"That's funny, Pirata."

"I mean it," I said.

"It's not just your decision no more," Chuy said. "I'm in this now. You get deported. I go to jail."

"I shouldn't have gotten you involved, Chuy," I said, exactly like one of those gringos I hate. "I'm a yo-yo."

"You go to the cops, you're a *tampón*." Chuy laughed. "*Tranquilo*, Pirata. I'll get *mi primo* José."

"Who?"

"My cousin," he said. "The guy is an expert on trouble."

16

Chuy's *primo* was an old-school Mexican fisherman, and probably the best boatman in the region. José López captained a twenty-two-foot panga that basically looked like a giant rowboat with a seventy-five-horsepower Yamaha outboard. The boat didn't come with life preservers or a Bimini top.

Three bench seats spanned the gunnels. A dirty plastic cooler sat open at midship, half-full of rotting fish chum. A homemade anchor was wrapped in a rusted chain on a small deck at the bow.

It was a bitch to push this boat off the beach and into the water. It was still raining pretty good, and the wet sand wasn't making it any easier. There were only the three of us, but even at that I was flipping out. This whole deal was becoming way too big a party.

"This is how you get caught," I said to Chuy. "No one can keep secrets—it's impossible."

"I can," Chuy said. "And José is *familia.*"

"But he's not mine," I said. "He doesn't have a dog in this fight."

I was talking about José as if he wasn't there, which was pretty rude, but I figured it was okay because I was speaking English.

Every cop show I have ever seen told me that most bad guys get caught because of some idiot confidant opening his yap. The crime-busting formulas are pretty simple, and a big ingredient is regret turning to panic. It's what the guys on *CSI* look for, and where I was heading. It made sense to me that the Mexican cops would follow similar investigative principles. They probably watched a lot of the same American TV.

"If this shit gets out, just watch," I said. "It's the gringo who'll get coughed up."

"Dude, it's your dead body," Chuy said. "We're just trying to help."

"I should have just left him in the cooler," I said to myself.

"And let that gringa get caught for this?" Chuy laughed. "If you can't close the deal with her now, it won't get easier when she's in jail."

"That's not what this is about, amigo."

"Yeah, right," he said, and laughed again.

After a chain gang of gut-busting heave-hos, we finally got the panga down the sand and into the water. The bow of the boat caught a wave and rose up. After it steadied, I jumped in. Chuy and José did the same, except that they didn't bang their knee on a broken oarlock.

Four or five fishing rods of various weights and lengths were lashed to the only working oar. There were two buckets full of nets, one for bait and one for real fish. Another bucket contained a coiled longline festooned with about a hundred hooks.

There was also a .357 Magnum bang stick propped against the transom.

I sat on the forward bench. José was throttling the Yamaha up and down as he maneuvered the panga through the breakers. Chuy was unbagging Winsor.

We were heading out to sea. The rocky wedge of Punta de Sabanita was to our left. The lights of town were directly behind us. It was raining like hell, and the wind was picking up. There was a lot of chop and white-water spray, and every minute or two I could feel the surge of storm swell.

It was very dark—except when lightning spiderwebbed across the sky, crackling like skeletons fucking on cookie tins and right on top of us. It wasn't necessary to count the seconds.

I was scared shitless.

"I think maybe we should turn back," I said all of a sudden and way too shrill.

Chuy laughed, and then I heard him say something to José about *tormenta y gringos*.

José laughed.

"I'm not trying to be funny," I said.

"Too late, Pirata," Chuy said. "We're going to Bin Laden this *pervertido*."

I had never said a word to José. He didn't talk to gringos. But I was frightened enough to try to change that.

"José, *¿su opinionato?*" I said. "*Su de experto.*"

"My opinion is, you should shut the fuck up until you can speak Spanish," he said to me in perfect English.

I'd no idea José spoke English. My mangled Spanish insulted him, and it should have. I had just talked down to him like some *turista* clod who's still afraid to drink Mexican tap water.

"I'm sorry, José," I said. "I'm the idiot here, I know."

But he just glared into the darkness.

Chuy had tugged pretty much all of Winsor out of the board bag and had him splayed across the middle bench, basically face up with his mouth wide open. He ripped off what was left of Winsor's clothes and tossed them overboard. There was a yellow Livestrong bracelet on Winsor's swollen wrist, but Chuy couldn't yank it off.

"Give me something to cut this with," Chuy said.

"But then it's no good," José said. "Fuck it."

Chuy dropped the wrist.

It was pounding rain. Winsor was being bathed.

"Do you want to say anything to Osama?" Chuy asked me.

"Let's just get this over with," I said.

We had passed Punta de Sabanita and were heading south. Chuy pointed at some standing waves that I could make out in the lightning flash. They were fifteen feet tall, from the backside and crashing onto shore.

Chuy grinned, and nodded at Palmitos—the left point break just off the edge of town. It was where Chuy had saved my life—and the reason I considered him my savior, instead of the devil's advocate he was playing now.

I'd had no business paddling into Palmitos on a big day. I'm a crappy backside surfer, and the wave generally eats up longboarders unless they're exceptional.

I'm not.

Chuy is.

He had told me it was a dumb idea to paddle out, but I had begged him.

"Eddie would go," I'd said, trading on the name of a revered big-wave surfer—and forgetting for a moment that Eddie Aikau had been lost at sea.

"Only kooks say shit like that," Chuy said.

I should have known better.

Palmitos is a *locals*-only break, and I'd been desperate to be recognized as a *low-cal* in the lineup. I was new, and it was my first time at Palmitos. But it'll never happen. I can be an amigo, but never a *local*.

I'd kept moving farther and farther to the inside of the peak at Palmitos to show the *locals* that I had balls big enough for this wave—and that I was just waiting for the right one. I'd feinted for a few, turning up my nose at the last second as if the wave wasn't up to my standard. But the reality was that when I looked over the lip, I was scared.

"Go or no," Chuy had called out. "Don't go and then no."

He'd been right. To surf waves as big as these, you had to commit and power down the face. If you picked a wave that was too big or if you started paddling too late or too early, you'd either slide off the back or pearl into the pit, and the whole wave would close out on top of you.

I pearled.

I'd gotten tired of hearing *fuckin' kook*, so I paddled blind down the face of a bomb, buried the board's nose, and catapulted heavily into the pit as twenty-four pounds of Red Fin smashed me in the head.

I was sucked up—triple overhead and flailing—and somersaulted over the falls. Then the wave hammered me to the bottom, and its churning energy bowled me across the ocean floor. I could feel the Red Fin tombstoning at the surface, ominously pointing toward the sky as I dragged at the other end of the leash below—until the leash snapped and I spun down even deeper, bashing against the reef. I clawed for the surface, but the water was so aerated with whirlpools and froth that there was nothing to claw against.

When I finally bobbed up, I was ready to drown—and looking forward to it.

I was only ten yards from the beach, but I was too exhausted to swim. I could barely float. I was being pummeled by the shore break.

I was going to die. I had no doubt.

Until Chuy grabbed me by my hair and shouted at me to breathe. I gasped and choked. He had ditched his board and was somehow able to paddle with one arm and still keep me afloat until the monstrous turbulence of the next wave sucked us up and launched us onto shore.

We hit the rocky beach hard, but Chuy held me close as we cartwheeled into a tide pool and I finally came to a stop, flat on my back. The tide pool's shallow water was cool, probably because of all the rain. It felt good. I didn't drown. *Thank you, Jesus.*

"You remember how crazy your first time was, Pirata?" Chuy said, still grinning about Palmitos. "The fucking wave you paddled for. I never seen bigger here."

"But I didn't make the wave," I said. "I was faking it."

"You can't fake that shit, man."

And no matter how many times I have told Chuy that my afternoon at Palmitos was less than honorable, he always gives me my props.

"Dude, I was there," Chuy said. "You paddled for it. That's all that counts."

José cut the engine. The panga lurched down the back of a wave and nearly swamped.

Chuy and I looked at him.

"*Dios mío,*" José said.

A hair-standing bolt of lightning lit up the entire bay.

And we could see that Winsor's eyes were open.

thought this motherfucker was dead," José said, impressing me even more with his command of the English language.

"He is dead," I said.

"He's waking up," Chuy said.

"He's *not* waking up," I said.

"The fuck he isn't," Chuy screamed. "It's this lightning—that can do it."

"Only in the movies," I said. "*Cálmate.*"

I switched bench seats so I was the closest to the body. Winsor's mouth was still wide open, and it was filled with rainwater. His eyes were bloodshot and blank, but his eyes were always sort of bloodshot and blank.

"You never heard of pennies on a dead man's eyes?" I asked.

It felt like we were sitting around a campfire and it was my turn to tell a scary story.

"No," Chuy said. But he didn't sound like he wanted to hear the story.

"Sometimes the eyes of dead people would open up," I said. "And it would freak everyone out at the funeral parlor." I was fumbling in my pockets for a couple of ten-peso coins. "So they would put pennies on the eyes to keep the lids down."

I found two coins. I closed Winsor's eyes and placed a coin on each lid.

"That's a total shit story," José said. "That's not even close to why."

He pulled the Yamaha's start cord. The outboard fired to life, and the coins skidded off Winsor's face.

"It was Charon's payment," José said. "That boatman in Hades who took the dead souls across the river of pain."

"Did you go to college, José?" I asked.

I was trying not to sound patronizing, but José didn't answer. He just moved toward Winsor and snatched up my twenty pesos.

I looked at the water pooling in Winsor's mouth. It was still raining.

Then Winsor choked.

And his eyes fluttered open again.

Then he coughed the water out of his mouth.

I couldn't see whether Winsor was actually breathing, but it sure looked like he was coming back to life.

Fuck.

We've all heard stories about people snapping out of really deep comas, or some stiff who sits up in his coffin just before the undertaker closes the lid. But I doubt that too many of those recovering dead guys recently had two inches of framing hammer claws embedded in their heads.

I mean, if Winsor wasn't totally dead in the technical sense, he was probably very brain-dead in the intellectual sense. I was already starting to plea bargain with myself. But Winsor wasn't going to help me out. He puked and groaned. I panicked.

"We have to take this man to a hospital," I said, squealing a little.

"That sounds like a way to get into a lot of trouble," Chuy said.

"I'll take full responsibility."

"You're just a fucking gringo, man. Nothing happens to you," Chuy said. "I told you that already."

"I'll bribe the doctors," I said, "to keep you guys out of this."

"This fucking *pendejo*'s got it backward, amigo," José said to Chuy. "He needs to bribe *us*."

"Winsor is a human being." I was pleading.

"He fucks kids," José said. "I ain't helping him."

"That's the rumor," I said. "But if he's not dead, we have to call the *policía*."

"That fucking rumor's why I'm out here with a fucking zombie," Chuy said. "You asked me for help. I'm giving it."

"We can't be the judge and jury, Chuy," I said. "It was

different when he was dead. We were just getting rid of a body. But now we have to do the right thing."

The hypocrite in me was trying to parse what little I knew about the Hippocratic Oath.

"First, do no harm," I said.

"To your family and your amigos," José said. "Yeah, that's right, don't harm them."

And then José simply picked up the bang stick and jammed it down on Winsor's chest, just above the heart. The .357 Magnum discharged, powering a short spear deeply into Winsor's sternum, arching him grotesquely as its razor-sharp tip exited his back and chipped the wooden bench. Winsor squirmed once and went still.

"*Jesús Cristo*," Chuy whispered.

José twisted the spearhead out of Winsor's chest.

"Okay," he said. "Now *I'm* the biggest dog in this fight."

Winsor's body slipped off the bench seat.

"Which makes us murderers, genius," I said. "Instead of accessories after the fact."

José glared at me. It was a warning.

"This isn't murder, Pirata," Chuy said. "It's just killing a dead guy."

"And you remember that if you ever feel like telling anybody about this," José said.

He hefted the bang stick. It was something he kept on board for sharks, but, as I'd just seen, he apparently had no qualms about using it on people. Gringos, specifically.

José knew that if this thing blew up, he'd be in deeper shit than I'd be. I'd get tossed out of Mexico, probably. But he'd go to jail. He had more reasons to worry about me than I had to worry about him—which exposed me some. I was a *cómplice*. But also a loose end.

And a witness.

As this became clearer to me, I started to tremble a little. I was hoping José didn't notice.

"But, you know," I said, "ninety percent of all crimes in Mexico go unsolved. So it's not like we've got that much to worry about."

José laughed. "We just tell that to the gringas so they feel like they need our protection."

And then he high-fived Chuy in a way that made me jealous and a little pissed off.

"Although that's just a statistic," I said.

I looked at Winsor and then back to José. He was smiling at me.

"Let's adios this guy," Chuy said.

José and Chuy wrapped Winsor in the rusted chain. I secured him to the anchor.

And we rolled his body overboard.

18

The tropical storm never quite got to *tormenta* status. It never made it to the big leagues. Nobody down here was going to be calling it an *huracán*.

Except me.

I was rocked by what happened with Winsor.

I was in the plaza, sitting on the concrete steps of the gazebo. Must have been about four in the morning—that no-man's-land between the heart of darkness and dawn. Everyone who'd been out looking for trouble or a buzz had either found it or packed it in, but none of the señoras was up and sweeping the streets yet.

I had been sitting there for a couple of hours.

Everything was very still—like the way it used to be when I was little and I looked out the window late at night at the intersection on my corner, when the stoplight changed from green to yellow to red and then back again, without any cars passing through.

José had gotten us all back to shore—without Winsor and without too much drama. We had to power over some really big waves, and he set a new boat beaching record. We must've been going about twenty miles per hour when we hit the sand, and we nearly slid into a palm tree.

We hopped out of the panga, and Chuy hugged me.

"Thanks for the board bag," Chuy said, and slung it over his shoulder.

"You're an asshole," I said.

"Would you chill? The fucking guy deserved it."

"There's a difference between a crime of passion and an execution," I said.

"Not when you're the one that's dead," José said, like an executioner might say it.

"You have to trust us, Pirata. We know more about these things," Chuy said, taking his cousin's side.

I looked at José and then finally offered him a nod of thanks, but he didn't nod back.

"So, okay, amigo—later, huh?" Chuy winked and gave me a thumbs-up.

I watched them walk off, jabbing at each other and then *fútbol*-ing an empty plastic bottle back and forth. Chuy wore the board bag like a cape. They were calm and collected, compared to me.

I started to think that maybe it was some kind of holiday, because I hadn't seen any *trabajadores*—the guys who get up super early to harvest the mango groves before sunrise, before it gets ungodly hot.

If I had seen any, I might have asked to borrow a machete—to slit my throat.

I had become a murderer.

It didn't feel great.

Though technically, I was just an accomplice.

It was going to take some serious mental maneuvering for me to get myself through this. It felt like a turning point, just as getting shot in the head had been a turning point. I mean, if killing someone isn't a turning point, you're probably a lost cause.

I'm not one of those guys who believe that good deeds can make up for bad behavior, but piling up some kindness right now might not hurt. I was very likely way overdrawn at the karma bank. I should probably make a deposit.

"What are you doing up so early?" Sarah said.

I turned. Sarah was standing at the edge of the plaza, under a streetlight. She had a small dog on a leash. It looked like a pit bull puppy—with mange and a bandaged rear leg. Since I had known Sarah, she'd gone through about thirty dogs. She was a dog foster mom.

"I can't sleep," I said. "I'm unloved."

"Rescue a dog," she said. "It'll love you."

Sarah sat down next to me on the gazebo steps.

"How did it go up at the sacred grounds?" I asked, a little like a smart-ass.

"There's been some progress," Sarah said, with an edge. "But it's a process, Nick."

Then she nuzzled her new dog and kissed it on the mouth.

"This is Captain," Sarah said. "He was poisoned."

"He looks like he's doing better, then," I said.

"There's a man who comes to Sabanita every year to poison the dogs."

"I've heard that," I said.

But I never believed it. Every few years, this rumor returns—*the man is here to poison the dogs.*

"He comes from Mexico City," Sarah said. "The government sends him. To poison the strays."

"He's doing a shitty job," I said. "We have more stray dogs than hungry kids."

"The kids are next," Sarah said.

It was the kind of wild rumor that could race through rural Mexico and get toy salesmen lynched. I was mystified about why so many gringos believed them.

"I wouldn't repeat that," I said.

"It's true," she said.

It was still pretty dark, but Sarah was sitting close enough to me that I could see her face. She was stroking the puppy, holding it as if she were breastfeeding. Sarah was wearing a little makeup, and her hair had been brushed. She wore a flower behind one ear.

I smiled at her.

She smiled back, and I could see that her missing front tooth had been replaced.

"Nice tooth," I said.

"Thanks. In Arkansas, that's a compliment."

"Here, too."

"I bought myself a birthday present for my sixtieth. I didn't want to be a toothless old crone. Just a regular old one." A great thing about Mexico is that the dental work is so cheap. I once got a root canal for fifty bucks.

"It's your birthday?"

"Yeah. Today."

"*Feliz cumpleaños.*"

"Thanks," Sarah said. "But you know what that means?"

"You're halfway to one hundred and twenty?"

Sarah tried to smile like she didn't care. "That I haven't been laid in a decade," she said. "Which would be funny if it wasn't so humiliating."

And then I remembered Sarah's over-sharing that sad fact when I bought the bindle last week.

"It's not humiliating," I said. "Celibacy is even, like, a thing now. A fad, sort of."

"Rubik's Cubes were a fad," Sarah said. "Never getting laid is just lonely."

It was probably pretty awful.

I felt sorry for the dog. Sarah was squishing it up against her chest.

"Go easy on that dog," I said.

"Fuck this dog," Sarah said, and let go of the orphaned pit bull. I had to grab the leash.

"What time of day were you born?" I asked.

"Why?"

"I'm an astrologist. I want to see if your seventh house is in escrow."

"Eleven seventeen in the morning."

"So you're not sixty years old for another four or five hours."

"What difference does that make?" Sarah fired back.

"It could make some."

"How?"

"Can I walk you home?"

Sarah looked at me. "What are you up to, Nick?"

"It's your birthday." I smiled and reached for her hand.

"Spare me the mercy hump, please," she said. "No charity."

"I wish it were that simple," I said.

I tugged on the leash and picked up the puppy. I offered a hand to help Sarah to her feet, but she didn't take it. Then she stood up and took my arm and we slowly circled the plaza, pretending we had nowhere to go.

A señora began to sweep out the gazebo. A *trabajador* with a machete dangling from a rope belt crossed the street. Sarah squeezed my hand.

"Walk me home," she said.

19

I was the only person to have sex with Sarah during her fifties and the very first person to have sex with her in her sixties. If I said I hadn't enjoyed it and that I was just jamming guilt coins into the good-karma slots, I'd be lying. Using sex as a distraction isn't exactly a new idea, but it sure helped me get over my initial anguish about Winsor.

Although it's not like my hands were any cleaner now. I was still just as culpable as I'd been when we wrapped Winsor up in that rusty chain—and when José blew a spearhead into Winsor's chest with the bang stick. My trying to guilt fuck my way out of that with Sarah was creepy.

And I was ashamed of myself for not feeling as bad as I thought I should. Maybe I had a little murderer in me. Maybe we all do—the coward who doesn't want to get caught. Or maybe it gnaws at you over time.

Or maybe you just end up forgetting about it.

Sarah and I did the elusive feat eight times over two days, and for a couple of people who could probably count on our hands how many times we've had sober sex, we were pretty good at it. We didn't have to worry about anybody getting pregnant, and Sarah had already assured me that she was a bad viral host.

I finally got back to my casa Wednesday afternoon. I hadn't been home since Sunday night. Someone had raked up the dirt, and there was a neat pile of leaves under the *higuera*. A small garden had been planted. I could see that those little seed envelopes were being used as signs. It was a spice garden. I hoped.

Meagan was standing on the front steps.

"I heard the car," she said.

I felt as if we had been married for ten years and I was coming home late from the bowling banquet.

"I was starting to think that maybe you got caught. Or that you ran away."

"The second one crossed my mind," I said.

"Where were you?"

"Where do you think?"

I climbed my front steps and stood close to Meagan.

"I'm not particularly good at getting rid of bodies," I whispered. "It's not as easy as you think."

"You should have called. It freaked out the boys."

"I didn't think you'd still be here."

"Where would we be?"

"Home."

"At Winsor's?"

"Well, that's where you live, isn't it?"

Meagan laughed. "Not anymore. The place is going to be haunted."

"Don't be ridiculous."

"That's what Jade thinks."

"Then tell him it's not true—that such a thing has never happened. You'll be doing him a huge favor."

I looked into the casa, and I could see both boys. They were sitting at the counter in the kitchen and maneuvering the mouse of my ancient iMac. There was a spreadsheet up on the screen.

"What are they doing?" I asked Meagan. "I have some personal stuff on that."

"Homeschooling," she said. "Jade's really good at math."

I could also see that Meagan had arranged some fresh flowers.

"Whose are these?" I asked.

"Yours. They grow all over the back of the house."

She held one to my nose and made me sniff it. But all I could smell was Sarah and me.

"I need to take a shower."

"There's no hot water."

"How is that possible?"

"You're out of *propano*."

"There was money in my drawer."

"It wasn't enough."

"Nine thousand pesos?" I said. "That's like five hundred dollars."

"But I had to use it to pay the rent."

"There's no rent. I own this place."

"On the Wave of the Day," Meagan said, and then whispered, "It's got to look like we think he's coming back."

Jesus.

"And, you know," she said, "stranger things have happened."

"No, they haven't."

I walked into the bathroom. Meagan followed me.

"*Mi baño, amiga*," I said and smiled as I tried to close the door.

"There's only one," she said and stuck her foot in the bathroom.

I pulled off my shirt and balled it up. Meagan gasped. She was pointing to the welts and bruises on my back.

"What happened to your back?"

I tried to calculate how much I should tell Meagan about my humiliating roadside encounter—but then I decided to take El Jefe's advice and simply tell the truth. "I was stopped at a checkpoint and lied about having drugs."

"*You* had drugs?"

"Yes," I said, without spin or varnish.

"What kind?"

"The wrong kind, apparently." I didn't feel like explaining my seizures to Meagan and going into my self-medicating defense. "So they beat me."

"You couldn't bribe them?"

"I brought it up—"

But Meagan cut me off with a glare. "What the fuck is that?"

She was pointing to a spot on my neck. I looked in the mirror. Sure as shit, I had a hickey.

"I was also choked?" I said, hiding a lie inside a question. "Choked *and* beaten."

"It's a *hickey*," Meagan said.

"I think so, yes," I said.

"And it's fresh."

"It is."

"You were just *with* somebody."

"I was," I nodded.

"Are you a fucking vampire?"

"I don't think so," I said.

El Jefe's theory about truth appeared to be falling apart.

"How the fuck can you kill someone and then fucking fuck?"

"That's a lot of *fuck*s," I said.

"I'm just warming up."

"But *I* didn't kill him, sweetheart." *And neither did you, now that I think about it.*

"So what, he deserved it."

"Probably," I said.

Meagan leaned in, but it didn't look like she was going to kiss me—she just sniffed.

"You need a shower," she said.

"I know," I said.

20

I took a cold shower. It felt great, if a little late. But the water really wasn't that cold. Every kind of liquid in Mexico ends up around room temperature, in the same way that all the dogs end up flop-eared and grayish brown.

I have this theory that eventually all the mongrel strays and neurotic cocker spaniels that have run away from their gringa nannies will breed into one genetically streamlined Mexican purebred. That's all you'll see down here—gangly gray mutts with long, droopy ears.

I hadn't had a shave or brushed my teeth for a few days, so I was taking my time with some serious primping. After all, it was my bathroom. I also wasn't crazy about having another face-to-face with Mother Meagan.

I took a closer look at the hickey on my neck, and I had to say, it was a thing of beauty. It looked like the state of Texas, but with too much blue inside the red. I don't remember Sarah sucking that hard, to be honest, but I'll never forget the gibberish she thought was sexy talk. It sounded like she was speaking in tongues, at least when she wasn't tonguing me in places that many people would find offensive and perverse—like I used to.

All I will say is, don't knock what you haven't tried.

I put on a clean T-shirt and alternated into my other pair of board shorts. I owned two pairs, one of which was always clean. In a perfect world, anyway. The pair I had just put on had a half-eaten candy bar and about a thousand ants in the pocket. I slipped off the shorts and snapped them hard against the shower tile, and most of the ants flew off. I took a bite of the candy bar but then dropped it in the toilet. I didn't want to spoil my dinner.

The front of my T-shirt said *Don't Ask*. The back said *Don't Tell*. I don't remember buying it. It just appeared one day. After a binge.

Don't ask.

I also put on a fresh eye patch. I keep a handful of them in the sink drawer next to my Good News razors. This one was white with a sequined peace sign. I also have a red one with a hammer and sickle, and then a few basic blacks and grays for formals.

"Too many *fucks*," Meagan said. "I'm sorry."

She was leaning against the bathroom door. I didn't know how long she'd been there, but it startled me a little. I wasn't used to the company.

"Mine or yours?"

"Just *yours* if you're going to be an asshole," she said, stepping a little too close. "But I do appreciate the help."

"You're welcome," I said.

Meagan took the Good News razor from my hand, expertly flicking off the excess lather and then drawing a smooth, clean line down from my sideburn to my chin. She quickly pushed up my nose and shaved above my lip.

"You're very good at this."

"It's not hard."

I began to wonder just what Meagan couldn't do—or maybe wouldn't do. But before I could give it much thought, she toweled me off and kissed me on the nose.

"How old are you, Meagan?"

"Thirty-two."

"Jade's thirteen?"

"Fourteen in February," she said. "I was knocked up my first year in college."

"So that explains the 'freshman fifteen'—it turns out to be a six-pound baby boy."

"You might be surprised just how unfunny being a young single mom is," Meagan said.

I realized I was being scolded a little.

"I was stupid enough to think it was an act of independence. I was in my feminist phase. Jade's dad was a senior."

"Where is he now?"

"Danny went back to Hanoi. But he *promised* to send for us."

"Danny?"

"Like Dan—with an *h*," she said. "But I Americanized him."

"Like secret Agent Orange, I'm sure."

"You're good with words," she said. "I like that."

"Used to be," I said, snapping the lid of my eye patch.

Meagan pinched my cheek—hard enough to let me know that she wasn't forgiving me.

"I made dinner," she said. "The boys said they want to eat with you. They want to pretend that we're normal."

Meagan left me to finish up in the *baño*.

I put on a different shirt, the only one I had with a collar, and I turned it up like Elvis. I didn't want the boys to see my hickey. They had seen enough unexplainable shit lately.

I THINK IT WAS THE FIRST TIME MORE THAN TWO PEOPLE HAD BRO-ken bread in my casa—or, in this case, folded a tortilla. Even though I didn't have enough forks to go around, it was obvious Meagan would have known exactly which one to use. I could tell by the way she sat in her chair and adjusted the paper towel in her lap that she hadn't been raised in Appalachia.

The aromas were delicious, but I had no idea what I was smelling.

"I thought we were out of gas," I said.

"I made a deal with the *propano* guy while you were in the shower."

Obsidian laughed, and Jade kicked him.

Meagan smiled.

"What kind of deal?" I asked, a little awkwardly.

"Whatever it takes," Meagan said.

"Yeah, Mom's a survivor," Obsidian said, probably from experience.

And then a phone rang and kind of saved us from the awkwardness. It was one of those old-fashioned rings, the kind from a phone that has a dial. They still use them down here, so at first I thought it was coming from somewhere outside. But then it rang again, and I realized that the ring was too loud. Either the phone was inside my casa, or it was inside my head and I was having an audio hallucination—which was possible.

"Um," I said, as calmly as possible, "does anyone hear a phone ringing?"

The boys were staring straight at each other. They didn't say a word. Meagan played dumb.

"Oh, my gosh, I do," she said. "If it's for me, I'm not here."

The old-fashioned ring rang again, and I glared at Jade.

"Answer it," I said.

Jade pulled a new iPhone out of his pocket and put it up to his ear.

"Hello," he said.

I had an idea where he had gotten this phone, and I wasn't happy about it.

"Winsor's not here," Jade said. "No. Nobody knows where he is."

Jade hung up the phone. I looked over at Meagan.

"Did you know about this?"

"I figured Jade deserved it," she said. "Kind of like the spoils of war."

"Give it to me," I said to Jade.

He handed over Winsor's iPhone. I got up from the table and walked into my bedroom. I put the iPhone in my drawer.

"This is my drawer," I called out from the bedroom. "It is off-limits. Everything in this drawer is a secret. And it's mine. So hands off the iPhone."

I went back to the table and sat down.

"My dad said that exact same thing about his drawer," I said.

"Your dad had an iPhone?" Obsidian asked, faking that he was impressed. It was the first time I'd heard him sound like a normal wiseass teenager.

"He didn't need one," I said. "He was a great shouter."

Meagan ladled out some kind of stew into a bowl and handed it to me. It was a rich, creamy broth with lumps of what could have been either fish or chicken.

"Do you have any allergies?" Obsidian asked me, wise-assing me again.

"Only to honest work."

"Work is the curse of the drinking man," Jade said.

I was pretty shocked at the quote. I had heard it a million times. It was kind of like the car salesmen's motto. I looked over at Meagan, and she smiled. I could see that she was proud of how smart her kids were.

"I'm not the best homeschooling mom around," Meagan said. "But we try to learn something we don't know every day."

"And that's Osmar Wilde," Jade bragged.

"I think it's *Oscar*," I said.

"But what if work is the curse of the *surfing* man?" Obsidian asked.

"It was for me," I said.

"And now you don't work, right?" Jade said. "See, Mom, he can pull it off."

"But you have to have an extra hole put into your head first," I said. "Which can be painful."

I rarely made jokes about getting shot. It undermined my victimhood. But I had to admit, I was enjoying the intimacy. I tasted the stew.

"Excellent."

"Thank you," Meagan said. "It's armadillo."

"You're kidding?" I said.

"She's not," Jade said, proud as hell—and what kid wouldn't be. "Mom's an exotic chef."

"I'm a chef like I'm a jeweler," Meagan said. "But I can cook."

21

There was still a little bit of daylight left, so after dinner I grabbed my board and walked down to the left break. No one was out, and there was a shoulder-high cleaner coming through.

A *pescador* nicknamed Cabezón was tossing his bait net into the shore break. A half dozen dogs were chasing an old pelican with a damaged wing. I thought that maybe I should step in and give the old bird a hand, but somehow he made it into the water on his own.

The dogs were all gangly and gray and a little wild. They started to sniff and growl around me a little bit, so I paddled out for safety just like the pelican had—and just like I do whenever I need to feel safe. The ocean does that for me.

I was harassing myself with a claustrophobic buzz I'd

apparently ordered as a side with the armadillo. I can't always be sure if it's the TBI or just me being neurotic that causes these episodes, and I had thought I'd deactivated this one with last week's binge. But it seemed to be hanging on. Maybe being surrounded by a family is a trigger because it reminds me of the one I used to have—and ran away from.

Either way, I wanted to resist ingesting any preventive medicines, so I figured I should get wet. If I can catch a few good waves, it usually settles me down. Maybe it's the lithium in ocean saltwater or the simple thrill of gravity, but surfing's roller coaster is how I get over my rough patches.

I also didn't want to go see Sarah again so soon—except for sex, maybe. But I certainly didn't need any more snortables, and my mental health triage would make for an uncomfortable ménage à trois. I didn't want to hurt her feelings—at least, not more than I'd probably hurt them already.

On my way out the door, I had hinted to her that despite my raves and her surprising flexibility, I was pretty sure our two nights' worth of a one-night stand was exactly that—a once-in-a-lifetime phenomenon. Like when it snowed in Mexico City.

The water I was surfing was barely two feet deep, and the wave, though small, was fast and hollow. My backside surfing is a little weak, and Sabanita's left only works on the lowest tides. So whenever I surf the left, it's always with a wall-to-wall carpeting of rocks just below the surface.

After I made the drop, I had to reach down and grab my outside rail to help crank a bottom turn. I'm a regular-foot surfer—which means my left foot is forward, and I face the wave when I'm surfing a right break and face the shore when I'm surfing a left. Once I trimmed the Red Fin down the line, I was able to stand up straighter, but any time I'm on a left, I always feel as if I am surfing like a kook.

A guy I paddle out with named English John told me, "The secret that enables regular foots" to surf shallow lefts is to go straighter on takeoff and not try to make the bottom turn so *briskly*.

"Go straight down the face and wait before you make your bottom turn," John would say. "Don't be frightened about it getting shallow—the rocks are your mates!"

The first time I took the Englishman's advice, I spent the rest of the day spraying Neosporin at the cuts on the bottom of my feet and looking for a new fin box. But he was right about some of it: "If you go straight at the thing you're afraid of, it gives you the advantage of surprise."

In English John's world, everything is alive. Scary waves can be surprised. Shallow shore breaks, thunderstorms, finicky toasters, and ATMs can be tricked and manhandled. Everything has a personality and a plan, and if you pay attention, you can outwit it.

"If I want my motorbike to start on the first try, I have to sneak up on it," he would say, kick-starting his old Jawa without warning and winding up the throttle.

He must have been from the watched-pot-never-boils

school of physics, but there was one thing the Englishman said that I knew in my gut to be true.

Going straight at the stuff that scares you is good advice. I just didn't have the courage to go there—or even the words to describe it. That's how big abandoning your kid is. It just makes you less of whatever you used to be.

22

By the time I got home, it was dark. I could see the red dot of a joint pulsate as I walked up the sandy path that connected my casa to the beach. Meagan was sitting on the front steps. I stood my Red Fin up in the crotch of the *higuera* and sat next to her.

There was a half moon and hardly any clouds. A swarm of lightning bugs blinked out their love signals.

"Pretty clear for this time of year," I said.

I could barely see Meagan nod in the darkness. She offered me the joint.

"I don't smoke," I said.

"Really?" she said.

"Yup."

I let that hang in the air for a little bit, seeing as how marijuana is Mexico's number-one cash crop. Maybe I had a particularly precious brand of TBI, but after my head wound, good bud always gave me the heebie-jeebies.

"What kind of deal did you make with the *propano* guy?" I asked.

"That I'd pay him when you got home."

"He gave you credit?"

Unheard-of. The gas guys down here, especially the delivery-truck drivers, are as ruthless as the Exxon execs north of the border.

"Sure did," she said.

"That's amazing. I once offered him my Red Fin as collateral—he told me to forget it."

My Red Fin was a certified original and signed by Hynson himself. It was worth two grand. Easy.

"You should have flashed him your tits," Meagan said.

"I don't have tits," I said, more defensively than accurately.

"And then I told him that if I don't pay him by Saturday—he can touch them."

"You're kidding?"

"He didn't think so. I got the gas," she said.

Meagan smiled and straightened her loose cotton top. "Pretty resourceful, huh?"

"Down here it's called something else," I said.

"You never heard of a pound of flesh?"

"I'll Google it," I said.

"Two pounds, actually," Meagan corrected, and then laughed.

She seemed so comfortable with herself that I wanted to laugh along with her.

"But what if I don't have the money?" I said.

"Oh, you'll find the money."

Meagan spit on what was left of the reefer and tossed the roach into the spice garden.

"Are the boys sleeping?"

Meagan nodded. "And thanks for letting them use your computer." She took my hand, and I let her hold it.

"No worries. I just don't want them to get it all bugged up."

"They won't. Jade's a computer nerd, just like his dad. He even hacked your passwords."

"Passwords are private." I was a little more pissed off than impressed.

"Supposed to be," she said. "That shows you how good he is."

Meagan began tracing little circles with her fingertips along the inside of my forearm. I'd had a high-school girlfriend who did that to me, and it made me crazy—crazy calm, if there could be such a thing.

"I told him not to make it a habit," she said. "But we needed to download the next level of this homeschooling program."

"Was it free?"

"I wish. We had to use your iTunes account."

"You mean, *I* wish. What makes you think you don't have to ask?"

"Well, I would have, of course, if you had been here. But you were out banging some dolly for two days, and I have kids to raise."

"She wasn't some *dolly*."

"We're never dolly to you guys," she said. "Once you're done."

"Look," I said, "has it occurred to you that a guy like me, whose entire criminal career can be summed up in shoplifting a KISS CD, might get a little stressed out over having to get rid of a *body*?"

"Keep your voice down," Meagan said, and nodded toward the casita.

"Don't worry about it. Your kids were there, remember?" And then I whispered, *"We ended up having to dump Winsor in the ocean."*

"I'm thinking you're trying to make it sound like it was a bigger deal than it really was."

"What?" I was incredulous.

"Yeah, so I'll feel, like, indebted to you. That's what men do. Usually."

"It was a very big deal. Trust me."

"No, it's not," Meagan said. "I've been there."

And it felt like the temperature dropped about ten degrees.

"Been where?" I asked, and I stopped her fingertips from making the tiny tingles on my forearm.

"Trying to get rid of bodies."

I shivered a little bit.

"With Obsidian's dad," Meagan whispered.

"His *dad*?"

"Jesus, take it easy."

"I'm trying to."

"Look—he was my drug buddy." She was whispering again. "Not just my *guy*. Okay?"

"Not really."

"And, well, I sorta let him OD."

"Sorta?"

"I stopped using. He didn't—couldn't, or wouldn't. So he kept spending all our money on dope. Our kids needed to eat. And Social Services was going to take them away if we didn't stop using."

"I'm trying to figure out if that's an alibi or an explanation," I said.

"It's both," she said and shrugged.

Then Meagan took my hand in hers and touched a finger against my eye patch. "We used to cook up our batches for each other. Back before I got clean. And yeah, maybe that last time I did use a tablespoon instead of a teaspoon. I wasn't used to doing it sober, so maybe I couldn't remember the recipe. Like I said, I'm not really a chef. People make mistakes."

Jesus.

Meagan moved to kiss me, but I turned my head.

"You don't believe me."

It looked like she was hurt.

"Of course I do," I said, and kissed her quickly on the cheek.

23

had decided to sleep on the couch on the porch, but first I tiptoed into my bedroom to check on the boys.

They were sound asleep in my bed, and angled in a way that made me remember this potato-skin game Marshall and I used to play on summer nights. Where we'd take potato peels and throw them over our shoulders. When one landed in the shape of a letter, we'd have to make a word out of it.

Jade was sleeping as straight as an uppercase *I*, for *ingenious*, maybe. Obsidian was comfortable in a smaller *c*.

I moved a dreadlock away from Obsidian's eyes and untangled Jade's arm from a pillow.

"It must be hard to miss this so much," Meagan said.

She startled me a little bit, and I jumped as I turned toward her.

"I thought you were sleeping," I said.

I was a little embarrassed.

"I thought you were."

I couldn't see Meagan well enough to know what she was wearing, but I could certainly smell her. She must have taken a shower after our little chat outside. She had that homemade-soap smell.

"Come to bed," she said.

"I thought I'd better just sleep on the couch," I said.

But Meagan had already left the room. I could hear her turn the fan up a notch and yank back the covers on the guest bed.

I took another look at the boys and walked out of my bedroom.

Meagan lit a candle as I stretched out on the bed. It was the size my parents used to call a double bed. Down here in Mexico, it's called a *matrimonial*. Meagan was naked. I have seen a lot of naked women. But I was pretty sure she was the most beautiful naked woman I had ever seen. Too bad I wasn't feeling very amorous.

"So how did you get rid of him?" I asked Meagan.

"Who?"

"Obsidian's dad," I said.

She blew out the match and jumped into bed, scrunching in between a couple of pillows.

"Yeah, that sucked," she said. "Nobody wanted to help me dump a body for free, and we didn't have any money."

"You and the kids?"

"Who else?"

"I'm just asking."

"So I had to leave him where he overdosed—in this crappy little apartment in New Orleans. The lease was in my name. I thought it would be wise to leave. The country, that is. I had already been arrested once for possession, and with an OD in the house I'd lose the boys for sure."

"You're from New Orleans?"

"Virginia," Meagan said. "Obsidian's dad was a roadie for the Dave Matthews Band—he was in charge of the guitars."

"So that's true," I said.

"And a very big deal, if you don't know—Jade and me got to tag along. The kids were the same age, so it worked out." Meagan stopped and nodded her head slightly, like she was remembering something nice. "But then my guitar tuner got fired after a show in Shreveport."

"What about Obsidian's mom?"

Meagan shrugged. "Maybe she didn't like hanging around backstage as much as I did. But I've never asked and Obsidian doesn't bring her up."

"That's considerate," I said.

"Yeah, sometimes our kids give us a break with the hard stuff."

"I wouldn't know," I said.

But it did feel like what she was telling me could be true—or maybe none of it was. I couldn't tell.

"And Jade's aunt really was the Napalm Girl?"

"That's what his dad told me," Meagan said. "They were boat people. Who knows—but I had to pass it on to Jade."

"What's Virginia like?"

"It's not for lovers," she said. "My stepdad was a dentist, specializing in back rubs. Mom's specialty was anything without me."

She began to knead the skin on her thighs, and I could see a network of thin gray lines, as if something had been written there once in some kind of hieroglyphs.

"And that's why you did that?"

Meagan covered up the faint scars. "Superficially," she said. "But I think I was really just trying to write my name."

Then Meagan pulled my head down with her free hand and kissed me. She slowly pressed her tongue between my teeth. She tasted like tea—the kind that wasn't coffee.

"That was nice," I said.

"Thank you."

"But isn't there supposed to be some kind of mourning period?"

"You should talk."

"I was vulnerable because of the sudden death of a fellow surfer," I said. "You were Winsor's girlfriend."

"I was a buddy with benefits—and he had satellite TV," Meagan said. "Anything else you hear is *chisme*."

It didn't surprise me that Meagan knew the *local* word for ugly gossip, and I reminded myself of the Mexican warning—*beware the gringo who speaks good Spanish.*

"But what happened to Jade is on me. Forever," she said.

Meagan kissed me again, signaling that the Winsor part of the conversation was closed.

This time, I kissed her back. She was delicious. Maybe this is why the English are so mad for tea. She eased me out of my surf shorts, and I rolled onto my back.

Meagan began to kiss my chest, trailing down and delicately putting her tongue into my belly button. One of her fingers started to trace those little circles again, but this time it wasn't on my forearm. She did this for a little while, and I stared up at the fan. I tried to count the revolutions, but in Mexico that's a big job.

"Are you okay?" Meagan asked.

"I'm great," I said, lying a little.

It was obvious to both of us that one of us wasn't getting an erection.

"No pressure," she said. "We can just snuggle."

"Thanks. That makes it easier."

I don't care how many touchy-feely articles women have read about this, there's no way that not getting your dick up doesn't totally bum a guy out.

"I have some Viagra in my purse," Meagan offered, in a voice that made her sound like a nurse.

I shook my head. The last time I'd loaded Señor Moment up on Mexican Viagra, I'd just about blown a hole in his sombrero. Dosages of bootlegged drugs are hard to figure. I was lucky I hadn't had a stroke.

"I thought you were a feminist," I said.

"That's why I have the Viagra," Meagan said. "I'm an equal opportunist."

"There's that resourcefulness again."

"It's all I got," she said, and leaned in to kiss me.

I held her off but then pulled her in a little closer. "What do you want, Meagan?"

She sat up and looked down at me.

"I want a real family. Have you ever had one?"

"Of course," I said. "I know about eggnog and Christmas and cleaning my room. I had a sister who kicked me."

"Well, that's what I want. For the boys."

It wasn't the worst idea in the world.

"It would be good for the boys," I said.

"And you could be their surf coach."

"Nah," I said. "I'm just an old longboard kook."

"They think you're a hero," she said, and began to trace those little circles on my chest.

I closed my eyes. *A real family*, I said to myself. Hard to imagine—but not impossible.

24

I woke up to the sound of the shrimp guy driving around Sabanita in his old pickup: "¡El camión de los camarones está aquí!" In fact, it sounded like he was driving through my bedroom. That's the kind of thing I love about Mexico— a fisherman bolts a loudspeaker onto his truck, and suddenly he's his own advertising agency.

I looked at the clock and yawned. It was nearly nine thirty. I hadn't slept this long since I was on Dilantin.

"Meagan?" I called out. And I have to admit, I smiled.

Meagan didn't answer, and it sounded like no one was home. Not that an empty house has a sound—but it sure has a feeling.

"Meagan?" I called out again, but then I just shrugged and got up. I had been hoping for a mulligan.

I put on some shorts and a T-shirt and headed out the

door. It was sunny as hell, and the whole town had a kind of freshly baked mud pie smell.

I looped down to the left to see if maybe the boys were out, but the surf was small. The flightless pelican was still there, though. Somehow, it had kept clear of the stray dogs and predatory fish and survived the night. Its broken wing had been plucked free of feathers and was dragging, raw and bleeding, at a hideous angle out to one side. I felt sorry for the old bird—but there wasn't much I could do about it.

I headed over to Wave of the Day. The front door had been propped open, and a steady stream of soapy water was cascading down the front steps. Meagan was balancing between two chairs and firing a power washer in short bursts like an Uzi. She was soaking. If this were a wet T-shirt contest, she'd win it easily. Meagan saw me enter and took a shot at my feet, raking a stinging stream of high-pressure water over my toes.

"Hey," I said. "That hurt."

"I just washed the floor," Meagan said, delicately stepping down from the chairs. "Watch your dirty feet."

I kicked off my flip-flops and nearly landed on my ass. The soapy concrete floor was like an ice rink. Meagan shut off the power washer and slid over to me, elegant as she did a little spin.

"You're a figure skater," I said.

"More like a hockey mom," she said.

She handed me the water gun and motioned for me to wrap up its hose.

"Where did you get this?" It was a pretty impressive gas-powered job, the kind that can take the paint off a wall or the skin off your toes.

"I borrowed it from the *policía*," she said.

"Did you have to flash them your boobs? Not that I care," I said, caring a little.

"Just my smile, darling," she said, smiling.

She did have a great smile.

"They need these to wash the blood off the highway after all the big wrecks."

"Or the shoot-outs," I said.

"Those, too."

Meagan had gutted the place. All the chairs were upside down on the tables. The posters were gone, and the walls had been blasted with soap and water. Both *baño* doors were open, and I could see that the toilets and sinks had been scrubbed down and sanitized.

"Where are the boys?" I asked.

"I let them hitchhike up to Vallarta. They wanted to sneak into the bullfights."

"Don't coddle them, Meagan."

And she gave me a hockey-mom glare. "I trust my kids to make the best choices."

"Between what? Dangerous and dumb?"

"It's not a perfect world. The sooner they know that, the better they'll be able to navigate it."

"I think they already know it's not perfect." It was going to be hard to continue this conversation without making Meagan feel guilty.

"You were the one who said people can get over stuff," Meagan said.

"We can," I said. "I've gotten over some doozies."

"Like what?"

"Like I'm so far over them I forgot."

I walked over to the walk-in cooler. I could hear the refrigeration unit running. And now that I thought of it, the lights were on and Meagan was blasting the stereo.

"How did you get the electricity back on?" I asked.

Meagan smiled. "You're not the only one around here with money," she said.

"Well, I was—up until yesterday, anyway."

"I sold my business. So I was able to pay the electric bill."

She was pretty proud of herself. *We have a new lucky breadwinner.*

"Your business?" I asked, a little confused.

"My jewelry business."

"That's, like, an umbrella with a plastic chair." It was a pretty mean thing to say.

"I had some precious stones, too. Some onyx. Some jade and obsidian. That was my medium. I was known for it. It's why I renamed my boys."

I didn't want to tell Meagan how high on the cringe-factor scale that was.

"For how much?" I asked.

"A lot," she said. "Two thousand pesos."

"Wow, that's *almost* a hundred and ten dollars."

"It was enough to get the electricity back on. So I think it qualifies me as a full partner."

"In what?"

"This place. The Wave of the Day."

"That's a pretty good deal."

"Oh, yeah? How much did you put up?"

Nothing.

"Don't I get points for getting rid of the body?"

"I think that's up to the jury," she said, smiling again.

We both seemed to be getting over the Winsor doozy pretty well.

"I've already forged my name onto the liquor license. And if you're good, I can forge your name on it, too."

Forgery is a cottage industry down in Mexico. It is why attorneys are less important than *notarios*—who do most of the forgeries. So Meagan was in good company.

"When?" I asked.

"When I know that I can trust you."

"Trust me?" I shook my head.

Then I opened the cooler's heavy door and looked down at Winsor's old spot on the concrete floor. I could smell bleach. The floor had been repainted.

"It's like he was never here," I said.

"As far as I'm concerned."

Meagan grabbed a chair in each hand and flipped them right side up and underneath a table. She grabbed two more and then looked at me.

"Are we partners?"

I nodded slowly. Meagan was pretty irresistible.

"Okay, then," she said. "Gimme a hand with these chairs."

25

It had been raining for a couple of days straight. The river through town was a raging mud funnel, and Bahía de Sabanita was chocolate brown. When the waves broke off the point, they had an ominous lavalike quality. It was a good day to skip surfing the home break—unless you wanted to beef up your viral load.

I'd been promising the boys I would take them to surf this spot on the other side of the peninsula called Surprises, so after Jade aced an algebra quiz online and I'd force-fed Obsidian another chapter of *The Outsiders*, we headed over to Punta de Mirador.

"Whenever you see a line of pelicans flying in low across the water," I said, driving too fast and dodging potholes, "get ready."

"For what?" Jade asked.

"To duck bird shit," Obsidian said.

He was stretched out across the back seat. Jade was riding shotgun. They both laughed.

"It means a wave set is coming in," I said.

"Is this, like, another quiz?" Jade asked.

"It's insider surfer information," I said. "Pelicans are lazy—like you guys with your homeschooling—so they look for the easiest way to get around. By riding on the air that's pushed up as the ocean rises when a set of waves is coming in, they get a free lift."

"Are you sure that's true?" Jade asked.

"It's total fact," I said. "Just watch next time you see some pelicans gliding just above the water—guaranteed, a few seconds later there'll be sweet waves."

And for a second, I thought back to that pelican I'd seen with his wing chewed off—that poor bastard wasn't going to be gliding anywhere. I hoped it had died.

"That kinda sounds like crap, Nick," Obsidian said.

But before I could debate him about it, an odd horse-laugh filled the Suburban.

Jade feigned obliviousness and looked straight ahead. Then the horse laughed again. It was another one of those custom iPhone rings. I stared at Jade for as long as I could without driving off the road.

The horse laughed once more.

"Jade, is that Winsor's iPhone?" I asked. I was trying to sound like a tough dad.

Jade nodded slowly. "Yeah."

"I thought I put it in my drawer."

"I borrowed it back. And I changed the ring so it wasn't his."

I held out an open palm, and he handed me the iPhone just as the horse laughed for the fourth time.

I answered it. "FBI Pedophile Division. How may I help you?"

Obsidian burst out laughing in the back seat.

"They hung up," I said.

I handed the iPhone back to Jade.

"You can keep that," I said, and then I nearly added *you earned it* but caught myself. "I mean, what the hell—right?"

"It doesn't matter. The battery's almost dead."

"I'll get you a charger."

I cracked open the window to let out what was left of Winsor's ghost.

"How were the bullfights?" I asked.

"We didn't go," Obsidian said. "We just told Mom we were going so she wouldn't worry."

"That's not cool," I said. "People always need to know where you're going in Mexico."

"Why?" Jade asked.

"So if you end up not coming home, at least we know where to start looking for you."

I tried to say it in a way that didn't sound too paranoid, but I think I was still suffering a little PTSD from my encounter with El Jefe.

"We went to the cockfights," Jade said. "Over in San Carlos. And that would have pissed Mom off."

"Yeah," Obsidian said. "Especially when she found out it was only with roosters."

Jade whirled and smacked Obsidian on the side of the head.

"Don't say stuff like that," Jade said. "I told you."

Obsidian backed off. I could see he was a little intimidated by his stepbrother.

"It was just a joke," Obsidian said. "She's my mom, too, you know."

"Not really, she isn't."

"Yes, she is. My stepmom."

"You're just borrowing her," Jade said. "That's all. It's not even legal."

Obsidian was very close to crying, and it wasn't because Jade had smacked him.

"Dudes, look," I said. "Real brothers and stepdads, moms and pops—it gets too complicated. It's really much more about how you treat each other, and if you care or not."

"I'm not caring if he's going to say perverted crap about my mom," Jade said.

They both looked out different windows and in opposite directions.

But then Obsidian surprised me. "I'm sorry, Jade," he said. It sounded like he meant it.

"Okay," Jade said.

I think the boys knew they needed to protect what little bit of family they had.

"I've never been to a cockfight," I said.

"They're pretty gross," Jade said. "But the roosters wear these razor blades on their feet, so it's over in, like, ten seconds."

"Did you bet?"

"Of course," Obsidian said. "It's not the freaking ballet."

He was a smart-assed little punk. I'd give him that.

"It's still pretty inhumane," I said.

"Why?" Obsidian said. "The winning rooster gets all petted and kissed. He probably gets laid. The losers get eaten. So what?"

"I thought the eggs got laid," I said. "After the roosters lay the hens, right? But what comes first?"

Jade laughed, and I knew it was coming.

"The chicken or the egg?" he shrieked.

"Good one," I said, with thumbs-up to Jade.

But Obsidian was way too cool for this. "What, you think chickens commit suicide just so you can eat them?" he said. "It's the food chain. Everybody's on the menu."

"If you were on the menu, I'd be a vegetarian," Jade said.

"If you were a vegetarian, I'd kick your asparagus," Obsidian said, and they both started to laugh like hell.

I was really loving hanging out with these guys. It was like a coffee break with car salesmen—everybody trying to outsmart each other, but everyone a little precious and thin-skinned, too.

Nobody wants to grow up to be a car salesman. It is always a second or third career choice. No kid asks to be an orphan, either. I never thought I'd be someone who *used to be* a dad. But all of a sudden, this didn't feel so *used to be*. It felt like that real family Meagan talked about—and for the first time in a long time, it didn't feel so bad.

26

The ocean was a lot closer to its standard aqua blue on the south side of Punta de Mirador, and the wave was pretty good. Surprises is a mostly sweet right point break with a little bit of a left that can roll off its backside. The wave starts out fat and slow, which lets you take off a lot deeper than you think you can, and then drops you into a *look-Mom-no-hands* glide, as if you were riding an old favorite beach cruiser.

The ride can be as long as the Huntington Beach Pier, but the wave can wall up and get nasty, too. On epic days, Surprises can even cough up head-and-a-half full curtain barrels—although I have never stood behind the privilege.

It was just the three of us for the first hour. Surprises is surrounded by a few all-inclusive, Mexican-style Vegas-knockoff resorts that cater to rich Mexicans and the cheap gringo *turistas* who are attracted to the 24/7 all-you-can-eat-and-drink buffets. These places are basically obesity farms. Very few surfers stay there, which was why I was surprised to see this dude paddling out from one of the private beaches.

As he paddled closer, though, it made more sense. He was floating on one of those ninety-nine-dollar Wavestorm soft tops sold at Walmart, the kind that anyone who's been surfing for longer than ten minutes calls a foamy. He was wearing a DayGlo rash guard with a hood that had a tinted visor attached. The guy looked more like a welder who repairs guardrails at night than a surfer.

He was also wearing rubber booties. Real surfers don't wear booties.

The boys waved. The man didn't wave back, but maybe it was hard to see through the tinted visor. He paddled around us and way off to the outside. Then he turned to face the shore, which is the exact opposite of what a surfer should do. It looked like he was watching us instead of keeping a lookout to sea for the bigger wave sets.

Surprises is known for this mutant rogue wave—which is the *surprise*, I think—that shows up out the back at least a few times a day. It doesn't matter what the swell direction is or whether the tide is high or low. If the break is working, you can count on an outside monster every few hours.

I've made it a bunch of times, and it's one of my all-time favorite waves. But it usually catches the shortboarders way inside. Which is a nice payback for guys like me. I was thinking that I should maybe paddle over and warn Mr. Wavestorm that he was sitting in a sketchy spot, but it wasn't really up to me to be this guy's waterman.

The first contest I was going to have the boys enter, now that Meagan had designated me the family surf coach, was the Mexican Junior Nationals, coming up at a break called El Tigre. What little I knew about competitive surfing is what I got from watching the World Surf League online.

The WSL is all about "speed, power, flow"—something we used to call "fast, strong, and smooth." Basic fundamentals. But now there's also a lot of vertical up and down on the wave face, with big snaps and fins above the lip— but who knows what the judges might be looking for down here in Mexico.

Obsidian was the more aggressive surfer, and his surfing had a lot of pop. He'd paddle into the riskiest takeoffs and go for the biggest airs. But Jade had a natural style, a lighter touch. There was an elflike quality to his surfing. Like a water spider, and he pranced rather than punched, with silky cutbacks and big round rail turns.

Jade took off on a head-high wave and linked up a couple of sweet roundies before snapping an air reverse into the closeout.

Obsidian hooted at his stepbrother, "*Sick.*"

And we could hear someone else cheering. I looked over to the guy on the foamy sitting on the outside. He was clapping like a seal—and completely unaware of the humongous wave rolling in behind him.

"Out the back," I shouted. "Go hard!"

The three of us began paddling like maniacs so we wouldn't have to take this outside bomb on our heads, and maybe one of us might even make it—but it wasn't going to be me. Because I kept stopping to raise both arms and wave.

"Hey, amigo, look behind you!" I shouted to the guy on the foamy. "Paddle!"

But the kook just waved back—until this mammoth sucked him up like a bug into a vacuum cleaner and he disappeared under a wall of detonating white water.

It was a crazy big wave, but Obsidian was just able to backdoor it into a pretty decent barrel. I took what was left on the head, and Jade belly-rode ten feet of froth to shore.

The DayGlo kook got the Neptune massage—platinum level—and was battered a couple of hundred yards down the beach.

I could see him sitting on the sand, wrapped up in some kelp.

I paddled over to him.

He had a bloody nose, and about the first six inches of foam had been snapped off his Wavestorm. The guy looked Japanese, and I wasn't sure if he could speak English. I don't see a lot of Asians down here, except for my stepkid. People tell me it's because Mexico isn't clean enough.

"Are you okay?" I asked.

The guy didn't respond. He was checking for loose teeth.

"¿Cómo está?" I said.

Finally, the guy nodded.

"*Bueno*," he said.

He stood up and examined the broken tip of his Wavestorm.

"Do you think the board rental place will charge me for this?" he asked, like a slightly obnoxious American.

Despite his bloody nose, I didn't have much sympathy for the guy. His energy was a little rude.

"Probably," I said.

"But wasn't that surfing?" he asked. "Shouldn't the board be able to do that without breaking?"

"That was tsunami-ing," I said, and shook my head. "The boards aren't designed for that."

He pointed a bootie at the jagged white foam where the soft top's nose should have been.

"Is that called a ding?"

"That's called a broken surfboard. They're going to make you buy it," I said.

"That's not fair," he said.

"Maybe," I said.

He started to walk off but then tripped over the Wavestorm's surf leash. It was still attached to his ankle.

"It's easier to walk if you take off your leash," I said.

"I know," he said, and uncuffed his leash.

He wiped some blood off his nose and looked out at the waves.

"Surfing is hard, isn't it?"

"Harder than it looks when it's done right," I said.

"Like those guys do it." He pointed toward Jade and

Obsidian. They were already paddling back out and effortlessly duck-diving through the breakers.

"Are they your kids?"

"Sorta," I said.

"They're good, aren't they?"

"I think so," I said, prouder than I had been in years.

27

A few days after our session at Surprises I figured it was time to go grab the rest of my new stepfamily's stuff, so I woke Meagan up and asked her for the key to Winsor's casa. Our moving in together was about to go public. The boys needed to change T-shirts, and I wanted my toothbrush back.

Meagan barely opened her eyes, but from her sleepy garble I guessed that she said the key was under the pot to the left of Winsor's front door—or if I find pot, to please bring her back some more.

I figured I'd better make a showing at Winsor's place anyway—just so his neighbors would know that the best friend Winsor had in Sabanita was still looking out for him. When Winsor would take off unexpectedly, sometimes he'd send me an e-mail and ask me to check on his place.

He didn't have any dogs or cats to feed, but one time he left his fancy Sony flat-screen on for two weeks. It had been tuned to one of those around-the-clock religious channels broadcasting a Catholic telethon with special-guest exorcists and singing nuns.

The place didn't have glass windows. No screens—just wrought-iron bars, so the whole neighborhood could hear the righteous witnessing twenty-four seven. It had nearly turned the guy next door into an atheist by the time I could get in and shut the TV off.

Winsor wasn't the most social guy around, and except for Meagan and the boys and me, not that many *locals* bothered to get to know him well enough even to say hola. The Wave of the Day catered to tourists, if it catered to anybody. Winsor was more about the gigantic quadruple-shot margarita than genuine Mexican chow. He'd rather sell I GOT HAMMERED BY THE WAVE OF THE DAY T-shirts than read travel blog raves about how authentic his tamales were.

He also hadn't had a lot of surf buds, because he was such an ampy prick in the lineup. Winsor was forever paddling out and sitting on your inside without waiting his turn, spewing some mysto calculus about being the surfer who was closest to the wave's peak, which justified his taking two or three or four of the best waves, one right after the other.

"If you just surfed two great waves in a row," I'd tell him, "one of them wasn't yours."

"If you want more waves, learn to surf better," he'd scream as he barged his way back to the front of the lineup.

Surfing isn't something surfers do on vacation. It's not zip-lining. Maybe that's why some surfers can get so territorial, because they've given up so much for it—good relationships and real careers. I started selling Chevys because the car lot was close to Swami's, and for those guys living off shaved ice and Hapa Browns on Oahu, it's a way of life. We called them the Wolf Pack because they were so hungry for waves and ready to chase off any stranger who got too close. I think Winsor had some of that in him and maybe it's why he ended up so crazy—and dangerous.

But after I hit that tree with my son in the front seat, surfing became more therapy than obsession, and probably the one thing that helped me survive myself. Dealing with this new head of mine has knocked a lot of the agro out of me. As if that bullet was dipped in aloha. Or maybe almost losing everything turns up the mellow in everybody. It's hard to tell.

28

Winsor's casa was a two-bedroom cinder-block pillbox with a steel roof and a small backyard filled with marijuana plants surrounded by electrified barbed wire.

The key was under the pot, but all the pot in Winsor's backyard had been plundered. The power had been shut off so none of the lights worked. The potlifters probably figured no one was home and trampled down his beloved high-voltage fence.

Winsor used to brag to me about his banana-sized marijuana buds, but there wasn't one left. If he hadn't been dead, he'd be in tears. But he was dead, thanks to me and my two accomplices—three, actually, if you count the original perpette.

And Meagan really had wanted Winsor to die—*unlike me, your honor.*

But then I remembered Meagan's statistic about how ninety percent of Mexican crime goes unsolved, and I felt better. I was still trying to forget José's telling me that the statistic was just something the *locals* made up to spook gringas into the safe arms of Mexican men.

The idea of José and Meagan building castles in the sand—with their feet—pushed my jealousy button a little more than I wanted to admit.

The Town & Country that Winsor had surfed at Gagger's was on the living-room floor. I had always coveted Glenn Pangs—there was something about the Hawaiian history of his boards that felt magical. But his shapes are too low-volume for a fat longboarder like me.

The two tiny bedrooms were connected off the living-room wall, and opposite was a kitchen nook. A military-style steel bunk bed was in one bedroom, and a plastic waterbed without sheets was in the other. The *baño* was dark and cramped, with a tile commode–shower combination and a metal wastepaper basket full of poop-crumpled toilet paper.

The whole casa couldn't have taken up more than five hundred square feet. I couldn't imagine four people living in this place for more than a weekend without wanting to kill each other.

Oops.

I grabbed a couple of pillowcases and began stuffing them with Meagan's bathroom junk—hairbrushes and toothbrushes, some black soap, a bag of makeup. Then I raked up a half dozen pairs of surf shorts and T-shirts for the boys, and yanked a few of Meagan's yoga pants off a bathroom clothesline.

It wasn't like these people had very much, so it didn't take me long to do a clean sweep. And on a wicked impulse I decided to snatch the TC Pang for Jade—more spoils from his war with Winsor. The board was a little big, but it would fit him better than the one he was riding, and he could grow into it. I also pocketed the iPhone charger.

Winsor's brand-new MacBook Pro was half-hidden under a ratty chair cushion at the kitchen table. It supposedly had all this hot new technology, which Winsor had bragged to me about after he'd smuggled it down on his last loop up to the US. He said the solid-state drive was the only way to go in our salty tropical air.

For sure this MacDaddy would get pinched once someone spotted it through the windows. I caught myself zoning out on the shiny white Apple logo for an oblong moment or two. I tried to shake it off and stuffed the laptop into a pillowcase—it felt like a miniblackout, and it made me a little jittery.

Then something started to smell—like wires burning somewhere—and I had this crazy taste in my mouth. It tasted like Bakelite.

THE SUN WAS SHINING DIRECTLY IN MY EYES. IT WAS STREAMING through a barred window, and for a second I wondered if I was in jail. But then I thought that maybe I had slipped in the shower and hit my head, because my face was wet. I wiped at it with both hands. I was a little clumsy, and my fingers felt numb and stiff. The wetness stung my eyes.

I looked at my hands. They were covered in blood.

I sat up.

The table in Winsor's kitchen nook had been knocked over. His infamous flat-screen was cracked. The two stuffed pillowcases were intact, but one of them was saturated with blood.

I got to my feet, went into the *baño*, and stared at myself in the mirror. I was white as a snowman. There was a three-inch gash above my good eye, and I had lost my patch. I looked back into the tiny living room.

There wasn't much space in there for a full-fledged fit thrown by a full-grown man. A bookcase was tipped on its side. The standing water pipe was broken.

That metallic taste and funny smell sometimes happen to epileptics right before a grand mal. Nobody knows why, exactly. What I did know was that I'd just had a really big one.

29

The four of us were sitting around the table at the front of my casa. The sun was setting. That *real family* vibe was a little strained. A teakettle started to whistle. Meagan had made toast.

I had replaced my missing eye patch with a basic black one. But the boys were staring at the gash on my forehead. My lip was still bleeding a little.

"I don't think that's deep enough for stitches," Obsidian said, breaking the ice and folding up a piece of toast like a tortilla and taking a bite.

"I do," Jade said.

"This feels like a family meeting," I said.

"Our first," Meagan said. "We were worried."

"Well, it's nice we're enough of a family now to worry, isn't it?" I said.

"Mom was worried," Obsidian said. "But I wasn't."

"I was," Jade said.

"There's nothing to worry about," I said.

Meagan got up, turned off the stove, and poured the boiling water into a teapot.

"I think you owe the boys a better explanation."

"About what?"

"Secrecy."

"So *I'm* the stepfamily expert on secrecy now?"

"We'll take turns with it, then," Meagan said. "You first."

I let Meagan pour me some tea.

"How much do you know?" I asked.

"I know that the binge therapy thing doesn't seem to be working out so well for you. Winsor told me about that. It sounds like an excuse to get high."

"Self-medicating isn't getting high. And it works. Smoking pot is getting high."

"Smoking pot is maintenance. And if self-medicating works so well, how come you have a big cut on your forehead and your lip is bleeding?"

I tried to laugh, but my throat was too dry.

"Mom says you're an epileptic," Jade said.

"Thanks, Mom," I said, glaring over at Meagan. "I thought you and Winsor weren't that close."

"We had our moments," she said, and then winked at me obnoxiously.

I looked back at the boys.

"Are you?" Jade asked.

"Who cares?" Obsidian shrugged at me like he was a comrade.

"I do," Meagan said.

"Well, then, no, I'm not—not officially. I mean, I wasn't born that way. I'm a TBI victim, which means that I can have seizures like an epileptic. But it's temporary."

"Sometimes it's temporary," Meagan said, like someone who knew how to surf the net. "But you have to take your meds regularly."

"And I would if they worked," I said, burning slowly.

"Is TBI like tuberculosis?" Obsidian asked.

"It means 'traumatic brain injury,' genius," Jade said.

"Very traumatic," I said. "I got shot in the head." I flipped up my patch and then held open my eyelid with two fingers. "And that's where the bullet went in—that hole right there."

My eye socket was an ugly red gouge of scarred muscle and leaky goo. I was hoping to freak the boys out, but they just leaned in closer to get a better look.

"Does it hurt?" Jade asked.

"Only when I cry," I said.

"Don't be an ass," Meagan said.

I took a bite of toast and pointed to my eye patch. "This is private, Meagan. There's personal stuff in here."

"Fine," she said. "But the boys are my personal stuff, and I don't want you to drive them anymore unless you go back on some medication."

"This was a onetime thing, Meagan."

"Two times, actually."

Meagan stared at me as I winced for an instant and recalled when Marshall and I hit that tree, the smell of sap and the ugly jazz of bending metal and shattering glass. "But you let them hitchhike to cockfights?"

"Bullfights," Meagan said. "There is a difference."

I looked over at the boys, and their look was begging me not to bust them. I let the opportunity pass. I was usually on their side, and I should probably stay there.

"What do I get?" I asked.

"You get to not have fits and drive the kids."

"No. I mean in standard-family *give-and-take*, what do you kick in?"

"Since when do we qualify as a *standard* family?"

"Pretend," I said.

Meagan sipped her tea. "I don't think I have to do anything."

I sipped mine and dipped a piece of crust. Dainty and smug.

"You could give up pot, Mom," Obsidian said.

"That would be great," Jade said.

"I don't smoke that much," Meagan said, as self-conscious as I had ever seen her.

"You're, like, the wake-and-bake Marley Mom," Jade said. "We're not dumb."

"This isn't about me," Meagan said.

"But all of a sudden it is, isn't it?" I was gloating. It was nice to be out of the spotlight. "It's something that would really make this family better. It's just a little thing. Pot's not addictive. You could do it, right?"

"Sure, I could," she said. "If I wanted to."

It was fun to overplay my hand. I was pretty sure Meagan wouldn't call my bluff.

"Yeah, I mean, she quit eating wheat," Obsidian said, taking his stepmom's side.

"Exactly," Meagan said.

"That's only because gluten can't get you high." I was grinning.

"Okay," Meagan said. "I'll quit."

I stopped grinning.

"It'll be good for the boys to see that I can do something like this."

Jade and Obsidian bumped fists. They were thrilled, and under different circumstances I would have been, too. But I had apparently just made a deal to go back on antiseizure medication.

"But you have to put your glass eye back in, too," Meagan said.

She might have been looking for an out. She was an inveterate pothead.

"How did you know about that?" I asked.

"Winsor told me everything." She glanced at the boys. "Almost everything."

"A glass eye?" Jade said. "That is so cool."

"It's an ocular prosthesis," I said. "But I'm not ashamed of the way I look. So what's the point of wearing it?"

"So you could stop being special?" Meagan snarked, tearing the crust off her toast as if it was a Band-Aid.

"There's nothing special about not having an eye," I said.

"Yeah, there is," Meagan said. "That patch gets every-one to back off. You get to keep your distance and do this whole *pirata* thing."

I was pretty stunned that I had let myself get sucked into this conversation and, even worse, agreed to a deal about my meds—and maybe even my glass eye.

"Does it look like a real eye?" Jade asked.

"Sort of," I said.

"Can we see it?" Obsidian asked.

"Maybe," I said.

30

I was pissed off. And it wasn't because going back on Epilim or wearing my fake eye again was any big deal. It wasn't. It was probably a good thing, even. I had been turning into a grumpy old gringo—one who didn't really care enough about how he looked or what he did.

What pissed me off was how easily Meagan had out-maneuvered me. How she had me throw in the free floor mats and the extended warranty *and* make her a deal below dealer cost.

But she was dead-on about the eye patch. It was part of my *sympathy* brand, and I did use it to stake out the space I liked to keep between myself and everybody else and to push off tedious obligations and that *be your own hero* bull-shit. I wasn't above faking a slipped disk as an excuse to skip big wave days and their inevitable hold-downs and flossings.

I hadn't always been like this. There was a time when hunting down sick bombs while scared shitless or hungover was the sweetest kind of winning—like selling an expensive car to a buyer who had a bad credit rating, or cheating on your wife without getting caught. There was an addictive challenge to it all. It was fun to pull off the tricks and pimp the kooks.

Then I got shot—and meeting Mr. Mortality face-to-face changed everything. When I shook his hand, I felt how weak my grip on reality was and how dumb lucky most of us are. If people knew how close we live to chaos and catastrophe—and how random it is—they'd freak. It's right next door.

I kept my glass-eye kit in this cooler I had stacked on a shelf in the back of my bodega. It was already about midnight, and Meagan and the kids had been conked out for hours. The night was moonless and pitch-black, so I had to be careful of scorpions as I rummaged through all my special stuff—stuff so special that I kept it in an unlocked bodega in Mexico.

It was mostly my passport and birth certificate, an old wedding ring, a fake Rolex, three Car Salesman of the Year awards, a Little League team photo, and a vibrator that I'd found in my ex-wife's golf bag—she told me it was her caddy's.

I located my glass-eye kit, which looked like a fake-leather man purse. Inside, there was a little velvet bag for the shiny little box that held the shiny, spoon-shaped ocular prosthesis—a sightless orb whose only advantage was that it didn't get bloodshot on drinking binges.

It's okay, officer, I was driving with my other eye.

My OP came with an instructional DVD, a short video that I was encouraged to review regularly in case I forgot how to put in my eye. But putting in a glass eye is about as difficult as putting on a condom. And it gets easier the more you do it—in the dark, standing or sitting, in a public john or in the privacy of your own home. Back in my prime, I could even put one in—or on—while driving.

But now I was probably a little rusty, so I slipped the man purse's handy strap over my shoulder. I didn't want to drop my eye in the dark and have it carted off by a tarantula.

I headed up toward Puerto Vallarta and Farmacia Guadalajara, an upstart drugstore chain that was open twenty-four hours a day, seven days a week. It was a great place to score some Vicodin or Percodan without a prescription, but tonight I was just hoping to cop some Epilim. If they didn't have Epilim, I'd settle for Topamax.

If they didn't have either, I'd go back to my old booze-and-blow regimen. I was sure Meagan would understand—and immediately spark a fatty.

I stopped at the Pemex about halfway to PV and ran into the *baño* while the Suburban was being filled up. The *baño* was spotless. I locked the door and took out my glass-eye kit. It had been a couple of years—at least—since I had worn this thing.

I'd never taken the necessary time to do the eye-socket exercises my oculist recommended, so I hadn't developed any muscle memory or directional control over my new eye. Whenever I saw myself in a photograph or a mirror, my fake eye always had a weird cast, like I was trying to look around a corner or down some lady's blouse.

Of course, the eye couldn't see—it was a decoy. But I still got my fair share of cold-shoulder glares from women who thought I was trying to steal a cheap look at their breasts.

The color of my glass eye matched my real one perfectly, and I had to admit that it appeared authentic—authentically cross-eyed, instead of half-blind, which was sort of a lose-lose.

I was going to give it another try, anyway. I rinsed off my glass eye with some cold tap water, something I was always told never to do.

But señor, this is Mexican *tap water.*

On the second try, I was able to massage my glass eye into place perfectly, just like the old days. I stared at myself in the mirror. Not bad.

"You look younger with two eyes," I said.

I tossed my *pirata* eye patch in the trash can and exited the *baño*. I tipped the *baño* lady two hundred pesos, and I winked at her with my new eye.

"Gracias, señora!"

But she just checked the buttons on her blouse.

I paid the gas guy, but he didn't seem to notice that I was now patchless. Maybe this was only a big deal to me.

I jumped into my Suburban, hit the gas, and headed toward Vallarta and the new Farmacia Guadalajara. I had to wake up the *farmacéutico*. He was asleep behind the counter, a Padres cap pulled over his eyes and iPod earbuds

stuck in his ears. I had to shake him a few times and un-
plug one of the buds.

"Dude, yo," I said.

The music was so cranked, I could hear it from the dangling bud. He was listening to a Spanish cover of Alanis
Morissette's "You Oughta Know," which made me consider,
not for the first time, just how universal the getting-totally-
fucked-over experience is.

"Por favor?" I asked.

I handed him a plastic pill bottle with a twist-and-turn
childproof cap and an old Epilim prescription pasted on
it—600 mg, every twenty-four hours.

"¿Seis meses?"

The *farmacéutico* looked at the bottle, shrugged, and
disappeared into a back room. I was hoping that he was
going to nod out again.

I did my best, Meagan.

But a few minutes later he returned with a small stack
of Epilim sample packages, the kind that doctors get for
free from the pharmaceutical sales guys.

"*Sólo tres meses,*" he said. "*Lo siento.*"

I assured him in fluent Spanglish that I'd probably know
before the three-month mark if I had run into any trees. At
least, that's what I thought I told him—by the look on his
face, he might have thought I was trying to explain *fútbol
de fantasía.*

Three months' worth of Epilim samples costs 3,000
pesos, about 150 US, a little more than a dollar a day—
pretty reasonable, really, to keep from throwing fits.

And it was nice not to get that *what's-with-the-eye-patch* look from the *farmacéutico*. Now I was just like any other droopy-eyed gringo buying pharmaceuticals without a valid prescription in the middle of the night.

I kept checking myself out in the rearview like someone with a new haircut. I had to admit, I liked the way my eye looked. It made me want to party. So I decided to wash down my first hit of Epilim with a shot of Cuervo Gold.

But then an old alarm clanged in my head. I took one of the Epilim sample boxes out of the bag and read the label: "Do not take with alcohol."

Shit.

There it was. That insatiable flag of restraint—waving right in my face.

31

Jade and I were playing hooky from homeschooling—off on a sort of stepfather-stepson surfing safari. We had the windows of the Suburban wide open, and a big, brassy Mexican march was blasting on the AM radio.

Obsidian was casa-bound with the Sabanita crud, a hybrid streptococcus–flu combo that victimizes nearly everyone in town at some time during the rainy season. A lot of bacteria floats around in the water systems down here in August and September, but I like to think that it inoculates the *local* immune systems against the coming gringo invasion—which would begin again at the end of October.

We were heading two hours south to Alacráns, an almost world-class left break when the summer swell is big. Winsor's old TC Pang would work pretty much like a big-wave gun for Jade, which was good because Buoyweather.com was forecasting fifteen feet. My Red Fin and I would have been thrilled with half that.

"It's going to be fun to work on your backside today," I said, and then immediately grimaced.

Jade was playing with a map app on Winsor's iPhone. It didn't look like what I said had rocked him much.

"Sorry, dude," I said. "Poor choice of words."

Jade shut off the iPhone.

"I'm still a virgin," Jade said.

I wasn't sure how to respond.

"Yeah, well, of course," I said. "Virginity is a state of mind, mostly. I mean, if someone forced you at gunpoint to climb Mount Everest, you couldn't really count it until you did it on your own."

Jade looked at me as if I'd just made the lamest comparison in the history of incomparables.

"I mean a *virgin*," he said. "A real one. Like Lady Gaga."

Exactly like Lady Gaga, probably—for appearances only.

"This can be any way you need it to be, Jade," I said. "No one is going to blame you for how you want to store this stuff."

Jade was getting frustrated. And I wasn't making it any easier.

"I was never penetrated," Jade said. "Winsor never—he never *f-worded* me."

He seemed pretty clearheaded about it.

"*¿Comprende?*" Jade asked.

I could feel the steering wheel getting a little slippery.

"What do you mean?" I asked.

"He just wanted me to take selfies without my clothes on," he said. "Then he took some of himself."

"That's what was going on in the cooler?"

"With his iPhone," Jade said. "He said people do it all the time—politicians. Everybody. Like it's no big deal."

"It's a big deal if you're thirteen and he's forty," I said. "It's a big-deal felony."

"I knew it was wrong," Jade said. "But if we *sextexted* our own pictures, it's legal."

"That's a lie," I said. "Why didn't you tell your mom that that was what happened?"

"Seemed pretty pointless. Winsor already had this hammer sticking out of his head."

I flashed to Winsor's execution on José's panga boat and then shook it off.

"So he didn't—*f-word* you?"

Jade shook his head. "He said he got money for pictures like that and he was going to give me some for mine. But he never did. Because Mom killed him."

"You have to tell her what really happened, Jade."

"Why?"

"Because the truth matters."

"Not more than she does. Mom was protecting me. I gotta carry this for her."

I was very close to telling Jade that his mom didn't kill Winsor—but I didn't have the courage.

Jade turned and looked at me. He was pleading.

"You can't tell her," he said.

"I won't," I said.

32

We hadn't said anything more to each other for about the next twenty minutes. Then I turned off the highway and onto a narrow jungle path that was barely wide enough for the Suburban. I had to pull in the side-view mirrors.

Jade had slipped back into his Maps app. He seemed to be a pretty tough kid and oddly squared away, given the circumstances and the bullshit in his life. I wondered if my son could be so tough, and how he might be handling the mess I'd left him. But I couldn't wonder about it for very long—I never could. It just emptied me out.

I busted the Suburban through a grove of dying banana trees and then pulled up to a small, rocky beach just behind the high-tide line. Alacráns was howling. Double overhead. Clean.

Jade and I grabbed our boards. We checked our leashes

for frayed loops and waxed up. Jade headed to the sand, and I followed him. He put down his board and started to stretch. It was a pretty serious routine, and I had never seen him do it before.

"When did you start stretching?" I asked him. My idea of a presurf warm-up is bending down to put on the leash.

"I saw it on YouTube. All the pros do it."

"And you guys want to be pros?"

"Obsidian does. I just love to surf."

Jade checked his leash one more time and snapped on its cuff. Then he made a special effort to slap-shake my hand with an added fist bump.

"Come on," Jade said.

"You go ahead. I want to get a good look at your surfing from the beach first," I said, trying to sound like a legitimate coach.

"Your loss."

Alacráns looked ready to go off even bigger than advertised on the surf report, so it was a little irresponsible for me to let Jade paddle out on his own.

"You don't have to surf this," I said.

"Are you crazy?" Jade said. "Of course I do." And in two steps he was in the water and hydroplaning down the back of the shore break.

"Surf smart," I shouted, like a pussy.

I was supposed to be coaching these kids, and we did have the Junior Nationals coming up—but the obvious reason I didn't go out with Jade was because when Alacráns gets this big, it scares me.

I was surprised that we hadn't seen any other surfers. Not that they'd be lifeguards. You always have to be your own waterman, but I'd rather Jade wasn't out there by himself. It wasn't one of my prouder moments—and then I had this sick-to-my-stomach feeling that maybe it was going to get too big for anybody who actually knew Alacráns, and that's why nobody was here.

I could see whitecaps about a half mile offshore, south of the point. The big sets were starting to stack up. It was near high tide, and usually that means the waves are smaller. Alacráns is a low-tide break. The wave gets bigger as the tide drops.

Unless the swell is really huge—like it was looking today—and then Alacráns can break gigantic on a high tide, and very close to shore. The place is an elephant graveyard for broken boards, and it's had its share of broken necks, too. There is blood in the water here.

It is also the sea urchin capital of Mexico.

Sea urchins are insidious baseball-sized globs of spines and slime that attach to rocks in the shallows. I have had the misfortune of stepping on at least a dozen of these ugly little pincushions over the years, and it has taken months to remove all the syringe-like spines that have broken off in my feet.

Jade was already a few hundred yards offshore, and it looked like he was having some trouble finding a channel out. I signaled for him to go around more to the outside, but I couldn't get his attention despite jumping up and down like a hired clown in front of a carwash.

A giant set came through, and Jade perfectly duck-dived under the first big wave. Then he barely scratched over the second one. But I did not see him come up after he dove under the third. I waited.

Jesus.

I grabbed my Red Fin and started to sprint toward the shore break. All I could think was that Jade had gotten his leash snagged on a piece of reef—which is how everyone figures Mark Foo drowned at Mavericks. And Foo was a real-deal Hawaiian waterman, not a thirteen-year-old boy whose *imbécil* of a *step*dad let him go out in monster surf all by himself.

I still couldn't see Jade, and I sprinted about a hundred yards up and down the beach, scanning the ocean and calling out for help. But it was useless. All I could see were whitecaps and closeouts—and what I was really trying to do was strap on a pair and man up. Finally, I just threw my Red Fin into the shore break and started stroking as hard and as fast as I could.

There wasn't time to try to find the channel. I had to go right at the heart of where I'd last seen Jade and just keep hammering toward the roiling white water and closeouts.

You can't duck-dive a longboard under a breaking wave the way Jade had on Winsor's old TC Pang, so getting out in big surf on something as floaty as the Red Fin can be a hard deal.

I had three choices as the sets came toward me. I could turn turtle, gripping the board over my head and angling it in a way that the wave *might* ride over me—generally a small-wave strategy. Or I could abandon my board and head to the bottom, holding on to my leash until the wave passed overhead, which is the smarter big-wave strategy.

Or I could paddle hard as hell up the face of the wave and try to smash over the lip and through the curling white water. This is known as the stupid strategy, and—not surprising, given the genius of my previous choices—was the one I went with. I wanted to keep my eye on where I'd last seen Jade.

It was a bad choice.

I never quite made it all the way over the lip of the wave, and instead I was hurled backward and down to the reef, collecting sea urchins with my ass as the shore break tumbled me back to the beach.

I ended up just a few feet from the sand. I grabbed my board and stood up. The water was barely knee-deep. I was standing on dozens of sea urchins—but I was so desperate to see Jade that I didn't feel a thing.

I scanned the horizon. There was a lull between sets. And then way out, maybe a half mile offshore, I saw a huge wave train—and then a tiny dot paddling down the face of the set wave.

It was Jade—absolutely killing triple-overhead Alacráns.

33

Dude, why didn't you come out?" Jade screamed as he rode the beach break onto the sand. "It was freaking epic!"

I was steadying myself on a palm tree with one hand and pulling sea urchin spines out of my left foot with the other. I had already finished with my right foot. But there was no way I could start on my ass without a mirror.

"I made one good wave and then got caught inside," I said, lying like hell. "But I saw you crushing it out there."

"I was okay?"

"Are you kidding? You killed it," I said. "But don't bend so much, and follow your hands through the turn."

As if I could see anything a quarter mile offshore. My critique was bullshit.

"You always tell me the same thing," Jade said. "You should have just come out."

Jade looked at my feet and then at the back of my blood-soaked board shorts.

"What happened?" Jade asked.

"I had an accident," I said. "I sat on some sea urchins."

"Why would you do that?" He was trying not to laugh.

"It was shallower than I thought."

"No, it's not. It's high tide. That's why the waves were so huge."

I shrugged. Jade could see that I had maybe been a little frightened.

"Were you worried about me?" he asked.

"Well, yeah. A little."

"Then why did you let me go out without you?"

"I figured it was time for you to challenge some big surf on your own," I said, lying like a phony. "I knew you could handle it. I was right here, though."

I wondered what the El Jefe rule was when it came to duplicity's first cousin—the *little white lie*, dishonesty's venial sin. The kind you use to not look like a coward to your kids, or when your wife asks you if her ass looks big.

"Thanks for believing in me," Jade said. He high-fived me and then hugged my neck.

"It was hard, but that's part of it, right? Part of you growing up." I felt like shit for not being up front with him, especially considering how brave he had been out there. "But I was scared, too," I said, in a blip of honesty. "I freak out surfing backside this big."

"Oh, yeah, right," Jade said, and laughed. "Like you're afraid of anything."

Jade picked up his board and wrapped his leash around the fins. "I'm starving."

"We can stop for tacos on the way home," I said. "Do you know how to drive?"

Jade went perfectly still. "Uh, no."

"Would you like to learn?"

"I'm not old enough."

"In Mexico everyone is old enough," I said. "And there's no way I can sit on this ass and drive."

I strapped my Red Fin to the Suburban's surf rack and put Jade's board behind the seats.

"Get in," I said. "On the driver's side."

Jade could barely contain himself. "I'm really driving?"

"Move the seat forward before I change my mind."

I knew this was just standard dad stuff—but it felt as pure and as wonderful as anything I have ever known.

"Have you ever taught anyone to drive before?" Jade asked.

He was nervous.

"I was a professional car salesman and auto demonstrator. You couldn't be in better hands."

"Don't let me hit anything," Jade said.

I let that one slide.

34

The Suburban's starter motor sounded like it was blending a batch of margaritas.

"Don't keep grinding it," I said.

Jade was holding the key fully forward as he floored the gas.

"Once the motor starts, back off on the ignition key." I reached over and loosened his death grip on the key.

"Sorry," Jade said.

"No worries. Everybody does it at first. And I'll bet your mom *still* does it."

I pointed to his bare foot, which was crushing the gas pedal against the floor. I slashed a couple of fingers across my throat.

"And cut the gas," I said. And he did. "Good driving has a lot of nuance, Jade. Subtle does it. Especially in a big tank like a Suburban."

I had put a piece of driftwood on the driver's seat to give Jade a boost.

"Can you reach both pedals?"

"Easy," Jade said. He pushed on the brake pedal with his left foot and nudged the gas with his right.

"Except that you use only one foot for both pedals."

"Why?" Jake asked.

"Nobody is sure," I said. "But just use your right foot."

"What should I do with the left one?"

"Tap it in frustration at the guy who's driving too slowly in front of you."

"Is that road rage?"

"In Canada, maybe," I said, and laughed.

Jade put on his seat belt.

"Okay, now, step on the brake pedal and move that shifter down into *D* for *Drive*," I said. Jade put his left foot on the brake, and I helped him with the shifter. "And don't forget, it's the right foot for both pedals."

"I'm an idiot," Jade said.

"Nah, it's normal." I was teetering on one knee to keep my ass off the passenger seat. "Ready?"

Jade nodded.

"Take your foot off the brake, and let the motor's idling start to move us."

The Suburban started creeping ahead at about two miles per hour.

"You're driving. See? No big deal."

Jade was mesmerized as he felt the Suburban rolling forward.

"This is fantastic," he said.

"Now add a little more gas with that same foot. The brake foot. Your right foot."

The accelerator pedal was a bit sticky, so Jade ended up stepping on it way too hard. The engine revved, and the Suburban lurched forward.

"Brake. Brake! *Brake!*" I called out, as calmly as possible.

And Jade pushed hard on the brake pedal with both feet. The Suburban jerked to a stop, and my head hit the windshield with a thud.

"I suck at driving."

"Don't be ridiculous," I said. "I once drove my grandmother's Rambler through her garage door. You're doing great."

After navigating five miles of jungle on the narrow dirt path, Jade had driving the Suburban down. He even wanted to turn the radio on, but I decided against it.

I had him stop just before we got to the paved highway.

"Look left and right and left again," I said, "and then turn north."

"How do you know what's north?" Jade asked.

"The ocean is on your left," I said. "If you're on the east coast, it's on the right."

Jade eased the Suburban into a big left turn onto Mexico 200.

"Where are we going?" he asked.

"That's up to you, boss," I said.

"Okay." He was beaming. "Are you hungry?"

"Starving."

"Tacos?" Jade asked.

"You're driving," I said, and held on for the ride.

35

We ate standing up at a taco stand on the shoulder of the highway, about ten miles below Malaki. I had a tongue taco for the first time—by mistake—because I was showing off my mad Spanish skills to Jade.

It wasn't really the taste that was weird. It was the texture. When I chewed it, it felt just like tongue, and all I could think of was Bonnie Gordon teaching me how to French-kiss back in seventh grade.

I was glad we were going to get home before dark, because we were in an area just on the edge of where things are still a little sketchy. The drug wars had gone from boil to simmer with the Peña Nieto presidency, but south of Guadalajara and along the Michoacán *frontera*, drug turf was being contested by a new-generation drug cartel called the Cártel de Jalisco Nueva Generación. The name had a bilingual kind of terror, despite its lack of originality. Murder was down, but kidnapping was up, and I still hadn't forgotten my lesson in linguistics with El Jefe. So the farther north we got, the better I'd feel.

Jade had been rock solid behind the wheel, and even though I was kneeling on my seat and looking backward, I was very *tranquilo*. But the sea-urchin needles in my ass were entering the insanely itchy stage. I needed some serious tweezer work.

"Don't let me fall asleep," I said, thinking wishfully. "I'm the designated dad on this road trip."

"Who can sleep kneeling?"

"Married guys and holy men," I said.

Jade laughed, but I knew he was just being polite. He adjusted his hands on the steering wheel. "How am I doing?"

"You could drive for Uber."

"Really?" He was thrilled. "My mom drove for Uber."

"She did?"

"Yeah, but she got fired for not having a car," Jade said. "And they wouldn't let her keep using rentals."

"The bastards," I said.

Jade laughed. I think he knew his mom was a little nuts.

"How did you think you did out there today?" I asked.

"That's not up to me to say, is it?"

"Probably not. Were you scared?"

"Heck, yeah. Wouldn't you be?"

"I was. And I was only watching you."

"Was it that big?"

"As big as I've ever seen Alacráns. Triple overhead. Easy."

"No way."

"It had to be close."

"But I'm short."

"Not that short. It was big. You could tell anyone that, and it would be true."

He smiled.

It looked like he was proud of himself. It wasn't something I was used to seeing.

"I wish someone had seen it," he said.

Ouch.

"Well, I saw it," I said.

Jade could see that what he'd just said zinged me a little.

"Oh, you know," he said. "But not a surfer. Somebody more real."

"Like who?"

"I don't know. Like a real dad, maybe."

At this rate, I was going to ask Jade to pull over so I could find a roof to jump off.

"What makes the difference between a real dad and a regular dad—or like a stepdad?"

Jade looked at me. "No offense, but I've had a lot of stepdads—buddy dads and *uncles*. I love my mom, and nobody's perfect. But it can suck."

Having such a *resourceful* mom probably wasn't much fun for a thirteen-year-old. I didn't want to think about how many men had shared a toothbrush with Meagan.

"Do you ever think about your real dad?" I asked.

"Yeah, all the time. But Mom won't tell me too much,

and when I creeped him on Facebook there were, like, a million guys with Vietnamese names."

"What would you have done if you found him?"

"Who knows? I mean, like, I don't really even know him."

"But what would you like to ask him?"

I was trying not to lead the witness, but his dad and I probably shared a similar despicability, and I'd often wondered what my son thought about me.

Jade was stressing a little bit. "I don't know. What would *you* ask him?"

And now I was stressing—more than a little.

"I'd probably ask him why he left."

"Yeah," Jade said. "That's a good question."

"I'd say," I said.

36

I must have dozed off somewhere before the village of Agua Caliente, because I remember passing through Malaki. But at the moment, I was being banged awake by someone pounding on the Suburban's hood. I had been sleeping in a kneeling position, with my ass up toward the dash and my chin hanging over the headrest.

I opened my eyes and looked over at Jade.

"I fell asleep?"

"I'm sorry," Jade said, with a face stiff with fear and taking way too much blame.

The driver's-side window was down, and there were two men with machine guns and wearing black ski masks. The masks' mouth openings had been ripped wider than designed, and I could see that the men were grinning at Jade. It was ghoulish. I didn't blame him for being scared—it was *fucking* scary.

The guy on my side was also grinning through the hole in his mask. He didn't have a machine gun and his ski mask was green, and through the left eyehole I could see a tattoo of a hangman's noose.

Oh, shit.

A roadblock had been set up for northbound traffic, and Jade had been pulled over onto an unpaved roadside spur. There were maybe a dozen masked men and a couple of pickup trucks with roll bars and roof-mounted machine guns.

Jade reached for my hand. I opened my palm.

"Don't touch that boy," said the man on my side.

"Okay," I said.

"Do you recognize me?"

"Yes."

"I must make a good impression," he said.

"You do," I said.

It was El Jefe, the sadist who had beaten me bloody with a bamboo reed. He yanked off his ski mask and smiled.

I looked over at Jade. "No matter what this guy asks you, Jade, tell him the truth."

Jade nodded slowly. But he was mostly gawking through the windshield at two poor bastards who were blindfolded and on their knees maybe only fifty feet in front of us. They were handcuffed with plastic cable ties and surrounded by a circle of armed men wearing black masks and camouflage pants. One of the handcuffed men was slowly shaking his head *no* as the other one quickly nodded up and down.

"What did those men do?" Jade asked.

"Do you want to make that your business, *mimado*?"

"No, he doesn't," I said. "What's the problem?"

El Jefe glared.

"Why the roadblock?"

"Cartel activity in the area," he said, coplike and official.

"Which cartel?" I asked, pretending that this was a normal conversation.

"The wrong one," El Jefe laughed. "Why the fuck are you sitting like that?"

"It's the only way I can sleep without getting carsick," I said.

"You want to start with the lying already?"

Jesus. What a wiseass thing to say. But maybe I was showing off a little to take away some of Jade's fear. I turned around and sat on the seat.

"I'm just still having problems with my back," I said. "It still hurts."

"So you remember the rule?"

I nodded. "In fact, I was just thinking about it."

El Jefe nodded back. "So?"

"Truth matters."

He grinned. I was a good student. Then El Jefe reached through my open window, turned my chin, and looked at me.

"You got your eye fixed."

"I did."

"Do you see better?"

"No," I said. "But I look better."

Jade stifled a laugh, and I motioned for him to shut up.

El Jefe pointed at Jade. "Who is this funny boy?"

But before I could get a word out, Jade answered.

"I'm his son," Jade said.

"He looks just like you, amigo."

Which wasn't true, of course. Jade was a brown-eyed Asian teenager with bleached blond dreadlocks, and I was a slightly graying white guy with blue eyes.

"He's going to be my stepson," I said. "I'm going to marry his mom. His real dad is Vietnamese. It was an honest mistake."

I could taste the bile backing up in my throat. I was terrified—but it was imperative not to panic.

"Okay. Next question."

"Thank you."

"Do you have any drugs?"

I pointed toward the glove compartment. "May I open this?"

"Slowly," El Jefe said.

I unlatched the glove compartment and took out the plastic bottle of Epilim. "I'm an epileptic—I mean, in a way, I am." I didn't want to come close to lying to this prick. "And I have to take these to prevent seizures."

"Does it work better than the coke?" El Jefe asked.

"I'm hoping it does."

El Jefe took the bottle and regarded the label. He shook out a pill and popped it into his mouth, and handed back the bottle. Then he whistled. The two men in cable ties were dragged closer to a pickup and then pushed down flat on their faces as a half dozen soldiers stepped into a semi-circle behind them. It was clear that the routine had been practiced—the soldiers knew exactly where to stand.

"Watch closely," El Jefe said. Then he raised his right

hand, and the soldier in the middle of the half circle leveled his gun. "*¡Hacer la primera de ellas ahora!*"

And the soldier shot the man farthest from us in the head.

"That's one," El Jefe said.

Jade started to vomit. He tried to push the half-digested taco back into his mouth with both hands, but most of it was spilling through his fingers.

"You want the next one, *mimado—el segundo?*" He was tormenting Jade.

"Please," I said.

"It's good to feel power when you've been surrounded by weakness."

"He's just a boy," I said.

El Jefe whispered to Jade, "*Ya es tiempo para ser un hombre.*" And then he whistled again and raised his hand. "Say it, *mijo!*"

Jade was trying to catch his breath. I couldn't let him be marked by this. I called out, "*¡El segundo!*" And the second man was shot dead.

A couple of soldiers yanked up the bodies and hurled them into the back of the pickup truck.

"That's what truth looks like. Spread it around."

El Jefe walked off and rejoined his men. I kept waiting for him to turn around and shoot at us or something—but he didn't. So we just sat there for a couple of minutes.

"Can we leave now?" Jade asked.

"I think so," I said. "Start to drive away slowly. And don't look back."

Jade started up the Suburban. He put his right foot on the brake pedal and shifted into Drive. We drove away—slowly—as Jade merged perfectly back onto Mexico 200, heading north.

I let out a long breath. Jade glanced over at me, squeezing the wheel. He was trembling.

"Huge courage, dude," I said and faked a smile, but Jade shook his head.

"Who were they?" he asked.

But I wasn't sure if he meant the two dead men or the soldiers and El Jefe, so I couldn't really give him an answer.

"Sometimes Mexico is just Mexico," I said. "And it's better not to know."

37

had commandeered some tweezers from Meagan's makeup bag, and I was squatting over a mirror that I'd positioned on the floor of my bedroom. Jade had passed out from exhaustion and trauma as soon as we'd gotten home.

"Are you okay to drive now?" Jade had asked me on our way back.

We'd made it about twenty minutes from the roadblock. Jade was still trembling. He was beyond tears.

"No problem."

Jade pulled the big SUV to the side of the road and let it roll to a stop. We switched seats. I put the Suburban in gear and stepped on the gas. The faster I drove, the less my ass hurt, mostly because I had to concentrate—the roads were shit and it was dark—something that also kept my mind off how I'd just become an executioner. Even if it was for the right reason.

I began to hate El Jefe in a way I hadn't known was possible—it nearly matched my fear of him. I hated him for how he'd terrorized Jade, and for how it had made me feel powerless.

"Do you think those guys are dead?" Jade asked.

I considered lying to him about what we'd just witnessed—but if truth mattered, it really mattered now.

"I have no doubt," I said. "They are dead. Yes."

"Were they bad men?"

"They could have been," I said.

Jade thought about that for a moment.

"So then it would be okay to do that. To shoot them," he said.

"What you just saw is never okay, Jade. Never think that it is."

I turned on the radio, but there was nothing but white noise. Jade turned up the volume, and we just listened to static for the next ten miles or so. Our Alacráns adventure had been consumed by a kind of speechlessness and unforgettable impossibility.

Just before we'd made it home, Jade's iPhone had crowed a roosterlike ring. He handed it to me, and I pressed the speaker button.

"Hello," I said.

"Please state your full name," a digitized voice said.

"Who's this?"

"This is the Federal Bureau of Investigation."

But this time, it was a real live voice.

I froze—and then looked over at Jade. He shrugged.

"So what?" he said.

I mouthed, "The FBI!"

"J. Edgar Hoover wore a dress," Jade shouted, like a graduate of Google U.

Then he snatched his iPhone back and tossed it out the window. It broke the tension, and we both laughed.

"I thought you had a lot of your songs on that," I said, a little shocked.

"It's easy to download more," Jade said, "and I got tired of having to skip over Winsor's stuff. The guy was an Amy Winehouse freak."

At the very least, I thought.

"Besides," Jade continued, "it had the Find My iPhone app, so the FBI could locate us if they ever felt like coming down here."

"But it's not like they know we've done anything wrong," I said, sweating the thought more than I would have liked.

"I haven't done anything wrong," Jade said. "Obsidian and I don't have to worry."

"I'm not worried."

"Oh, yeah, just like Mom isn't," he said, and laughed.

Back at the casa, I'd let Jade take a shower first, and then he hit the sack while I put away our boards. Meagan had left a note on the *higuera* informing me that she and Obsidian were having tacos in the street and they hoped the surfing was great.

I WAS ABOUT THREE FOR SEVEN WHEN IT CAME TO PLUCKING THE SEA urchin spines out of my ass. It was difficult; I had to look down between my thighs to a reflection in a mirror that only a proctologist could love—face-to-face with the outer rim of my inner self. It wasn't pretty.

I broke off the back end of a sea-urchin spine.

"Damn," I said.

My legs were cramping, and my back was killing me. But then Meagan came through the door, and my humiliation trumped everything.

"You could have knocked," I said.

"I'm sorry. I thought I lived here."

Meagan looked down at me, and at my ass reflected in the mirror. She smiled.

"Are you trying to find your head?"

"That's what I love about you, Meg," I said. "Your sensitivity."

I stood up, and for some reason I had a bit of an erection. I was at half-mast—at least.

"Oh, my, what's this? Were you expecting company?"

"I was trying to get a couple of dozen sea-urchin spines out of my ass," I said.

"With my good tweezers?"

"I didn't know they were your good ones."

"Jesus, Nick," Meagan said. "I use these on my eyebrows."

I handed her the tweezers. "Sorry," I said.

"How was the surf?" Meagan asked, shaking her head as she rinsed off the tweezers and put them back in her makeup bag—the contents of which I had scattered out on the top of the polished concrete counter.

"Your son killed it," I said. "You would have been really proud of him."

Meagan smiled. "How did you do?"

"It was too big for me. I was afraid to go out."

She turned cold. "You let Jade surf alone?"

"I did," I said. "But I was on the beach watching him."

It was a hedge—but no way was I going to tell Meagan about El Jefe if she was already going all helicopter mom over Jade surfing alone.

"You were too *afraid* to paddle out?"

"The boys have passed me by, Meagan. They've got the stoke. They're really good."

For some reason, I hadn't lost my half erection. In fact, it was no longer at half. It was heading toward three-quarters.

Meagan looked down at it but didn't appear to have much of an opinion. At least, not yet. "Are you waiting for me to hang something on that?"

"I guess that would depend on whether or not you have any hang-ups," I said, with a glibness that recalled my car-lot days.

"I don't have many." She took the scarf from around her neck and began to gently—very gently—buff and polish my penis as if it were a shoe and she was a shoeshine boy.

"In the porn industry, this is called fluffing," Meagan said.

She was sexy as hell, and as embarrassing and odd and funny as this was, it was wonderful.

"Were you a fluffer?" I asked.

"Not professionally," she said.

I couldn't believe how relaxed and comfortable she

was in her own skin. It didn't seem as if there was a self-conscious bone in her body. It calmed me down quite a bit.

"Let's see what we can do about those sea urchins," she said. "Lie down on your stomach."

"I don't think I can do that," I said. My erection was pointing toward the ceiling. I hadn't been this hard since I slow danced to "Nothing Compares 2 U" at my senior prom.

"Oh, I'll make it so you can lie down," Meagan said. "Promise." She turned around and motioned to the buttons at the back of her thin cotton dress. I unbuttoned the first three or four, and she easily slipped out of the shoulders. Meagan never wore a bra. She didn't have to. Her breasts were perfect. She kicked off the dress and slipped off her panties.

She turned around and faced me. And then she touched herself. I could see that she'd recently had a full-Monty wax job. Her fingers glistened. She put the middle one in my mouth.

"Suck me," she said.

And I obliged. Then Meagan turned and locked the door. "The boys are sleeping," she said, "but just in case."

Meagan squatted in front of me—straddling the mirror—and I had to admit that I preferred her reflection to the recollection of my own. She cradled my cock with one hand and began to masturbate with the middle three fingers of the other.

I had a very good view of the mirror. I was sort of mesmerized. Then Meagan French-kissed my belly button.

"Do you like oral sex?" she asked me.

"I do."

"Me, too." She put my cock in her mouth, and I closed my eyes.

In too short a time, I was able to lie on my stomach. And Meagan went to work on removing the sea urchins.

She must have been some kind of ass-repair expert, because she was able to manipulate out virtually all of the sea-urchin spines. Meagan barely had to use the tweezers, but once or twice she applied that old cowboy standard, the snake-venom suck.

"Sorry," I said. "He can be persistent."

I had another erection.

"We'll see," Meagan said, pulling me close to her. "My turn."

"What's fair is fair," I whispered.

I kissed Meagan as lightly as I could, hovering just above her lips, barely touching them, and then I licked out for her tongue until I found it. I kissed her chin and then her neck and then the nipples of both breasts.

"I don't like gentle," she said, a little breathlessly.

"That's just where it's going to start," I said. "Give it a chance."

38

The sheets were soaked and twisted. We had somehow knotted ourselves together like two sneakers flung over a telephone line.

Someone was banging on the window. I opened my eyes. It was already dawn.

Shit.

"Hola, Pirata!" It sounded like José. I pulled back the curtain and saw him standing next to Chuy. Chuy looked like he'd seen a ghost. He was obviously freaked. I opened the window.

"What's up?" I asked.

"We got trouble," Chuy said.

Meagan groaned. I went back to the bed and whispered in her ear, "I'm going to go surf the early session, honey."

It was my first real lie of this new relationship, and I wasn't happy with how easily it slipped from my lips.

"Have fun," she whispered.

I put on some surf shorts and a FREE FIJI T-shirt and met José and Chuy in my front yard. They both stared at me in disbelief.

"What the fuck," José said.

"Jesus," Chuy said.

"What's the matter?" I asked.

"What's the *matter*?" José said. "How about what the fuck?"

He was laughing. A rare thing to see. Whatever it was, José thought it was very funny.

Chuy was pointing to my left eye.

"Are you seeing better now?" he asked.

And I realized that this was the first time these guys had seen me wearing my glass eye.

"No," I said. "It's just for appearances."

"It's a good disguise," José said. "You could rob banks with that shit. The *policía* would all be out looking for a one-eyed *bandito*."

"You always see the positive in everything, José," I said. "That's a great quality."

"You make work what works," he said. "But you get something shot out down here, amigo, you are on your own. Nobody's passing out fake eyes for free."

"This wasn't free," I said. "It cost me twenty-two hundred dollars."

"*Muy guapo*, Pirata," Chuy said. "But it looks crooked."

"That's how they all look," I said. "Do we need to drive?"

"We can walk," Chuy said.

"Fill me in," I said. "Because you just yanked me out of heaven."

"And now we are all going to jail," Chuy said, a little panicked. "*Un cuerpo muerto* washed up on the beach at Libros."

"A *what?*" I asked.

"A dead body," José said.

"Oh," I said.

Libros is a small beach and stand-up-paddle break just above Sabanita, between San Carlos and our north beach, named for the booklike stacked reef that emerges at low tide.

"Why is that a big deal?" I asked. "If we don't know him."

"But what if we *do?*" Chuy interrupted. He was starting to spool up. "José saw the body when he was out getting bait this morning."

"But it's okay, Chuy," José said. "I called *la policía.*"

"Why the fuck would you do that?" I was incredulous.

"So they would know I wasn't involved because I'm not worried."

I shook my head. "Do you guys know how they catch arsonists?"

We were walking down the beach and getting very close to the little rocky point that separates Sabanita from Libros. A helicopter was circling low and about to land. There wasn't a SUP surfer in sight.

"No," Chuy said. "How?"

"They go into the crowd of spectators that always shows up to watch a fire—and they arrest the guy who's got a hard-on."

"What's a *harden*?" Chuy asked.

"A hard-on," I said. "A boner. An erection."

I pointed at José's crotch and made an Arm & Hammer fist—which José took as a direct assault on his heterosexuality.

"I'll fuck you in the ass with my boner, *bizco*," José hissed.

"All I'm saying is that things aren't as connected as they look," I said. "Synchronicity is a crock. No way the cops would put us with some dead guy without your help. And the possibility that it's our dead guy is ridiculous. It's a big ocean. We dumped Winsor miles from here."

It was low tide, so it was easy to wade around the point. The helicopter had landed, and there were a couple of cops and a coroner huddled around what looked like a bloated, beige couch cushion. It must have been the body.

"So it's just dumb to drag me into this," I continued, keeping my voice low.

"Oh, so that's it," José said. "Even if this is your mess?"

"How would this be my fucking mess?" I didn't know if it was the Epilim or some kind of postcoital bravado, but I was feeling clearheaded and ready to throw down, although, considering the look on José's face, that might be a mistake.

"José thinks the dead guy is a gringo," Chuy said.

"Why?"

"Because of his *pulsera*," José said.

"Relax. It's probably stolen," I wiseassed.

José's look turned contemptuous. He didn't like the cheap shot I'd just taken at his compatriots. And he was right. It was a shitty thing to say.

"*Lo siento*, amigo," I said to José.

The cops saw us coming. They even separated so we could get a better view of the body, as if we were somehow official and entitled to a closer look. Maybe it was gringo privilege and they figured I was a tourist. Or maybe they recognized José as the fisherman who had reported the dead guy at Libros.

"*Buenas tardes*," I said.

"*Buenos* días," José corrected me.

Everyone smiled—*estúpido gringo*. But I was instantly relieved when I got a closer look at the body. No way it was going to be identified; it was barely recognizable as a human. Crabs had cleaned the entire carcass of hair and fingernails and a couple of crustacean hangers-on were still gnawing on an earlobe.

The body had blown up, rotting from the inside out and stretching against skin so tight that it looked as if it was about to explode. I stepped back and picked a place to take cover. What was left of the face had swelled into something about the size of a sunflower and cartoon hands with hideously fat fingers reached out from ridged arms.

I was trying to hold my breath. There was a horrific

smell of sweet gas and seaweed, like a bizarre kind of sushi-fart. But then I exhaled and gasped.

A bright yellow Livestrong bracelet cut deeply into the dead flesh that circled one wrist.

Uh-oh.

It was Winsor, after all. He'd put on weight—but mostly water-weight.

I looked at Chuy and José, but they were too busy star-ing down at the body.

"This guy puts the *float* in *flotsam*," I said.

I really needed to learn to watch my mouth. The coro-ner looked up at me. He sort of glared but then smiled. I was lucky he didn't speak English.

We stepped back to give the guys room to zip up Win-sor's body bag, which fit him about as good as the surf bag had. Winsor was hoisted into a body basket attached to the helicopter's landing skid.

One of the cops slap-shaked José's hand and, from what I could make out, thanked him for making the call. Then he pointed at me. José said something. The cop laughed and then walked off.

"What did you just say to him?" I asked José.

"I told him I was taking you fishing," José said. "And that I hoped you were luckier than my last customer."

I didn't think that was a particularly funny or smart thing to say to a cop. Neither did Chuy.

"We're going to jail," Chuy said.

"*Cállate*," José said. "Grow up."

The helicopter took off, and we watched it bank north-east toward Guadalajara. I couldn't imagine that anyone was going to have much luck trying to identify the body. It's not like they keep dental records down here. But even if they did, Winsor hadn't been reported missing.

For all anyone knew, he was still perving around up in the States.

39

I walked the beach back to Sabanita after leaving Chuy and José to drink beer with their cop buddies—which made me a little nervous. It seemed like half the people in Jalisco were related, and the rest played *fútbol* against each other. Mexico was a small town. I made a loop around the plaza, and I could see that the *locals* were already whispering about what had washed up at Libros. Then I headed to the bar.

Meagan was making herself a margarita. The Wave of the Day opened at eleven for the morning happy-hour crowd. Meagan's idea was to give the expat drunks a feel-at-home hangout, so she came in around nine to cook up a pot of Chicken Soup for the Liver.

We'd been open for a week but had served only nine customers—there was a lot of soup left over. But not as much tequila.

"The boys want Wi-Fi in here," Meagan said. "Is that expensive?"

"It's not free," I said. "And you have to have a phone first."

"Well, we need a phone, too. For credit cards. I can't believe Winsor doesn't have one."

"Didn't," I said.

"And it'll make the boys' homeschooling much easier. They can do it right up here with me."

"A homeschool on the barstool. Sounds quaint."

"Smart people can learn anywhere. Dummies need to go to Harvard."

I couldn't imagine having that kind of self-confidence. I wondered when the last time was that Meagan thought she had gotten something wrong.

To be fair, Jade was smart as hell. That was for sure. And he needed the Wi-Fi thing because he had recently hacked into Stanford's fifteen-*thousand*-dollar-a-year home-schooling program. He was getting all the lectures and taking the tests—and he was patiently walking his step-brother through the prep-school curriculum, subject by subject. They were a heck of a team.

"I'll look into it," I said.

"Telmex said they could have someone here by two."

I shook my head. Meagan smiled and then leaned over and kissed me.

"I could love you, you know," she said.

"When?"

"When do I have to?"

"You're such a romantic," I said.

"You grow out of that," she said. "How was the surf?"

"I didn't go surfing."

"No waves?"

"It didn't matter," I said. "I knew I wasn't going surfing when I told you I was."

Meagan looked up at me. "Okay," she said, a little confused.

"I lied to you," I said. "I'm sorry."

Meagan topped off her margarita. "Would you like one?" She wasn't exactly rocked by my confession.

"I can't. I'm back on meds."

Meagan knew I couldn't drink, but maybe she was testing me.

"Yeah, well, if you think I'm giving up reefer *and* margaritas, you are out of your mind. I have *two* thirteen-year-olds."

"I don't," I said. "But I am sorry I didn't tell you the truth."

"I know. You should always save lying for the important stuff."

She handed me a Diet Coke.

"Winsor's body washed up at Libros," I said.

This slowed Meagan down. She dabbed a few grains of salt off the bar with her little finger and tasted them.

"Are you sure it was him?"

"Yeah."

"Did it look like he had suffered?"

"He was dead before we dumped him overboard, Meagan," I said. "But he didn't look great."

"He deserved to suffer." Meagan poured herself a little more margarita. "Are we in trouble now?"

"I don't think so. He was pretty hard to recognize. I only knew it was him because of that Livestrong bracelet he wore."

"That he stole from me because he thought it was cool," she said. "Cheap prick."

I couldn't blame her for hating on the guy. I was pretty low on fond memories myself.

"The *chisme* is, it was a murder—that the cartel is out for revenge in Sabanita."

"Revenge for what?" Meagan asked.

"For nothing. That's how rumors work. People make up whole fantasies out of tiny pieces of reality."

"My modus operandi is the exact opposite of that."

I couldn't tell if she was being honest or making a joke.

"But I think it might make sense to get the boys out of town," I said. "Junior Nationals are at El Tigre this weekend. We could surf Pacuinas on the way up—make it kind of a vacation. It would be fun for the family to get away. Don't you think?"

I was suddenly thrilled by the idea of the four of us vacationing like a real family. Next year, we could go to Disneyland.

"I'm not sure it's so great that when a body turns up, we close down Winsor's place and head out of town. I mean, he's still missing. How's that going to look?"

"He's not missing, Meagan. He's dead."

"Well, yeah, that's what I mean."

And then something pinged—just a blip.

"Why don't you and the boys go?" Meagan continued.

"Just us?"

"They'd love it. I'll stay here and run the Wave. I need the practice. Before you know it, it'll be tourist season."

"Will you be okay here all alone?"

"I'm an expert at all alone," she said. "And it's just going to be a couple of days, right?"

"Yeah, just for the weekend—maybe a day more if the boys make it through the quarterfinals."

"They'll make it—they're my kids," she said. "And you're their coach."

Meagan took both my hands in hers.

"I love this," she said. "You and my boys on a road trip. It's perfect."

"Okay," I said. "If that's what you think we should do."

"It's exactly what I think you should do," Meagan said.

40

We left Sabanita an hour before dawn. There wasn't much traffic on *el* 200 heading north, and during off-season, Puerto Vallarta is pretty much a *turista*-free zone. So we blew right through it and were already on the other side of Bahía de Banderas as the sun rose.

Meagan had still been sound asleep when we left, but I'd made each of the boys kiss her on the cheek and leave an "I love you, Mom" note next to the teapot. I'd left one, too.

Pacuinas was going to be about a six-hour drive. But we'd be driving during daylight so it should be cool.

"This is a real *guys'* trip," I said. "There is nothing more special."

"Why?" Jade asked.

"Well, first," I said, "zero chicks. So our whole world is going to be like a tree fort. No girls allowed."

I looked at Obsidian in the rearview mirror as he shrugged at his stepbrother. Jade was riding shotgun. These guys didn't know what a tree fort was.

"When I was your age," I said, "guys had their own places—where females weren't allowed to go, like locker rooms and fraternities. Girls didn't sue the school so they could play tackle football. And you'd hardly ever see them in a surf lineup."

"What happened?" Obsidian asked.

"The Supreme Court said that girls get to do all the cool shit, too," I said.

"But that's good," Jade said.

"In the long run," I said. "But for the next few days, we can do whatever the fuck we want."

"So we can swear?"

"Fuck, yeah," I said.

I was planning that our surf trip might end up being a little bit of a facts-of-life tour, too. I was guessing that Jade and Obsidian hadn't had too many man-to-man talks—at least, not with the right kind of men.

"Here's all you need to know about cursing and swearing," I began, lecturing a little. "First, there is only one word that is off-limits—sometimes even with men, but ALWAYS with women. It's the nuclear-option word. The one you *only* use when you want to get expelled, get punched out, or permanently end a relationship."

"Which word is that?" Jade asked.

"Guess," I said.

"Bitch," Jade said.

"That word is, like, a two. I'm talking about a word that's, like, a *thousand*," I said. "Do you know the word I'm talking about, Obsidian?"

"Cunt," Obsidian said. He said it a lot easier than I would have liked, though, to be fair, I had asked.

"Bingo."

"I've heard that word," Jade said. "What does it mean?"

"Well, that depends on who you ask," I said. "But usually somebody who'd cheat on you and steal your money and then beg you to take them back."

"Who'd ever want someone like that back?" Jade asked.

"You'd be surprised," I said. "But don't use words like firecrackers, just for the shock factor. Some people freak out about f-bombs and crude talk, so out of respect, don't use profanity when they're around. And make sure you know enough about a swear word to use it in a sentence—so you don't just look like a kook with a bunch of bad words who doesn't really know what they mean."

I wasn't sure if Jade was getting my point, but it looked like his stepbrother was. He had that wise-guy gleam in his eye.

"All women are cunts except for my mother," Obsidian said. "But if you ask my father? He's not so sure." He was laughing at me. "You mean like that?"

"I thought your father was dead," Jade said, coming to my defense. "And my mom isn't a cunt."

"I was being hyperbolic," Obsidian said, showing off.

"Ooh, big word," Jade said.

"Better than *abandoned*," Obsidian said, just as Jade took a swipe at him.

"Guys, hey, that's my point," I said. "Words matter, and they can hurt."

"What's the second-worst word?" Jade asked.

"Probably cocksucker," I said. "And that's usually a guy who fires you from your job, or cuts you off on the freeway."

"Or Winsor," Obsidian said.

And I winced at the name that now sounded more profane than any of the words we'd been batting around. I looked over to Jade.

"I told him what really happened, but he doesn't believe me," Jade said.

"Why not, Obsidian?" I asked. "Jade wouldn't lie to you."

"Because then Mom's made a big mistake," Obsidian said.

"She did," I said. "And I'm not big on secrets, but this is one we have to keep."

"We do," Jade said.

"Okay," Obsidian said, and shook Jade's hand.

"But, you know, guys," I said, "sex is actually pretty fantastic."

"And noisy," Obsidian said, being snide—and reminding me how small my casa was.

"Do you even know what sex is?" I asked.

"Don't be ridiculous," Obsidian said.

I was sure these two had seen Internet porn, but I wondered if they knew that sex wasn't usually about three guys and a cheerleader.

"What is it, then, big shot?" I asked. "Fill me in. Pretend I don't know."

"You mean pretend you're Jade," Obsidian said, laughing awkwardly.

"I know what it is," Jade said. "Don't lie."

"So tell me," I said.

"It's what you do nude. With a girl," Obsidian said.

"Not always with a girl," Jade said.

"That is so gay," Obsidian said.

"No, you can do it with just yourself, too, genius," Jade said.

"He's right," I said. "And that's called masturbating. Totally normal—and a single man's best friend. Unless he has a fuck buddy. And then that person immediately attains best-friend status."

"It's also called jerking off," Jade said, "which is easier to spell."

I had to laugh. The kid was funny.

"So," I said, "how do you get a girl pregnant?"

They just sat there.

"Okay," I said. "You guys should have had this talk when you were about ten—so now I'm just going to be blunt and burn through it."

"Is this going to get weird?" Jade asked.

"You'll see," I said.

I caught Obsidian's eye in the rearview, and then I looked over at Jade. They looked ready.

"Men have cocks," I said, "or dicks or rods. Doctors and gym teachers call them penises. When you get sexually excited, your cock gets hard. That's called an erection. If I were having this talk with you guys when you were ten, we'd call it a stiffy. When it's stiff—and you have permission— you can put it anywhere you want. In your hand, for example, like Jade said."

"Masturbating," Jade said.

"Exactly," I said. "Or you can put it in someone's mouth or their vagina—or even in their butt, if they're into it, too. It's always better to do this with someone who is about your own age." I took a breath and let all that sink in.

"When you have an orgasm, sperm comes out. That's called *cumming*—spelled with a *U* and an extra *M*—or ejaculating. And, as you probably know, it feels fantastic," I continued. "If cumming happens when you're inside a vagina, your partner could get pregnant. If you're inside their mouth, they might get pissed off."

I looked in the rearview mirror. Obsidian was mesmerized.

"It's basically okay to do whatever feels good as long as everybody agrees and nobody feels like they're doing something they don't want to do," I said. "It's *always* better if they're digging it as much as you, and when you like them a lot."

"Boys or girls?" Obsidian asked.

I couldn't tell if he was fucking with me, but it didn't look like he was.

"Yeah," I said. "Boys or girls."

At this point, I would have opened one of the Suburban's windows, but all of them were already open.

"So," Jade said, "do you like my mom a lot?"

"I'm crazy about her," I said, mostly meaning it.

"Is there anything else?" Obsidian asked.

I probably should have told them about how being a slut sucks and about condoms and STDs. But I didn't want to ruin the moment.

"That's all I know, Obsidian," I said. "The rest of it comes down to style and attitude. The kissing and the warm-up and the wanting—that stuff? That's going to be your own mystery."

We pulled into the parking lot of a restaurant that was right on the beach by the break at Pacuinas. We could see good waves, and there were already about a dozen surfers out.

It was midmorning. The tide was rising. We had timed it perfectly.

"It's big," Obsidian said.

"That's why we drove all the way up here, dude," I said.

I was feeling confident. Maybe it was the Epilim, or maybe it was because these kids needed a role model and I was happy to do it—or maybe I was ready to admit how much I'd missed being a dad.

I turned off the ignition and opened the Suburban's door.

"Follow me," I said.

41

A lot of Aussie watermen were in the lineup, so we had to be polite. Maybe Qantas was having a winter's-end sale. Pacuinas is a bucket-list break for a lot of serious surfers so there are always people in the water when it's on, and it's competitive as hell. I have sat out there all day and never had a chance at a decent wave.

But on this day, for some reason, the cosmic surf calculus was in my favor. I must have been exactly the right weight, and my Red Fin precisely the right shape, for this particular wave. I was killing it and doing my stepkids proud.

Obsidian was stalking Pacuinas's big slabby lefts—which are heavier and meaner than the juicy pigs I was snacking on. A small crowd had gathered on the beach, and a few people were even taking vids of Obsidian's stoke and show.

Jade was having a tougher time. There was a big, sweet wave that showed up on the right side about every ten minutes, but Jade kept getting snaked by this Muscle Beach bully. No matter how far inside Jade sat, this idiot—who had a pretty impressive rendering of *The Last Supper* tattooed across his back—would go even deeper inside and steal the wave.

The rule is that the deepest surfer, the guy closest to the peak, gets the wave. But there were plenty of waves today. And it wasn't a fair fight. Jade was thirteen and maybe 120 pounds, wet or dry. The inked-up Aussie looked like a retired pro. He could have let Jade have a wave once in a while. But he wouldn't.

So I paddled over and sat next to him and watched as he snagged another one of Jade's waves. The guy could surf, no doubt. My kid was pissed. He punched the water and bit his lip.

"Let me handle this, Jader," I said quietly.

The prick from Oz paddled back out. I smiled. He didn't. He was all game-faced and grim.

"That's a heck of a tattoo," I said. "*The Last Supper*. Wow. Incredible work."

"Tattoolicious in Waikiki," he said. "In the winter I'm on the north shore. Mostly at Pipe."

For a guy so core, he seemed to drop a lot of names.

"So you travel a lot," I said.

I could see Jade smiling out of the corner of my eye.

"I'm a messenger for Jesus," he said.

"That'll do it," I said.

"I surf for Christ."

"Okay, then, what about a little Christian charity for the grommet here? Let him make a wave, okay, pal? You've had, like, ten. He hasn't had any."

"Charity is a Catholic lie, mate," he said. "Good works are a trap. Accepting Jesus as your savior is what matters. If your grom can't make his own waves, it's God's will."

The guy was a nut—and a wave hog. He started to paddle for another set wave, but I motioned for Jade to go for it.

"This one's his," I said.

"If he can make it," the Aussie said.

I spun my Red Fin around and paddled after the Jesus freak. I hooked his leash with the nose of my board and we nearly collided, but it slowed him down enough for Jade to make the wave—and then a magnificent rail turn into a big-time Pacuinas barrel.

I flipped the Christian a middle-fingered shaka and then dropped in on the next bomb, bottom-turning a little to my left and pushing him into the closeout. It was a nice wave. I trimmed up the Red Fin and took her home.

I joined Jade onshore. He was smiling.

"Dude, what a wave," I said.

"What an ass-cork," he said. "What was with that guy?"

"There are two kinds of Christians," I said, "the real kind and the kind you don't want sitting on your jury. *Ass-cork* is right."

"I made that up," Jade said, enjoying the permission to be obscene.

"It works," I said.

But I was secretly hoping that this guy was also the turn-the-other-cheek kind of Christian, because he was riding in on the cleanup wave from the last set. And I could tell even from this distance that he was furious. He made it to the sand and stormed up to me. He took off his leash and tossed his board. And then he waved a fist in my face.

"I paid a lot of money to come here and surf this wave, you cross-eyed prick," he said, just about spitting. "So if your little concubine takes another one of them, I'll kick his arse, and then kick yours."

He stood there, glaring at me. I could see that Jade was frightened, but I was really pissed off about the concubine insinuation. And what's with that *cross-eyed* shit?

I turned a little sideways so I could see him better—and then I punched him square in the face. My fist caught the Aussie flush and knocked him flat to the sand. He looked up at me, just as amazed as I was. He tried to scramble to his feet, but I stepped on his wrist.

"I live down here, mate," I said. "If you ever fuck with my kid again, I will have you killed."

This was the toughest tough-guy thing I could think of. I hoped it would work. This Aussie was a lot younger than I was, and a shitload more fit.

I could see Obsidian running toward us.

"Obsidian!" Jade screamed. "Dad just knocked this fucking guy *OUT*."

But I couldn't tell whether Jade was proud or panicking. A few *locals* I had surfed with at Pacuinas over the years began to circle in. I nodded to a couple of them, and I hoped they remembered me. I was lucky that they nodded back.

Then some of the Jesus freak's Australian buddies jogged up and helped him to his feet. There was a lot of stink eye going around, but nobody knew quite what to do, so we all just tried to look big and badass.

I could see that some of the Aussies were ready to throw down, but then one of the *locals* stepped in. He pointed to them.

"You *chicos* ever hear of a Mexican standoff?" he asked, in pretty good English.

Then he motioned back to his amigos, who were standing in a half circle behind him. "This is what it looks like," he said.

Every Mexican on the beach laughed. If they didn't understand English, they sure got the body language. There was no way these Australians were dumb enough to get into a brawl down in Mexico—with Mexicans.

"Leave it in the water," one of the Australians said.

Another Aussie picked up the wave hog's board, and they all walked off, murmuring and kind of laughing. I think they knew that their fellow Down Under man was a dick.

Obsidian and Jade were staring at me.

"Holy shit," Obsidian said, "I didn't know you were like that."

"Me neither," I said. "I think I hurt my hand."

42

I ran into a bump trying to register the boys at the Mexican Junior Nationals at El Tigre. The contest organizers were telling me that the competitors had to be Mexican, and they wanted to see birth certificates or passports to prove it.

They wouldn't buy my story that Jade and Obsidian were born in Tijuana to a Vietnamese UCSD exchange student on a spring-break binge down in Mexico. But as luck would have it, I could buy the organizers for 1,000 pesos each.

When you bring kids who are used to being the hot-shit groms at their home break to a national surf contest, it's often the first time they're competing for waves against young surfers who are just as hot shit as they are. Jade took this a lot better than Obsidian did—who kept telling me he had a stomachache.

There were sixty entries in the fourteen-and-under division—twenty heats, three surfers per heat. Because of the sign-up hassle and, no doubt, the boys' questionable nationality, Obsidian and Jade were relegated to the final heat.

I didn't expect the boys to win this thing. I just wanted them to experience organized competition at a national level. I wanted to show them that the world was a bigger place than they probably thought it was, and how nobody was all that special or different.

But as we sat on the beach and watched the opening heats, all I wanted for my boys was that they wouldn't be humiliated. There were *gromeros* here in ragged shorts, riding waterlogged boards with missing fins and dinged-up rails, who were absolutely owning hollow overheads and pitchy barrels. The kids down here were hungry, and it showed.

The heats in the opening round lumbered on, Mexican-style, but at least the swell was holding up. In fact, it looked like it was getting bigger. Jade was dozing on and off. Obsidian fidgeted. The beach was muggy and bug-ridden. I was nervous.

And then, right around dusk, Ali Nereida and Jade Lutz and Obsidian Lutz were announced over the screechy PA. I had used my expired FM3 as Mexican ID and claimed to be the boys' real dad, so they had to use my last name— and I puffed up a little at the sound of it.

The boys snatched up their boards and sprinted into the ocean. I was barely able to nod good luck. The shore break was pumping, but Obsidian and Jade easily powered their way through it. The final heat of the day would begin immediately. It would last twenty minutes and probably end in the dark.

A competitor's two best waves are scored at a maximum of ten points each. Two perfect waves would make twenty, but that's an unheard-of total at a Junior Nationals. A good score here would be around fifteen. A combination of sevens and eights could win the heat.

Jade was in a white rash guard. Obsidian was wearing blue. A young lady was in red. Ali Nereida was a girl, what surfers call a *wahine*, and immediately after the horn sounded, she pounded down the face of the first makeable wave and leaned into a backside barrel.

I wished I had binoculars, but even from where I was, I could see that Obsidian and Jade were head-smacked and staring at each other. Then Jade chased down a smaller wave but missed it. I could see that he was pissed at himself.

As the next set was coming in, the girl in red was sitting on Obsidian's outside. My kid had priority because the girl had just paddled back to the lineup, but she charged hard for the next wave anyway, forcing Obsidian deeper than he wanted to go. Then she backed off—suckering Obsidian into making the drop—and smiled as the wave collapsed on his head.

Ali Nereida was kicking ass.

Jade made a wave, barely staying on his feet as he boned a cutback. It was clear that he was in over his head, and I began to think that I had made a mistake entering my guys into a competition this heavy.

But then Obsidian made a huge wave with a big drop into a delicious string of rail turns. He tried to finish with an amazing reverse air—but missed it, and then flipped into the shore break closeout. The tip of his surfboard jammed into the sand, and it snapped in half.

Obsidian waded out of the water, the remains of his board dragging behind him on the leash like a drowned dog. The top of his right foot was bleeding.

"Dude, so sorry," I said. "You had that dialed."

"Yeah, good wave, huh?" he said, surprisingly zen. "I was just starting to figure it out."

But his day was over.

"Come on, Jader!" Obsidian screamed, waving a fist at his stepbrother. "Up to you, bro."

So far the judges had scored the wahine 9.6 and 9.1, which sort of shined the shit light on my wave-scoring theory. But they scored Obsidian's last wave a 6.6, which I thought was generous, seeing as how he blew his air.

Jade's only score so far was a 2.7, and now he was paddling hard after a set wave—he nailed it and made the drop, linked up two sweet roundhouses, and then stuck a perfect one-eighty.

But instead of paddling back to the lineup, he rode the white water into shore.

"Dude, get back out there," Obsidian said.

Jade uncuffed his leash and handed the Glenn Pang to his stepbrother.

"I'm getting crushed," Jade said.

Obsidian looked over at me as Jade hugged him and then rapped a lucky knuckle on the TC Pang. "You need to go," he said.

I nodded at Obsidian, and he sprinted into the surf.

"Put the leash on!" I yelled.

The judges gave Jade's wave an 8.1. I put my arm around him.

"Nice," I said.

But *la dama de rojo* had Obsidian comboed with an 18.7. He needed two waves, both big 9s—pretty impossible—to win it.

High tide was just about peaking—it was nearly dark, and I could barely make out a wedge of dots against the darkening sky. It looked like a skein of pelicans swooping low across the water.

The girl paddled in a slow circle, staying close to Obsidian and protecting her lead. It looked as if Obsidian had given up. He was just sitting on his board and staring out to sea—but then I realized he was watching the pelicans.

Obsidian paddled toward the lazy birds as the ocean started to rise and lines of waves began to fatten and show themselves. Jade looked at me.

"Dude, you were right," he said.

"Sometimes," I said.

Obsidian made the backside set wave with a free-fall drop into a bottom turn so full of torque that he had to grip his outside rail with both hands. Then he carved up the face and snapped off three vertical hits in a row, fins above

the lip and ripping down the line as the wave walled up—
barreled—and then blasted him out in a ball of spray as if
he had been shot from a circus cannon.

He raised his fist—claimed the wave—and fell sideways off his board. Done.

"Holy shit," Jade whispered.

"No kidding," I said.

All three judges gave Obsidian's final wave a ten. The
only perfect score of the day.

43

S o what are we supposed to do now?" Jade asked.

"Cry," Obsidian said. "I got beat by a wahine."

"Get used to it," I said. "But right now—we bask."

We were heading away from the ocean, it was drizzly and dark, and the dirt road was more of a ditch. I clicked on the high beams. Jade was riding shotgun. Obsidian was slouched in the middle seat—totally bumming. He knew he could have done better.

"Bask?" Jade repeated.

"In our glory," I said. "It's like being baked—but in the juices of victory."

"That's *baste*," Jade said.

"Look," I said. "Obsidian comes from out of nowhere in the final minutes of the final heat to bang out the only perfect wave score of the day—tens by *all three* judges."

I flashed ten fingers three times as if my hands were a scoreboard.

"And you knocked down a solid eight, my son," I said.

"An eight point one," Jade said.

"And then you honorably handed over your weapon to your bro, the stronger warrior," I bragged. "This is mysto surf stuff. Half of Mexico must be talking about it already."

"We still lost, Nick," Obsidian said. "To a girl."

But I could see that he wasn't exactly suicidal. Both of the boys looked like they were enjoying how stoked I was.

"It was a victory," I said. "Anyone who knows what losing is will tell you that." I looked at Obsidian in the rearview mirror. "You need to be able to recognize a victory when you get one. They can be hard to come by. There'll be long stretches in your life without any. And then sometimes they'll come in streaks—so you have to be ready. Today was a victory, guys."

"Do you ever have any?" Jade asked.

"Of course," I said.

"Like what?" Obsidian said.

"Well, today is sort of a victory for me, too. I'm proud I helped get you guys down here and sign you up." I wanted to be careful not to barge in and take credit for who these boys were as surfers. I had very little to do with it. "And I think that if what your mom and I are thinking about putting together works out, that would be a victory, too."

"You mean the Wave of the Day?" Jade asked.

"That was Winsor's," Obsidian said.

"I mean, like, this sort of a family thing we're talking about—*us*," I said. "That could be a victory."

This was delicate turf.

"Any victories that didn't happen this week?" Obsidian asked, pimping me, but he probably wanted to know a little more about me, too.

"I've had some," I said. "But I don't like to baste."

We were heading back through the city of Compostela. I dimmed my lights and tried to count the victories I had had since the one big defining defeat of my life. There weren't many. I was a divorced former car salesman—with a head injury, no family, and occasional substance-abuse issues. If I'd been victorious at anything these last six years, it'd been racing to the bottom.

"Should we drive home or crash somewhere around here?" I asked, letting myself up off the mat.

"Can we go to a strip bar?" Obsidian asked.

"No," I said.

"Why not?"

"Because strip bars are a crime against women," I said, caught off guard.

"Why?" Jade asked. "Mom danced when she needed the money. She said it was nothing to be ashamed of if you weren't slutty and the men couldn't touch you."

I was going to need to back out of this alley—it was a good thing the Suburban had four-wheel drive.

"Your mom is like an astronaut discovering new planets," I said. "But for regular girls, taking their clothes off for money can be a bummer."

It would be smart to change the subject.

"How would you guys like to get a tattoo?" I said, nominating myself for the Irresponsible-Stepdad-of-the-Year Award.

And then all I could think of was that kook from Oz with *The Last Supper* tattooed across his back.

"Are you kidding!" Jade said. "That would be so cool."

"Yeah," Obsidian said. "I want a skull—on my neck."

"I was thinking of something a little different, maybe," I said. "Like 'death before dishonor' or 'peaceful warrior'—in Chinese. And small—like maybe on the bottom of our heels."

I had just driven down another alley I needed to back out of.

"How about if we design our own?" Jade suggested. "Something for just the three of us that's symbolic."

"As long as it has a skull," Obsidian said.

"It's not going to have a skull," I said.

"How about a surfboard?" Jade asked.

"Maybe a surfboard," I said.

"Do you have something I can draw with?" Jade asked.

"In the glove compartment," I said.

got tatted at an all-night parlor on the plaza in La Peñita. I was now the proud owner of a Jade Phuc original tat. It was a miniature surfboard with *Meagan* inked across the bottom in green, white, and red, the colors of the Mexican flag and the only ink the tattoo artist had in his kit.

The *Meagan* surfboard took up about six inches on the inside of my left forearm, and it hurt like hell. It was still bleeding a little, and I was supposed to stay out of the ocean for at least a week.

"It's a great tribute to an amazing person," Jade had said, finishing up the tattoo design he was drawing on a paper towel. "Mine and Obsidian's will say *Mom* and yours *Meagan*—and it's on a surfboard, like a family coat of arms."

"So it's sort of like an adoption," Obsidian said.

"It's even better," Jade said.

He'd been working on the design for about an hour,

and for some reason I'd gotten caught up in the energy. I was longing for Meagan. I'd just had a great day with her kids. I felt a little like a real dad again. We'd all been bunking together. And I had always wanted a tattoo. Or maybe the Epilim and exhaustion had somehow morphed into a lovestruck mania.

But *what the hell*. I rolled up my sleeve.

The boys wanted me to get tatted first because they were a little freaked out by all the horror stories they'd heard about painful needles and how bloody it was. And they were right. The process was bloodier and more painful and took longer than I had expected. But that's probably because tattoos are inked in to last a lifetime—something that hadn't totally dawned on me, not at first.

Jade sucked it up and raised his hand to become the next tattooed member of our new family tribe. The tattoo artist wanted to see proof that Jade was at least sixteen, which is apparently the age of consent for tattoos in Mexico.

"Why didn't you tell us that before I got my tattoo?" I asked.

"I'm busy-ness man," the artist said, in so many words and some impressively broken English. "Me talk first, you no buy."

Nobody likes to lie in front of their kids—unless there's a good reason. So I told the guy that Obsidian and Jade were both *almost* sixteen and Irish twins, and that I was their birth father—and I was giving him permission to scar my children for life.

He still shook his head.

"*Lo siento*," he said. "No crime."

I would have offered to bribe him, but I had used up my extra cash buying off the organizers of the surf contest.

"Maybe this worked out the best way," Jade said.

He had stretched out on the Suburban's middle seat and was gazing up at the stains on the roof liner. Obsidian was in the very-back seat, already asleep.

"How?" I asked.

"You're older, Nick," Jade said, "and better at making the important decisions. I mean, who knows if in ten years, or even two, I'd want *Mom* tattooed on a surfboard permanently on my arm. I might not even like surfing anymore."

"But you'd still love your mom, right?" I said. "And it's marking our bodies with a memory—an epic one. I think we should see if there's a tattoo place still open in Vallarta."

Stepdad or not, I didn't want to be the only one coming home wearing a dunce cap.

"Not if it's illegal, though," Jade said. "And as I think this through, I think I'll wait. But I'm honored that you tattooed *Mom* on you—for life. She's going to freak."

"But it doesn't say *Mom*," I said. "It says *Meagan*."

We got back to Sabanita around four in the morning after deciding to drive straight through from La Peñita. I pulled up in front of my casa and parked. All the Suburban's windows were down. It wasn't that hot, and it was going to be light out soon, so I decided to let the boys sleep. We would unload the surfboards later.

There was a strange dog tied to the *higuera*. A big mutt

that looked like a sweet gene combination of black lab and maybe golden retriever, or Irish setter.

She was stuck somewhere between growling and wagging her tail, so I held out the back of my hand and slowly walked toward her.

"It's okay, gorgeous. I live here."

The mutt licked my hand as I tiptoed up the casa's front stairs. I was being very quiet.

The door to my bedroom was locked, but I could hear the fan going full blast. It made a pretty good racket. I took out my key and opened the door to my bedroom. And there was Meagan, sound asleep—gorgeous and naked. She was sleeping on her stomach. Her hair was cascading around her shoulders and floating a little on the wind from the fan.

A man I did not recognize was sleeping flat on his back next to her—also naked.

I was pretty sure he wasn't a *local*, because he didn't look Mexican. And he wasn't a white guy, either. It was also obvious to me—and likely to Meagan—that the man could use some fluffing.

But it was the damnedest thing. As I glared at him, this bastard started to look familiar. And then I realized he was the kook from Surprises—the Japanese guy who had paddled out on the foamy and gotten pounded by that outside bomb.

I leaned down close to Meagan and kissed her on the cheek.

"Hi, honey, I'm home," I said.

Meagan opened her eyes just as I slipped out the bedroom door.

45

know what you're thinking," Meagan said.

"I doubt it," I said.

Because killing both of them had crossed my mind—except that the name of my recently deceased girlfriend would be freshly tattooed on my forearm. It's doubtful that even a Mexican jury would believe that the two adulterers had bludgeoned themselves to death with a Mike Hynson Red Fin while I watched and cheered them on.

I had been sitting outside the bedroom for about twenty minutes. I wasn't trying to listen, but I did hear some intense murmuring and then some crying—and even a little laughing, which made me crazy.

When Meagan finally came out, she was wearing my favorite Watermark Fins T-shirt. Her eyes were red, and it was the first time I had ever seen her looking like shit. It made my heart sing.

"That's my favorite T-shirt," I said.

"I was hoping you'd let me take it with me."

"*What?*"

"It has your smell," she said.

This woman was from a galaxy far beyond the one I was trying to live in.

"The guy surfs a Wavestorm," I said. "A *foamy*."

"He doesn't surf."

"Tell me."

"He just paddled out that day so he could watch you guys."

"So you know him?" I wondered how long I'd been a sap.

"He's Jade's father," Meagan said.

That stopped me cold. I had thought the Wavestormer was Japanese—but he was Vietnamese. If I'd guessed that at the time, I might have put some pieces together, and this cuckolding wouldn't have been such a stunning punch to the heart.

"He's been looking for us for years," Meagan said. "And then Jade found him on Facebook."

"Jade knows about him?" I felt betrayed. I started to cry—not sobs, just tears.

"No," Meagan said. "But that's how Danh was able to finally find me. He started chatting with Jade online, and Jade said his mom's name was Meagan and that he was half-Vietnamese."

I remembered that Jade had told me he'd searched Facebook for his dad, but there were too many Vietnamese guys to really narrow it down.

"But Jade said he couldn't find his dad," I said, desperately hoping this was somehow just a crazy mistake.

"Danh wanted to tell him in person," Meagan said. "That's why he came down to get us. Jade's going to get his real dad back, Nick."

"As opposed to me—the cross-eyed fake dad?"

"That's not what I meant."

"How do you know he hasn't just escaped from prison—or a mental hospital?"

"He owns a software company in San Francisco," Meagan said.

"So the fuck what," I said. "Everybody up there does."

"I have to do this."

"You don't even know him anymore, Meagan—but you know *me*."

I looked over at an empty bottle of wine in the kitchen sink and shook my head.

"This is the first time in my life that the truck loaded with all the goodies didn't just run me the fuck down, Nick," Meagan said. "You've seen my life up close. You think I don't know what a shit fest it is—how messed up I am? I do. I suck. I'm a shitty mom. But I love my kids. And Danh says that's all I have to bring with me."

"You're taking Obsidian, too?"

I was so flipped out about Jade, I hadn't even considered that Obsidian would be leaving me.

"Of course," Meagan said. "I'm his mom."

"Well, it is nice to see that morality and integrity have finally begun to raise their heads inside your black soul," I said, like a spokesperson for recovering aphasia victims.

"Oh, Jesus, Nick, step away from the ledge," she said.

"I already jumped off the ledge, Meg. I got rid of your boyfriend's body, remember? You pulled sea urchins out of my ass." I extended my hand. "Have we met?"

But Meagan wouldn't shake it and glanced toward the bedroom. She wasn't crazy about the secrets I was broadcasting—but that was the point.

"I got thrown a rope," Meagan said, as calmly as possible. "And I'm going to grab it."

"And let go of me," I said, a little wimpier than I would've liked.

"Nick—we've lived together for, what, a *week*? You'll get through this. Unless all that stuff you said about surviving ourselves was just bullshit."

It sounded like she had been taking notes.

"When does this happen?" I asked.

I thought I saw her lip start to quiver, but that might have been optimistic.

"There's a flight out of Vallarta every day at eleven forty-five," she said.

I motioned for Meagan to come closer. She didn't hesitate. I put my arms around her waist and then wiped the tears from my one working eye with my favorite T-shirt.

"I promised Danh we'd leave as soon as the boys got home," Meagan continued.

"Is there a chance I could change your mind?" I asked. I hated groveling—but I'd be willing to do it.

"No," she said.

I stood up. Meagan flinched. This wasn't the first time she'd been in this movie.

"Ever?"

"Nick—let's just try to get to tomorrow. I'll go wake the boys."

"I don't want to see them."

"You have to say good-bye."

"Says who—Super Mom?" I was suddenly seething. "I *never* want to see you again, Meagan. I don't care if you're being chased by Borneo headhunters. Don't fucking run in my direction. Tell them I took off because I found something better—it'll be easier to forget me that way. Because that's exactly what the fuck I'm going to do about you."

I had been flailing my arms, and Meagan was looking at my new tattoo. "And don't think this means anything," I said, covering up the fresh ink. "Because as soon as it's dry, I'm going to have it changed—to *Pagan*."

I stormed out of the casa and down the front steps and tripped over the dog. I fell flat on my face, and once again the dog didn't know whether to growl or wag her tail.

"And take this fucking mutt with you," I said, getting up.

"It's Danh's," Meagan said. "He rescued it."

"And I rescued you," I said softly.

She was standing behind me in the doorway and twisting up the front of my T-shirt. "I won't forget that."

"Try," I said.

"Can we leave her here? She could help you with your loss."

"Whatever works for *you*, Meg," I said, and kept walking.

I peeked into the Suburban. The boys were still sleeping. I whispered that I loved them. Then I headed to the beach.

46

I was sitting in Sabanita's birthing tree on a corner of the beach at the far edge of town. All that was left of *el papelillo* was its gnarled trunk and a few twisted limbs. For generations, *local* mothers had given birth to their babies while hanging on to a branch and squatting over a smooth, damp hole that had been scooped out in the sand. Chuy and José were born here.

But my two boys were leaving town.

I was old enough to have known better than to fall for a woman like Meagan. From the first moment she'd knocked on my heart, I'd known there'd be trouble. I had no one to blame but myself.

I'd miss her—just for the sheer madness of it. But I was heartbroken about the boys. I had no delusions over who got the best deal with the three of us getting to know each other.

It was very possible that Jade and Obsidian would be leaving my life for good. And I knew from experience that if I couldn't forge some kind of closure, the continuing regret would be impossible for me to endure—I could only run from it. I needed to say good-bye.

Meagan and the boys and Wavestorm Danh would have to be at the airport two hours before departure. That meant they had to leave for the airport by nine, and it was probably already after that. When I got back to my casa, the rescued mutt was still tied to the *higuera*. I was in too much of a hurry to let it bum me out, but I did fill her water bowl.

Winsor's MacBook had been left out on the kitchen table. There was a note taped to it from the boys. A piece of printer paper was folded in half, and there was a math formula inside: $8.1 + 10.0 = 100\%$ U.

It was a score I did not deserve.

I jumped into the shower, rinsed off and toweled down, pulled on my formal khaki pants, and put on a Hawaiian shirt patterned with hot dogs and gas stations.

I was dressed to impress, and I flatfooted the gas pedal all the way to Vallarta.

I parked in the passenger drop-off zone and sprinted into the *aeropuerto terminal*, hoping to catch the boys before they got past security, and I had already missed check-in. But then I found the latest revision of Meagan's happy family sitting at the Starbucks adjacent to where the line starts to the X-ray carry-on.

Obsidian saw me first.

Jade was lost in an iPhone. He had its buds in and was

playing *World Surf Tour.* I slowly walked toward them and then just stood there until Meagan noticed me. I could see that I had caught her by surprise.

I smiled, not wanting her to think I had come to cause trouble.

"I just wanted to say good-bye to the boys," I said simply.

Jade looked up at me—and then at his dad. His face was blank, but Obsidian was grinning with relief.

"*Dude,* I am *so* happy," Obsidian said.

The kids were wearing brand-new yellow-and-silver Puma runners and plaid cargo pants. Their WE LOVE PUERTO VALLARTA T-shirts were a matching blue. They were a little self-conscious in the new duds, which made them look about ten.

"Nick, this is Danh," Meagan said, "Jade's dad."

"Whose name will go back to Kim as soon as we land in the States," Danh declared, standing up.

It was clear that switching Jade back to his Vietnamese name had already been discussed—and settled.

"What about Obsidian?" I asked.

"Right now he wants to keep it, but it'll go back to Wayne if I decide to adopt."

"So he's kind of getting a tryout?"

"Of sorts," Danh said, a little too cheerfully. "But he's a heck of a prospect."

Danh wasn't very tall, but he was fastidiously dressed. I was happy I was wearing my best khakis. I couldn't see a wrinkle on this guy's face, or in his shirt.

"You're the surf coach?" Danh said, shaking my hand

firmly. "What I saw at Sorpresas that day was impressive—even if I wasn't." He used the Spanish word for Surprises, probably so I'd know he was cool and surf-aware. I tried not to cringe. "And I hear you've been a wonderful surrogate uncle, too," he continued.

I looked over at Meagan. She smiled at me, pleading.

"I do the best I can with what I have," I said. "But I'm not much of a coach."

"I want Meagan to take up life coaching in the Bay Area," Danh said. "She could teach single moms how to support themselves."

I smiled back at Meagan.

"Sounds like a perfect fit," I said.

Danh nudged Jade and pulled an earbud out of his son's ear. "Kim, say good-bye to Nick," Danh said, smiling down at his son. "He just got his first iPhone, so he's a little carried away."

Not his first, I thought.

"Can I have a couple of minutes with the boys?" I asked.

Danh looked at Meagan, but she still had just that same pleading smile on her face.

"Just surf coach, surrogate uncle stuff—nothing serious," I said.

"Sure," Danh said.

And then he seemed to get it. It was nice to see that he wasn't a total dick. Danh took Meagan's hand, and she stood up. "We'll go check to see if the flight's on time," he said. They walked off, and I sat down with the boys.

"Man, talk about lucky," I said.

Jade couldn't look at me. He was really torn. Obsidian was just confused.

"You guys are going to be surfing the best breaks in North America," I said. "Steamer Lane, Ghost Tree, Mavericks—that's some epic shit. You'll forget all about three-foot Sabanita."

"No, we won't," Obsidian said. He wasn't so confused anymore and wiped away a tear.

"I just never even thought that my dad would ever really come back," Jade said, "and if he did, that we'd just stay down here or something." He was pretty jumbled up. Everything was coming out in spurts.

"And he said we can only surf on weekends," Obsidian said, "because we have to go to *school*."

"That's the real world, Obsidian," I said. "Everyone should live in it for a while. To see if they like it."

"What's not real about you?" Jade said.

"Lots," I said. "Like this eye, for instance." I popped up my lid and evil-eyed them. It got a little smile.

"I just came up here to tell you guys something that you really need to know. And it's not like how good you surf or how funny and smart you guys are, or how brave—or how I know you have my back, because you know I have yours. It's none of that. What I want to tell you is, even if you weren't all those things and we didn't have that stuff—I would still love the hell out of you both, just like I do now. And I need you to know that."

Now I was the one who was crying.

I could see Danh and Meagan coming back to Starbucks.

Danh arrived at the table first. He put a hand on each of the kids' shoulders and then looked me in the eye.

"Thank you for taking care of my boys, Nick," Danh said.

It seemed like he meant it. Meagan must have filled him in a little.

"You're welcome," I said.

The boys stood up. I gave them both a hug, and I held them as tightly as I could for the two seconds I had them in my arms. Then I kissed them each on the cheek.

"Adios, amigos," I said. I shook Danh's hand. "Nice meeting you," I said. "You're a lucky man."

"I know," he said.

I looked at Meagan. She still had that stupid smile on her face—it looked as if the survivor inside her had finally surrendered.

"And now I just need to talk to Meagan for a minute," I said.

"I don't think that's a good idea," Danh said.

"It's a very good idea," I said.

"No," Danh said.

I looked at Meagan and then back at Danh. Jade took his father's hand. "Let him do it, Dad," Jade said. "He deserves to talk to Mom."

Danh looked at his boys, and then Meagan snatched her passport and ticket out of his hand.

"I'll see you guys at the gate," she said.

Danh nodded slowly—*he would deal with this later*—and I watched him walk the boys to the security line. Then

I turned back to Meagan, took her by the hand, and led her over to a more private part of the airport.

"I need to tell you something," I said.

"I know—I'm a horrible person and you're going to hate me forever. I get it, and I don't blame you."

"That's not who you are to me," I said.

This wasn't going to be easy.

"I need to tell you that what you thought happened to Jade—didn't happen. Not exactly."

"What do you mean?" Meagan asked, and stepped back a little bit.

"Winsor never raped Jade," I said.

"You don't have to lie to me, Nick."

"It was fucked up. Some weird pictures and shit—" I took both her hands. I was whispering. "Jade couldn't tell you. He was afraid you'd hate yourself for doing—what you did."

"Oh, god," Meagan said, and closed her eyes.

"You didn't kill Winsor—and I never should have let you believe that you had. I'm very sorry."

Meagan squinted and squeezed my hands.

"He was still alive when we took him out in the boat," I said. "Maybe we could've saved him—but we didn't . . ."

I kissed her on the cheek.

"So don't drag that around with you for the rest of your life. Leave it down here with me."

Then I turned, and I walked out of the terminal.

47

I hadn't had any sleep since the surf comp at El Tigre, which was only the day before—but felt like last Christmas. I was deeply fried. Once I saw United Flight 806 lift off safely into the sky, I honked my horn twice and drove home.

I slept eight hours straight. It was dark out when I woke up, and I was starving. I looked out the window, and I could see the orphaned dog sitting under the *higuera*. She looked lonely. I decided to take her with me to go grab a bite. The mutt really was a beauty, so I figured I'd keep her, at least until . . . *until Meagan came back?*

So I named her Tilly—the rescued dog that could win Best in Show in Mexico.

Tilly walked to my right and just in front of me. She was well trained. I never once had to tug on the surf leash that I was using as a dog lead. I wondered how such a well-behaved dog had ended up in Sabanita. Meagan's ex probably rescued her from some wealthy Mexican's backyard—so he could pass himself off as a compassionate gringo.

We turned south on the beach. The lights of El Gecko were blazing about a half mile down the sand. It was probably the only place open, and I had been feeling shitty about dropping out of Sarah's life without any kind of an explanation. It wasn't like what happened was a serious hookup, but two old tugs who had crashed together in the night shouldn't have to worry about navigating away from each other. Sabanita was too small a pond.

I took my usual table and put my feet up on the short concrete beach wall. Tilly sat down next to me—straight and royal. She looked like the kind of girl who could ride English. I should probably stop tying her to a tree.

A señorita I had never seen at El Gecko poured me some ice water and put down a bowl of chips and some salsa. It was a nice touch, and a new one. Maybe this joint had changed ownership.

"Gracias," I said. But the new girl only smiled.

I craned my neck to see if I could spot Sarah, but I didn't see her. There was a couple canoodling at a corner table, doing tequila shots and whistling lime seeds into each other's mouths. Other than that, the joint was empty.

I'd ordered the *relleno especial* and had pretty much slammed all of it but the *frijoles* when I saw Sarah walk out of the kitchen. I barely recognized her. She was newly blond with a bit of a tan, and was wrapped in white linen. I was stunned by how pretty she was.

"Sarah," I called out.

I smiled and waved. She looked at me, hesitating for just a second.

"Amigo," Sarah said, finally.

Amigo?

Sarah came over to my table and kissed me on each cheek—quick and Euro-trashy.

"I am so sorry I disappeared on you," I said. "But I was on this surf trip to El Tigre, and then I—"

"Hey, no worries, Nico," Sarah said, glancing back toward the kitchen and faking a smile.

Nico?

And I was waiting for her to notice my eye.

"Yeah, well, it's a shitty thing to do," I said.

"It's fine."

At first I thought I was making Sarah nervous, but then this just started to feel awkward.

"What do you think of my eye?" I asked, a little too loud.

"Oh, my god," Sarah said, "I knew something looked different. I thought you maybe got a new haircut."

"Thanks for noticing," I said.

Apparently, I'd lost a little juice with this lady.

"Can I buy you a drink?"

"Look, Nick, if you want to party, I'm out of the business."

"I don't want to party," I said. "I just felt like seeing you."

"That's nice," she said. "But I'm not really seeing people anymore."

Or *most* of my juice, actually. Sarah looked to the kitchen again and held up a finger. Then she turned back to me.

"Nick, I owe you, I know," Sarah said, and then slid out a thin fold of peso bills she had tucked under her wrist bandanna. She counted out ten and handed them to me.

"I'm not here for the money," I said. "Keep it."

"I pay my debts," she said.

I quickly put the money in my pocket. It felt like we were being watched.

"You opened me up and let me feel real again, Nick," she continued. "And I will always be indebted to you for that."

"I'm happy I was able to help out," I said.

Sarah's linen top was so sheer I could see the tattoo of the unicorn she had on her stomach, although the last time I saw it, it had looked like a rhinoceros. She must've been on a fast.

She looked pretty trim—and then Sarah pointed to a large diamond ring on her left hand.

"I got married, Nick."

What?

"To who?" I was stunned—but I probably shouldn't have been.

"Fernando," she said. "I'm Mrs. Castilian now."

"Who's Fernando?"

"*Nando*," she said, pointing at the kitchen.

The only guy I could see was the cook who'd been cooking at El Gecko since my first meal here six years ago. He was still wearing the same T-shirt—but it had finally been washed, and his Che Guevara mustache was trimmed to match his slicked-backed, pitch-black hair. Nando suddenly looked like Zorro.

"The *cook*?"

"He'd been chasing me for years," Sarah said. "When I finally stopped running, he caught me." She was proud of herself. "But Nando's not just the cook. His family owns most of the beachfront in Sabanita."

"So you're rich?"

"Not exactly," she said, tossing her hair. "But I do have my own business now."

"Let me guess—*jewelry*," I said, figuring Sarah for one of the few gringos in town who would be nuts enough to buy Meagan's plastic chair.

"Detox Yoga," Sarah said.

"Of course," I said.

"It can cure cancer," Sarah said.

"How about incredulousness?"

Sarah laughed. "Never lose that sense of humor, Pirata."

She waved at Nando, and he blew her a kiss. I gave him the finger.

"It's all I got," I said.

Then I stood up and shook Sarah's hand.

"You make a lovely couple."

"We do," she said.

48

I was sitting on a hunk of driftwood and staring out at my little piece of the Pacific just north of town. I could see lightning on the horizon. The shore break was big, cresting and then crashing, bashing thousands of stones onto the beach as they nicked off little pieces of each other, making sand.

I might have been coming off my Epilim, because it felt a little like I was experiencing another absence seizure, those mini-space-outs that only last about a minute—but they put me in the ozone. If I saw a plane crash during one of these, I wouldn't remember it.

It was probably what was happening when I hit that tree with my son in the front seat. Grand mals have more drama, but absence seizures are more insidious. It's hard to tell when someone is having an absence seizure. It can just look like they're daydreaming.

Or maybe my current mental thickness was just the blowback from losing Jade and Obsidian, and getting dumped by Meagan. I was kind of bouncing between bumming and blacking out—like everything was moving forward, but I was still going backward. I mean, Jesus, even my drug dealer had retired—and then gotten *married*. I really *was* on my own.

I whistled for Tilly and then panicked a little until I could make out her shadow sniffing around a beach wall made of boulders. From the sounds of her growling and digging, I could tell that she had something trapped.

There was an ungodly croaking sound. And whatever it was, I didn't want Tilly to get stung on the nose. A lot of lethal shit shows up at night in Mexico, and I would hate for anything to happen to my new roommate.

"Easy, girl," I said. "Leave it alone."

But Tilly was really agitated, so I jogged over and then freaked.

What was croaking—and almost croaked—was my old friend Señor Pelícano. His broken wing had been chewed off, and the poor bastard was basically featherless.

I probably should have let Tilly put him out of his misery, but I didn't want her first lesson from me to be that it's okay to kill birds on the beach.

"Leave him alone, Tilly," I commanded. Sure enough, she backed off.

I still had the surf leash in my hand, so I tied Tilly up to my driftwood bench.

"Stay," I said.

Tilly sat down.

I went back to the pelican. It was hideous—skinny and bleeding. Part of its bill had been broken off, there was a hole in its pouch, and most of the webbing had been torn from its toes.

I needed to suck it up and wring the bird's neck. I couldn't let it keep suffering like this. I was ashamed I hadn't ended this bird's agony back when it was being harassed by the stray beach dogs.

I picked up the pelican, gently gathering its remaining wing in my left hand and folding it back to its body. I cradled my other hand underneath the dying bird's bare belly. He was squishy and slippery and leaking pus. I wasn't very good at this. I gagged.

I'd never done any neck wringing. I didn't have a clue about how to do it. I knew it involved grabbing the bird around its neck and then swinging it in a circle, which seemed horrifying. I tried it anyway, but apparently too slowly, so all I did was splatter myself with bloody pus—and a glob of this awfulness actually landed inside my mouth.

Blech!

I gagged again—and then just hurled the dying pelican into the sea. There. I was done with it.

"I'm sorry you had to see that," I said to Tilly as I spat into the sand and spritzed my mouth with ocean water. But just as I was about to untie her leash, I heard a croak. And then a splash.

And then more splashing and croaking. This must have been Rasputin's pet pelican. I sat down to wait for the reaper, hoping it wouldn't take too much longer and that something would eat the old bird. I had the over/under at five minutes. I looked over at my new dog.

"I'll take the under," I said.

But the splashing and croaking continued and then got even louder. Tilly started to bark.

"Just go with it, señor. It's time. Don't fight it."

Easy for me to say.

"Shit," I said.

I stood up and kicked off my flip-flops, pulled off my T-shirt, and dove over the shore break. I started swimming hard toward the sound of the croaks. I couldn't see a thing.

"Where are you, Señor Pelícano?" I shouted, as insane as it sounded.

The croaking was now farther out to sea, which shouldn't have surprised me, because this end of the beach is infamous for its riptide. But the ocean was my home; I wasn't worried.

I heard more splashing, and I swam faster. The croak was now a cry. I did notice now, though, that the lights from town were dimmer and a little farther away.

"I'm here," I said.

I had to bob up and down between swells, but I was finally able to reach for the bird.

The pelican was about three feet tall and would've had a five-foot wingspan if one of them hadn't been gnawed off. Its bill was nearly half that long. I had watched these magnificently cartoonish creatures guzzle foot-long bota fish in one gulp. But when I lifted this dying bird gently by the neck, all I could think of was a broken umbrella.

I probably should have just held the big bird underwater until he drowned, but I couldn't even do that. I was going to have to swim back to shore and let Tilly finish him off. At least I would be teaching her about the survival of the fittest.

But there was no way I'd be able to swim back to shore with one arm, not while holding a dying pelican in the other. In fact, the riptide was so strong that there was a possibility that I might not make it back even using both arms. I was pretty sure I was being swept out to sea. And it was pitch-black.

This wasn't good.

"Tilly!!!" I wailed.

I started to sidestroke, trying to break out of the rip's surging current. I knew I should swim parallel to shore and then power toward the beach once the riptide released me. If I didn't break through, I'd be swirled back out to sea. Which was what kept happening.

I should have let go of the bird. But I couldn't.

It occurred to me as I fought to hold on to this dying bird that I might drown, an idea I found as ridiculous as it was terrifying. I tried to imagine what Jade and Obsidian might think. I hated the thought of leaving them with the memory that I was a shitty waterman. And then I wondered if my son would ever know what happened to his dad.

I heard more splashing and croaking, but it wasn't Mr. Pelícano. He was high and dry in my hand—and the croaking was mine. The splashing was Tilly. She was swimming out to rescue me, trailing the surf leash and the chunk of driftwood behind her. My new best friend circled around me, and I was able to grab the leash.

"Good girl," I gasped.

I delicately put the pelican aboard the driftwood and then frog-kicked and pushed as Tilly dog-paddled us sideways out of the rip and then toward shore.

It was after midnight when I was finally able to roust Sabanita's one and only veterinarian. And he was really pissed off when he found out why.

Dr. Ramos was in his underwear, and I could smell beer on his breath. I might have prematurely ignited his morning hangover. He didn't speak much English, but he didn't have to.

"I can't kill this pelican," I said.

Dr. Ramos nodded slowly.

"Could you do it for me?" I asked.

"*¿Por qué?*"

"He's *suffering*."

I handed him the pelican.

"How much you pay?" Dr. Ramos asked.

"Whatever it takes," I said. "Just do it."

That might not have been the smartest thing to say to an animal health-care provider in Mexico, but at that moment I was pretty happy just to be alive—and relieved that Señor Pelícano's blood would be on someone else's hands.

49

Early the next morning, I took Tilly for a run on the beach. We made it all the way to where I'd almost been drowned by Señor Pelícano and then back to town for a smoothie at the Magic Mango, a popular gringo hangout on the plaza that specialized in two-thousand-calorie avocado-and-coconut milkshakes. It was off-season, so I was the only customer.

It poured rain for the rest of the day and kept raining for the next two weeks.

Most mornings I surfed head-high muddy Surprises while Tilly waited patiently for me on the beach. During afternoons, I took extralong siestas and tried to dream up new menus for the Wave of the Day. The local rivers were peaking, and *tormenta* had just about finished flushing Sabanita's excess trash into the Pacific.

"Slow down, Tilly," I said as I juggled my board and reached for her to steady myself. The runoff into Surprises was still raging from a predawn thunderstorm, and it had flooded the path to the beach. But the sky had cleared—first light was crystal. No wind, and the waves sounded exactly right.

We made it to the sand and looked out to sea as lines of perfect head-high cleaners stacked up and then released toward shore. Tilly pointed—someone really *had* trained this dog.

"I see her," I said.

And there she was, the 1975 ISP longboard champ, gracefully paddling into the silky face of a perfect left. Sarah stepped back on her Red Fin, wheeled the board into a textbook cutback, and then cross-stepped up to its nose—standing tall and hanging ten. I watched her in awe. It was true. She surfed like a champion.

"Let's go," I finally said to Tilly, and we slipped away unnoticed, leaving Sarah alone in her world.

If I missed a morning surf, I'd skip the siesta and head straight to the Wave of the Day. I had to admit that during Meagan's brief tenure in the cantina business, she had done a hell of a job. There wasn't that much for me to do. The toilets flushed and the lights stayed on.

The Wi-Fi had been activated, so I'd signed up for Facebook. I was hoping that the boys might friend me. But so far they had not. It bummed me out, but deep down, I knew what was going on. Having started over from scratch myself, I knew the kind of relationships that had to be severed.

I decided to change the name of the bar to Pirata's. The Wave of the Day was a kook slogan that you see on countless surf school T-shirts and coffee mugs. And it was also impossible for me to say it out loud without thinking of Meagan and the boys—and that bang stick and Winsor with a spear through his chest.

I drove up to Home Depot in PV and bought a four-by-eight-foot sheet of plywood. I painted it in the Mexican colors—to match my Meagan tattoo and to attract the *local* loyalists.

In the center of the middle white stripe, I fancied up *Pirata's* in an amateur attempt at Old English. It was nearly unreadable. I also drew a pirate with an eye patch and a Captain Jack Sparrow bandanna.

"I think *pirate* is spelled with an *e* at the end," a man said.

I turned and saw a guy standing in the doorway, but he was backlit by the sun, so it was hard to make him out.

"It's *pee-rah-tah*," I said, phonetically. "Which is how you say *pirate* in Spanish. And it's spelled with two *a*'s."

"Well, that's how you can spot the tourists, I guess," he said, moving just inside the door.

I got a better look at him. He was wearing a blue windbreaker and hard-soled brown shoes—and had short hair and long pants.

"That, and your shoes," I said.

This guy was either a Jehovah's Witness or a cop.

"Are you open?" he asked.

"I could sell you a beer if you want," I said.

"Sounds good," he said. "And a shot if you've got one."

Okay—so he wasn't a Jehovah's Witness.

The man stepped up to the bar. There was a directness about him that was a little disconcerting. He was maybe thirty-five years old and pale in an office cubicle sort of way. But he also had the low-fat face of a gym rat.

"Sorry, I don't have any lime," I said, handing him a Pacífico. I also poured him three fingers of tequila, which he slammed in one gulp.

"Gracias," he said.

I could see him ogling the big-wave gun Winsor had left hanging up on the wall.

"How do you like Sabanita?"

He shook his head. "I don't. Too much rain. Too many Mexicans."

I couldn't tell if he was joking or just being ugly in that American sort of way.

"That's why we call it off-season," I said.

"*Tormenta*," he said. "Mexico doesn't have a word for *monsoon*."

He had obviously read the handy tourist guide.

"Well, at least the flights to get down here are cheap," I said.

"That doesn't matter. The US taxpayers pick up my tab."

"Must be nice." I swallowed. This guy was a cop. Likely a Fed.

"I'm looking for someone," he said. "Maybe you can help me out."

"Maybe. Depends who you are, I guess."

"Lloyd Jeffries, FBI."

He actually took out his wallet and flashed me his ID. I pretended that it was the kind of thing that happened to me every day. I nearly yawned.

"Federal Bureau of Investigation," I read, a little sleepily.

"Ever hear of us?"

"I think so." I laughed—but it was a nervous laugh. All I could think of was Jade telling me about the Find My iPhone app and throwing Winsor's old one out the Suburban's window. Holy shit—it looked like somebody had found it.

"I'm looking for a man named Nick Lutz," he said.

I gave Agent Jeffries my very best car-salesman smile. "I'm Nick Lutz."

I couldn't tell whether he was surprised or if he already knew. The guy had a killer poker face.

"That was easy, huh?" he said.

"I've got nothing to hide," I said, like a married guy trying to explain the condom in his wallet to his wife.

"Any idea what brought me here?" Jeffries asked. "Why I'd come all the way down to Mexico during the hot and shitty season?"

"Not really."

He had this weirdly triumphant look on his face—as if he was having a little fun with this. My heart was pounding through my chest. I was sure he could see my T-shirt pulsating.

He finished his beer and motioned for another one. I handed him his second Pacífico.

"Go ahead. Take a free kick," he said. "No penalty."

It was obvious to me why Agent Jeffries was here. The Mexican cops had somehow identified Winsor's body and notified the US.

"You probably came down here to talk about the owner of this place," I said, heavy and slow.

"So *you're* not the owner?"

The guy could play dumb like a genius. I was being Columbo'd.

"I'm just running it for him," I said, soaking through my shirt.

"But you're Pirata, the gringo with one eye, right?" Agent Jeffries smiled, feigning confusion.

"Not anymore," I said, pointing to my glass eye. "I'm a miracle of modern technology."

"Then why the new sign? Why change the name?" He took a tiny sip of his Pacífico.

This guy was slick. I forced myself to smile.

"I think you're looking for Winsor Baumgarten, actually," I said, ignoring his last two questions completely. "But no one knows where he is. I don't. No idea. None."

I think it was the first time I had ever said Winsor's whole name out loud. I fully expected Agent Jeffries to arrest me for murder, and I felt as if I was going to pass out. I nearly held out my hands to be cuffed—and I immediately began thinking about what kind of plea deal I should try to make with the FBI before Chuy and José teamed up to send me to the gas chamber.

"Who?" Agent Jeffries asked.

"Winsor Baumgarten. That's who owns this place."

Fuck.

"I'm just running it for him until he gets back," I said.

"From where?"

"From here, behind the bar." I was talking way too much and making very little sense.

"Never heard of him," Agent Jeffries said. "And I'd remember a name like that."

Jeffries took another tiny sip of his beer and then nodded his head almost imperceptibly. For some reason, I started nodding along with him—or maybe I was shaking. I gritted my teeth. This guy was definitely up to something. I couldn't tell if he was good cop, bad cop–ing me—or if maybe José and Chuy had already confessed and they had blamed killing Winsor on me. I was nearly hallucinating with stress.

"We found the guy who shot you, Mr. Lutz. He's being extradited from Florida this week." Agent Jeffries had that triumphant look on his face again.

"What?" I wasn't too sure what he had just said. I was trying not to hyperventilate, and I gripped the bar with both hands.

"The guy who shot you." Jeffries pointed to my glass eye. "Remember?"

"The *carjacker*?"

I felt like I had just been pardoned from death row. I had to fight off an urge to kiss him as he took another drink of his Pacífico. I had thought for sure I was about to be arrested for Winsor's murder. I tried not to smile too much.

"But he wasn't a carjacker," Agent Jeffries said.

"He was so. The guy jacked an Impala. It was fully loaded."

"He was a hired hit man," he said.

"No way," I said, even though I was very relieved he wasn't here to pop me for Winsor.

"Yup, he was. A pro," he said. "He admitted to being hired to kill you because he was trying to plead down another murder-for-hire beef down in Miami. He passed the lie detector and everything."

"That sounds a little ridiculous," I said. "Don't you think?"

"It doesn't matter how it sounds," he said. "That's the reality of it."

"I was a car salesman. Nobody puts a hit on a car salesman. I mean, who would do that?"

"Well, apparently a wife would," Agent Jeffries said. "At least, she would if she was banging the assistant manager, and the husband had a two-million-dollar life insurance policy."

He took another long drink of his Pacífico. I stepped out from behind the bar and slumped down into a chair.

"*My wife?*" I asked softly.

50

From the way Agent Jeffries was looking at me, I thought that maybe I'd just had an absence seizure. Somehow I was drinking a glass of water. I had no idea how much time had passed, but Agent Jeffries's beer was still half-full—so it wasn't like I had blacked out and confessed.

"She hired someone to kill me?" I said.

"With an accomplice," Jeffries said, as if that might ease the blow. "Her boyfriend, apparently. Who was your assistant new-car manager at the time."

"Steve Levine?" Holy shit. "He was a *buddy* of mine."

"You didn't know that they got married?"

"They got *married*? I didn't even know Julie and I were divorced."

My brain felt like it was being caned.

"Hey, you abandoned her, right?"

"I didn't *abandon* anybody. Living with a hole in your head is an incredible bummer. I was miserable. So was Julie. So I took off. It was what was best for everybody."

Jeffries started with the tiny nodding again.

"But that hole in your head is because Julie and Steve hired a guy and had you shot. Your *buddy* ended up with your old job. Your new house. And your ex-wife."

"Jesus," I said.

It was starting to sink in.

"Motive is a big part of how these things get figured out," he said.

It was impossible to comprehend anyone hating me that much. Julie and I had a crap marriage, and I won't deny playing around when an opportunity got teed up. But she wasn't exactly the heartbroken housewife, either. After I'd gotten shot, it got even worse.

But I never wanted her dead.

We had talked about divorce—in fact, it was the *only* thing we talked about. We just couldn't figure out how to King Solomon our kid, who was the only person in the family who mattered to both of us.

Then I ran into a tree, and that pretty much decided who got to look after our son.

"What's going to happen to her?" I asked.

Jeffries shrugged. It was obvious.

"Jail?" I asked.

He laughed. "Oh, yeah. Attempted first-degree murder and solicitation. Grievous injury. The new hubby's already agreed to testify. It'll be hard for her to PMS out of this one."

I stood up. I was light-headed, and I reeled a bit. I leaned against the back of a chair and then reached out to shake Agent Jeffries's hand.

"Thank you for telling me all this."

"Sit down," he said. "I'm not done."

I sat back down.

Agent Jeffries removed a small photograph from his pocket and handed it to me. It was a color snapshot of a boy wearing a San Diego Chargers jersey and holding a skateboard tied with a blue ribbon. The boy looked about twelve. And then I had this horrible flash that maybe this was about Winsor, after all.

"Do you recognize that kid?" Agent Jeffries asked.

I was hesitant and very frightened. "He looks familiar."

"He should. That was taken at his last birthday."

And then it crashed down on me that I was staring at a photograph of my son, Marshall. I hadn't seen him in six years. I was startled to see how grown-up he was.

"When the Marshman turned twelve years old," I said softly.

It felt as if the volume had been turned down on the whole world. I could barely hear.

"What do you want to do about him?" Agent Jeffries said.

"I'm sorry," I said. "What?"

"Where do you want them to put your son?"

"How is that up to me?"

"His mom's in jail—probably going to stay there. Your in-laws are passing on the boy. They don't want him. If you

don't, he goes to Child Protective Services and then probably some kind of foster care."

All I could say was, "No."

"Well, it was a big thing to ask, I know. But that's why
I came all the way down here. I figured your kid deserved
the effort."

"I meant, no foster care." I looked at the photograph.
My hand trembled.

Jeffries smiled and nodded. "I'll bet he'll be happy to
hear that," he said, and gave me his card. My in-laws' address was scribbled on the back. "There's a Ward of the
State petition in progress, which is a bitch to get out of,
so you don't have a lot of time—but for now he's staying
there." He nodded at the address on the back of the card.

"How long do I have?"

"Depends how screwed up CPS is," he said. "But his
grandmother wants him out of the house."

"I'll leave tonight."

"Okay." He smiled. "This was worth the trip, then."

I stood up, and Jeffries shook my hand.

"Take care of him."

"I will do my best," I said.

Agent Jeffries finished the last inch of foam in his
beer and then walked out the door. I looked back down at
the photograph of Marshall. I had forgotten how beautiful
he was.

It was hard to breathe.

51

For the last six years, I'd pushed back against the night-mares and negotiated down my responsibility for the fits and the accident—trying to disown the memory of regaining consciousness just in time to watch my seven-year-old being loaded into an ambulance.

We had been coming back from a victory dinner at In-N-Out Burger. Marshall's Little League team had just crushed the Mini Padres. The Marshman had hit a triple with two RBI, so I was letting him ride up in the big-boy seat next to me—even though California law is very clear about car seats in the back seat for kids under eight.

"Just put that seat belt on and you'll be fine," I told him.

Marshall was always more worried about breaking the rules than I was. But tonight we were pretty full of ourselves, and I was getting a kick out of treating him like a superstar.

The arresting officer had told me that Marshall had been jettisoned from under the big-boy seat belt on impact, and when the airbag deployed, it had broken his neck.

I had been warned about driving with a TBI while off my meds, so I couldn't really blame Julie for trying to kill me—even if I've been too chickenshit to finish the job ever since.

This was the crazy loop that kept circling in my head. But I had it backward—something I would just be able to grasp and then instantly lose sight of.

The reason I even had a hole in my head and all these fits and seizures was that I'd been shot. Agent Jeffries told me that my ex-wife and her boyfriend had hired someone to kill me. Julie and my old pal Steve "The Machine" Levine—they were responsible for the hole in my head. Marshall's mom didn't put a hit on me because I'd nearly killed him in a car accident. *She* bought the bullet that caused my TBI in the first place.

I had been off my meds, and I will always own that—but I shouldn't have ever been on them.

I was finally able to assemble the bits and pieces of this nightmare in a way that made some sense—even if it would only hold together for a few seconds. But I was having moments when the impossibility of it all was at least manageable.

I didn't have a Mexican credit card and my SSDI installment didn't come in until the first of the month, so I was going to need gas money to get up to SoCal. And who knew how long it would take me to get settled and find a job and a place for Marshall and me to live.

I packed my one pair of long pants and six T-shirts. I needed a dog sitter and someone to watch my casa—and, I figured, about $1,000 in cash. Which was about 20,000 pesos, or two months' income for a hardworking Sabanitan— an impossible sum to have saved up during the off-season.

"Pirata," Chuy said, "I'm giving you food if you are hungry and a bed for sleep, but I don't have no big dollars like that."

"Yeah, and who lends money to a gringo who's running away back home?" José asked.

I could see José under the shadow of a mango tree at the edge of Chuy's front yard. He was naked and covered in blood—masterfully butchering a cow with a machete and stacking up large slabs of bright-red meat.

Chuy was barefoot and shirtless, with both his hands shrugged apologetically into the giant pockets of his cargo shorts. I was dressed for the road in my long pants and a Billabong hoodie. I was even wearing my leather flip-flops.

"I'm coming back, amigo," I said.

"Oh, yeah, *now* I'm your amigo." José snorted.

"Why do you need so much money, Pirata?" Chuy asked.

I shrugged—I wasn't ready to talk about my son. "You just have to trust me."

"But we know each other's everything," Chuy said. "We carry the same sins."

"Those sins didn't even come up in the conversation," I said.

"That's what you say," José said. "No one knows what the fucking FBI said."

José hosed himself down and pulled on some pants.

Then he walked over to me and mumblety-pegged the machete between my feet. I didn't flinch, which disappointed him a little.

"Don't make me come find you—or that cow will look good compared to you," he said, in that great way he had with the English language. "I'll lend you the money."

"You will?" I tried to pull the machete from the dirt between my feet—but it was buried halfway to its hilt and wouldn't budge.

"And I don't give a fuck why you need it," he said, yanking the machete free with ease.

"Thank you," I said.

"But I live in your casa until you pay me back," he said.

I tried not to smile. No one messes with José. My casita would be safe while I was gone.

"Only if you take care of my dog," I said.

José turned to Chuy. "Is this *pendejo* negotiating?" José asked, laughing.

"Tilly's a great dog," I said.

"I know," he said. "Maybe I meet her already."

José winked at me just to piss me off and then slipped the machete through a steel ring hanging from the rope slung over his shoulder.

"Chuy and Yohana run the Wave of the Day. All the money they make when you're gone, they keep," he said. "No percentages."

"That's bullshit," I said. I was smiling.

"It doesn't matter," José said. "You need the money. And if you no come back, we keep everything."

"I get the Red Fin," Chuy said.

"Fuck," I said. But I said it like a man getting laid.

I couldn't have hoped for a better deal, but I think José knew that. He could tell I needed help, and he was willing to help me—no questions asked. He just didn't want it to look like the gringos were getting their way with the Mexicans again.

52

It took 2,000 pesos to fill up the Suburban at Sabanita's Pemex. But at least it had a four-hundred-mile range. If my bladder held out, I could take Highway 200 all the way to Tepic and then México 15 up to Mazatlán without stopping. Then I'd head straight toward the border on the toll roads, with just one more pit stop before crossing over.

Sabanita is about fifteen hundred miles due south of Nogales, Arizona. It's a hot and hellish thirty-hour drive to the border. I was hoping to pull off an unassisted all-nighter and then grab a few hours of sleep on the side of the road in the safety of the States late tomorrow night. I planned on slogging the Tucson-to-San Diego leg the next morning.

I didn't kid myself that I had any good karma to cash in, and I'd already been boned buying US dollars for twenty-two pesos each at the *cambio*. But the trip *el norte* was pretty much a snore—until I decided to exit México 15 North just past Culiacán.

The new *cuota calles* that are under construction all over boomtown Mexico were slowing me way down—single-file, bumper-to-bumper bullshit—and costing about ten bucks an hour in tolls. I was losing time and money.

So I took a freebie two-laner that cut up just west of Hidalgo del Parral—which is El Chapo Guzmán's old neighborhood, but he's in jail now, so it's not supposed to be that sharky. I figured, what the hell, I could make up some time.

It was a mistake.

Ten miles later, I was at the back end of a long line of cars inching toward *another* nightmare checkpoint. Mexico is Mexico, and it always requires a third eye—although even then I'd be one eye short, so I had to be even more cautious than the average gringo idiot. But tonight, I wasn't. I was in too much of a hurry to see my son.

As I crept closer, I could make out a wooden lookout on the driver's side of the road. It was three steps tall, and a man wearing a dark suit was perched on its small platform. Just below him, a soldier slung with a machine gun and bandoliers was questioning the occupants of each car. The man in the suit held a spotlight.

It took me about an hour to reach the soldier. He was being very thorough.

My window was already down and I tried to fake a smile, but my Adam's apple kept jumping with each beat of my heart—so I just gritted my teeth.

"*Buenas noches,*" I said, about three octaves higher than normal.

Even though it was dark, the soldier wore sunglasses. It was hard to gauge his mood. I squinted up at the man in the dark suit but was blinded by the spotlight he was pointing at me. I could see a handful of soldiers milling around a fruit stand on the other side of the two-laner.

All I could think was how close I'd been to seeing my son again, and how I'd put all that on the line just to save a little toll money. I've never felt more regretful, or like a bigger fool.

"*Documentos,*" the soldier demanded.

I leaned over to the Suburban's glove box and reached to open it.

"*¡Pirata!*"

I immediately recognized the voice. El Jefe clicked off the spotlight, and I was able to see him standing on the wooden platform.

"I'm on my way *el norte*—to see if any gringos are sneaking across the border," he said.

He looked proud. I was terrified.

"I'm trying to sneak back out," I said, faking a laugh.

El Jefe didn't crack a smile and I recalled how tricky his sense of humor could be. He was wearing a red tie with his dark suit, a white shirt, and polished shoes. A rose was pinned to his lapel. "Actually," he continued, "it's my *sobrina's quinceañera* in Culiacán."

"*Felicidades a su familia,*" I said.

"Gracias, Pirata," he said. "I'm a little drunk—I ate too much *tres leches. Por favor perdóname.*"

"No worries," I said, taking a shot at what he meant.

"Maybe just a few," he said. "I have to check *mis tropas del destino, ¿y tú?*"

I had to guess again.

"It's good to see you, too," I said.

And El Jefe went cold. "Don't lie."

Fuck.

"I'm sorry," I said.

Every time I ran into this guy, it was the game show from hell.

El Jefe sniffed at his boutonniere and started to list. He was pretty drunk, and he grabbed at the platform's handrail to steady himself. "Where are you going?"

I was starting to panic. This guy was nuts enough sober.

The soldier moved to stand in front of the Suburban as he clicked the safety off his machine gun, and I wrestled with whether or not to tell El Jefe the truth.

"To the US," I finally said, measuring the opening between the soldier and the roadside and El Jefe listing on his platform. I was going to have to run one of them down, and then, very likely, I'd be shot to death by the other soldiers—all of whom were now paying close attention as they stood at the ready in front of the fruit stand. I started to weep. I'd let Marshall down again.

"*¿Por qué?*" El Jefe slurred.

"Family business," I said, trying to hide my tears.

It was the only thing I could think of that didn't sound like a lie—besides the fact that it was actually true. It seemed to please him.

"*Respuesta perfecta,*" El Jefe said softly. "It's all that

matters." Then he delicately removed the rose from his lapel and tossed it at the soldier. "*Déjalo pasar*," he sang, with a grandiose wave of his hand, "*¡apúrate!*"

The soldier backed away from the Suburban, and I slowly drove away.

Jesús Cristo, what an unpredictable motherfucker.

But I wasn't bitching.

I have never believed in luck—bad or good—and maybe you don't have to for it to work, because I'd just caught a big break from a three-alarm maniac.

But my luck changed again when I arrived at the border the following night, reminding me why I'm a nonbeliever.

As soon as I crossed into the country of my birth, I was dragged out of the Suburban by a couple of my fellow Americans. Once the border agents had seen that I was a gringo driving a Mexican vehicle with five-year-old plates, they had waved me into a special lane.

"Your passport is expired, amigo," one of the idiot customs agents said.

I had assumed the position across the hood while another agent conducted a bumper-to-bumper search of the Suburban. A team of drug dogs circled and sniffed.

"I know, sir," I said, maybe a little too obsequiously. "One of the reasons I'm coming up is to get it renewed."

"Don't call me *sir*," he said. He was going through my wallet and testing for cocaine residue on the edges of my expired credit cards. The other agent had begun opening up the Dakine surfboard pads that he had stripped from the roof rack.

"And my FM3 has expired, too," I said.

"Shut up," the first agent said.

Then he handed my wallet and passport to an agent who was standing at a computer in a glass booth.

"What's the purpose of your trip?" the agent in the glass booth asked, without looking up.

He was typing my old California driver's license number into a computer.

"I don't need a purpose," I said. "I'm a US citizen."

"That's the old days," the agent said. "You're a Mexican resident now."

He was a little less of a hard-ass than the others and appeared to be the boss on this shift.

"With an expired FM3, too," he continued.

"I'm sending in all the stuff to get that done," I said. "There's, like, a three-year wait."

"But you can't beat the *al pastor* street tacos," he said, like someone who'd been south of the border and liked it. "What's in the States?"

He walked over to the Suburban and motioned for me to get off the hood.

"My son," I said, dropping every piece of ass-kissing bullshit. "He used to live with his mom, but now I have to take over."

"Why?"

"She's in jail," I said.

"That's tough," he said.

I was hoping he wasn't going to ask me the details.

"How old is he?"

"Almost thirteen," I said. "I haven't seen him in six years."

"You won't recognize him," he said. "But you have a bigger problem."

"I do?" I started to go through a not-so-short list of potentials in my head.

"I can't let you drive across the border. You have a reckless under-the-influence in California. Your license to drive has been revoked."

"Well, actually," I said, "I *wasn't* under the influence. I was off my seizure meds."

"It was a felony," he said. "There were serious injuries."

"I remember." I took a breath. "I have a Mexican license."

But he just laughed. "To practice medicine, or drive?"

Shit.

"And your expired passport is going to take a couple of days, too," he continued. "I can't let you cross until I get a temporary stamp from Phoenix."

"I *have* to get to California."

"I'm sorry. Maybe in a few days you can take the bus."

He motioned for a couple of his guys to move my Suburban out of the special lane.

"I totally get that you have rules and that this is Arizona," I said. "But could I try entering at Tijuana?"

"Too late, brah," he said.

Brah? It was pretty old-school surf slang, and he probably didn't get that now it made him sound like a kook, but maybe he'd been in the lineup back in the day.

He picked up the Dakine surfboard pads that the

other agent had stripped and dissected, and tossed them through the passenger window and onto the seat.

"These are the kind, dude," he said. "Don't lose them."

The kind? I knew I was grasping, but *Da-kine* was Hawaiian pidgin for "the kind—the best." It *was* surf talk, no doubt. Maybe this guy was secret-coding me.

"Do you surf?" I asked.

Not that surfers were all from the same tribe, but sometimes there is this sense of aloha when we run into each other inland instead of out in the lineup.

"No surf in Arizona. Got a lot of kooks, though." He smiled. "I grew up in Encinitas."

"Beacon's?" I asked, flashing back to some surf breaks up in San Diego County.

"Boneyard and Seaside Reef," he said. "Black's when I got brave, and Swami's when it got big."

"Sweet spots," I said.

"Then all of a sudden I was too old to ride a shortboard—but I got transferred here, so it worked out."

"That's why I ride a Red Fin."

That stopped him.

"Did Mike Hynson shape it for you?"

"I didn't know there was another kind," I said.

He opened my passport and looked at the date again. He frowned. "My parents sent me to summer camp in Idaho when I was fourteen. For two weeks, I hid out in the lodge and watched *Endless Summer.*"

"That doesn't sound like a bad vacation," I said.

"Not now."

"But Hynson didn't ride a Red Fin in *Endless Summer*," I said. "That came later. In the movie, he rode a Hobie."

"With those stripes and that sick middle stringer," he said, measuring out more than an inch with his thumb and forefinger.

"I remember," I said.

He narrowed the gap between his fingers, as if to show me just how close a call I was asking him to make. And I suddenly realized how much of our future this stranger held in his hand. He had to decide whether my son was going to get to live with me or in a foster home among strangers, while betting I wasn't a drug dealer or a terrorist and simply the dysfunctional surf bum I claimed to be. And he had to make that bet almost instantly. Lives depended on it. I couldn't imagine that kind of pressure.

"Okay," he sighed, shaking his head slightly as he stamped an extension on my passport and stapled an official-looking document to my California driver's license. "I wouldn't do this if you didn't know what a Red Fin was," he said.

"If I didn't know what a Red Fin was, I wouldn't be living down in Mexico," I said.

He nodded. "That's probably true."

I crossed into the United States of America for the first time in nearly six years, and headed west on Interstate 8.

53

I turned onto the street where my in-laws had lived ever since they moved out from Iowa so Julie's dad could work for Hughes Aerospace. Their two-bedroom stucco bungalow with the turquoise gutters and Astroturf front lawn was typical of the homes at the western edge of the Inland Empire, that vast, air-conditioned nightmare known as the 909—which was the original area code for what is considered one of the most heat-stricken and tedious neighborhoods in Southern California.

Not much had changed since I'd lived here. It looked a little more tired and run-down, maybe—just like I probably do. SoCal was still crowded as hell, but I had missed its everythingness. How all the street lights turned on and the toilets flushed. I liked that the police weren't going to shake you down or shoot you—at least, not a chubby white guy like me. I hated the chronic politics and the online badgering of America's chattering class, but I had to admit I missed backyard picnics and the sweet sixteen.

I just wasn't sure I could live here again.

My son was standing in the driveway. He had a backpack slung over one shoulder, and he was holding a skateboard as if it were a guitar. I would have preferred that his instrument of choice was a surfboard, but the closest beach *was* an hour away by bus. His hair was much longer than in the photograph, and he looked about two feet taller, too. But for sure, this was my son, for real and for the first time in almost six years. It felt like I was paddling into a wave that could either drown me or take me to shore.

I pulled into the driveway just as the bungalow's front door closed. It was pretty clear my in-laws didn't want to see me. They probably figured that what their daughter had done was reasonable, considering what a crappy husband I was.

Marshall and I looked at each other through the windshield. He was skinnier than I'd thought he was going to be. His jeans were ridiculously tight—and short. When I was his age, we would have called them *floods*. He was wearing a TONY HAWK FOR PRESIDENT T-shirt. I liked him already.

I started to get out of the Suburban, but Marshall motioned for me to stay inside. He looked back at his grandparents' house and sort of rolled his eyes.

I got it.

He climbed in on the passenger side, and we both kind

of fumbled around. Then he handed me his skateboard and backpack, and I tossed them onto the rear seat as if I had been doing it every day for the last six years.

"Hi, Marshall," I said.

He wasn't sure if he should hug me or shake my hand, so I leaned over and kissed him on the cheek and put my arms around his shoulders and squeezed. He felt strong, and I recognized his smell.

"Nobody calls me Marshall anymore, Dad," he said.

"I'm sorry."

"It's okay." He waved at the drapes in the front window. "Can we go?"

"Are they watching?"

"They watch everything. I even have to pee in a cup after every weekend."

"Put on your seat belt," I said.

"Okay," Marshall said, and then buckled himself in almost instantly—as if to keep the moment as small as possible.

I backed out of the driveway—pretending that driving with my son in the front seat was no big deal. But it was a very big deal. The last time I had taken my son for a ride, I'd nearly killed him. We were both faking that the memory wasn't hogging up most of the seat between us—and we weren't exactly pulling it off.

"So, what *do* people call you these days?" I asked, trying to pop the boil.

"Usually Marsh."

"You mean like a swamp?"

I bumped him on the knee to make the joke, but nothing was feeling very funny.

"Like the *Marshman*, Dad," he said. "Like you used to."

But it did sound like he was getting a kick out of calling me Dad, and that felt good.

He pulled up his sleeve and showed off a tattoo—it was a skateboard with *The Marshman* inked in gothic script just above his left bicep.

"That'll last forever, Marsh," I said, a recent expert.

"And I got it when I was eleven, so it's even longer."

"Who lets an eleven-year-old boy get a tattoo?!" I asked, faking shock and disdain.

"Me and Uncle Steve got them in Tijuana," Marshall said.

"He's not your uncle."

"Well, I don't know what else to call him."

"How about an accomplice to attempted murder?"

It was a cheap shot, and it stung a little more than I'd wanted it to. Marshall seemed unsure how to respond.

"What's an accomplice?"

"Usually a guy who can't say no to a bad idea," I said, on uncomfortably familiar ground.

"Oh," Marshall said.

He started to bite a thumbnail. I could see that his fingernails were bitten down and a little bloody. Marshall caught me looking and crossed his arms to hide his hands. He was embarrassed.

"I used to bite my fingernails," I said.

"You did?"

"Yeah, all the way down. I couldn't stop."

"Why not?"

"Because, who knows—maybe the world made me nervous." I hadn't given biting my fingernails that much thought. "But I liked pushing the part I bit off through my teeth."

"I do that," Marshall said. "But Steve told me it's because I'm a pussy."

"That's not a word I'd use."

"I know what it means."

"I'm not surprised," I said.

I was hoping my son wasn't going to hurl the C-word as easily as Obsidian had.

"It means 'wimp,'" Marshall said.

"You're not a wimp," I said.

Marshall clicked his thumbnail against his front teeth. It was quiet and we just sat there, trying to figure out the shapeless space between us and whether we should push into it or lean away.

"Have you talked to Mom?" Marshall finally asked.

"No," I said.

"I didn't think you would," he said. "You guys hate each other."

I let out a breath. "You do know what they're saying, right?"

"What?"

"That your mom tried to *kill* me."

"I know they're saying that," he said.

Marshall reached into the back seat and took something

out of his backpack. I couldn't see what it was, but it didn't look as if he was hiding it from me.

"Your mom and *Uncle* Steve hired some guy to shoot me in the head," I said, as if he might have missed my point the first time.

But the Marshman only nodded.

"What do *you* think?" I didn't want to start sounding like I was interrogating him—but I was. "I'm sure you have an opinion about this."

"I'm glad that the guy was a lousy shot, I guess," he said.

"Not about the guy who did the shooting," I said. "About your mom."

Marshall reached over and turned the ignition key. Then he pulled it out so the steering column locked. I had to let the Suburban glide to a stop.

He looked at me.

"I don't want this to be the first thing we talk about, okay," he said, wiser than his father.

Marshall handed me the photograph that he'd just taken out of his backpack. "Do you remember this?" It was a picture of Marshall and a lopsided chocolate cake.

"It was your birthday. You were five," I said.

"And who made the cake?"

"We did."

"You and me and Mom did," Marshall said. "And I wished you were gonna come back for my birthday every year."

My lower lip was stiffening up. "Well," I said. "Here I am."

We were both breathing in the exact same way. I began to bite my thumbnail.

Marshall took the photograph back and delicately slipped it into his backpack.

"So where are we going?" Marshall asked.

"Well, I should probably go find a job."

"Oh—so we are staying up here."

I looked over at Marshall. I couldn't tell if he was relieved or disappointed.

"What kind of job?" he asked.

"Something that I am very good at," I said, maybe a little too cocky.

"Can I come?"

"I got this," I said. "Where can you hang until I close the deal?"

"Anywhere but here," he said.

"Okay," I said. "But you're going to have to narrow it down."

I figured that what I had seen was disappointment. But then Marshall smiled just a little bit.

"Go west on the 78 to the 5 and then go south."

54

I was standing at the edge of a gigantic concrete skate bowl and watching my son throwing ridiculous air. I had dropped him off at the Encinitas YMCA skate park while I went to interview for a job at Jacobs Chevrolet, the same dealership where I'd been the new-car sales manager before getting shot.

"The business has really changed," said a twentysomething in a shiny suit that looked like it was about two sizes too small.

He pointed to a chair in his office, and I sat down. His pants were flood-length, just like the Marshman wore his jeans, and he had a pink-and-black pocket square that matched his knit tie.

It was a smart move that I'd swung by the Gap for a pair of black cotton pants and a crisp, gray rugby jersey with a white collar. Mr. Shiny didn't seem like the Hawaiian-shirt type.

"What was your best year, Mr. Lutz, when you worked here at Jacobs?" he asked.

"Oh, I don't know," I said. "I don't like to brag."

"I can check," he said. "But I'd rather you tell me."

"When I was in straight sales? Probably two hundred K, at least," I said. "When I was the new-car manager, probably another fifty because I got a taste of everything that went over the curb. And I pushed hard."

"Our best man doesn't make half that," he said, like he was proud of it. "And I'm the *new* new-car manager. My salary is one hundred thousand dollars a year—no *taste*—counting a health-care buy-in and a take-with pension plan."

"Jesus. I thought Obama saved General Motors." I laughed.

Mr. Shiny didn't.

"Our customers search the Internet for the lowest possible price on the *exact* car they want to purchase. And if we don't sell it to them at that price, they'll go to a dealership that will."

"Jesus," I said again.

"We're not salesmen anymore, Mr. Lutz. We're automotive demonstrators. Vehicle introduction hosts. Product knowledgists."

"Knowledgists?" I said.

"For lack of a better word," he said.

"*Experts* is a better word," I suggested. "My guys knew every option combination and the gas mileage and available warranties on every vehicle in the entire GM line. They sent birthday cards to their old customers and a bottle of champagne to their new ones."

"That would be a waste of time and money in today's market."

"Dude, it's only been six years."

"Well, maybe I'm not a *dude*."

"I'm sorry," I said.

"And I'm afraid that considering your special circumstances, Jacobs Chevrolet won't be able to employ you at this time," Mr. Shiny said, with an obnoxious glint in his eye.

"Special circumstances? You mean like how I was Salesman of the Year for three years?"

"No. I mean the felony reckless you have on your revoked California driver's license."

"I have a Mexican driver's license now," I said. "It's valid here."

"For full-time Mexican residents in the US on tourist visas, yes," he said, like a wannabe lawyer who never got past community college. "But if that's the case, it means you're not a California resident—so we can't hire you, anyway."

"Do you know why I lost my license?" I asked, and not very nicely. "The guy you replaced was banging my wife. The two of them hired a hit man to assassinate me."

"I'm staying out of all that," he said.

"It's how I got this fake eye, and why I had fits and ran my son into a tree." I was starting to raise my voice.

"Let's leave that to the jury, Mr. Lutz," he said, shifting in his seat.

"The Machine was your buddy, wasn't he?"

"He was a mentor," the shiny suit said. "I don't mix business with buddies."

"Well, he was *my* buddy," I said.

"Which is why I don't."

I wanted to kill this guy.

"And despite how unfair this might be—and I think it is," he said, "a car salesman who can't take his customers for a demonstration drive wouldn't be much of a salesman, would he?"

The Marshman spotted me standing at the edge of the skate park. I waved and he skated over, impressively balancing on the two back wheels of his skateboard.

"You want to try it?" Marsh asked, kicking up his skateboard and catching it in one hand.

"I'm a surfer," I said.

"This is a concrete wave, *dude*—overhead every day."

"You don't surf," I said. It wasn't a question.

"I'm a nine-oh-niner," my son said, about as antiprecious as possible. "And we only go to the beach to wreak havoc and rage."

I wasn't surprised that my kid had some smart-ass in him. I laughed and tweaked the back of his neck as we walked toward the Suburban.

"Ow," he said.

Then with my index finger I traced the jagged scar at the center of Marshall's forehead that ran down and around the back of his neck to where his upper spine had been fused back together.

"Does that ever hurt?" I asked.

"Now it tickles," he said, and shrugged it off. "How did the job thing go?"

"Not so good," I said. "The car business has been taken over by an inefficient gang of efficiency experts."

The Marshman laughed. "Mom told me you were funny."

"As a hole in the head," I said, and felt bad about it as soon as I did.

"Don't keep doing that," he said.

"Okay," I said.

We got into the Suburban, and I pulled out onto Saxony Road.

"Do you have a plan?" he asked.

"Yeah," I said. "I plan to win the lottery."

"Let's start with an easier one," Marshall said. "Like where're we gonna live."

"In the Suburban," I said.

There was no *easier* one. Three days ago I was an expatriate licking my wounds in Mexico, and today I was a single dad with a teenager. Life might not be a dress rehearsal, but it's not supposed to be just an improv, either. I was clueless about the next step. I thought I'd get my old car sales job back—but that idea blew up before lunch.

"We can panhandle at Huntington Beach," I continued.

"I *hate* Huntington Beach." His disdain was palpable. "I'd rather live in Mexico."

"Mexico is *not* like here, Marsh."

"That's why I would," he said.

I was actually hoping to bring up Mexico at some point—it was always my bailout strategy. The cut and run if I still hadn't found a decent job when José's front money was gone.

"But you have school," I said.

"Our family shit was on the news, Dad. The kids in school all know."

I couldn't imagine how hard it would be to have to go back to the eighth grade after your mom had just been arrested for hiring a hit man to murder your dad.

"You'd be willing to try Mexico?"

"Nobody would be talking about me and pointing their fingers every ten feet." He shrugged. "I mean, it's not like *I* shot you."

I glanced at the middle seat and nodded at Marshall's backpack and skateboard.

"Do we have to go get any more of your stuff?"

"No," the Marshman said. "I've got everything I need."

55

We entered Mexico a little after midnight at the No-gales border crossing where I had just exited the day before. My passport was still expired, and Marshall didn't even have one. But it didn't matter. I had slowed to a stop for the Mexican customs guy and rolled down my window, but when he saw the Jalisco license plates, he just waved us through.

"That was easier than I thought it would be," I said. "I had this whole story ready about how we were with the Census Bureau."

"They probably think we're smuggling guns."

"Maybe."

The Marshman searched for something on the radio, eventually zeroing in on a Mexicali hip-hop station that blasted an obnoxious mix of white noise and profane Spanish slang. I turned it down.

"Was I that bad?" I asked.

"About what?" Marshall shifted in his seat and turned to look out the window.

"At being a dad."

"I didn't think so."

"But your mom did."

"I don't know what Mom thought," Marshall said. "We never talked about you."

He turned the radio back up. He didn't want to talk. Or he wasn't ready to. I couldn't blame him. I was pretty speechless about this whole mess, myself. Like how I apparently had a weakness for women who wanted to kill their significant others—and maybe how that says as much about me as it does about them.

It's not the first thing I look for in a woman, but at the end of my last two relationships it's the most obvious thing that's left over. I had to face that. Meagan and my ex had different reasons for what they did, but they'd both intended to kill somebody. Which is different from being a good cook or fun in the sack—the first things I'd tell you I wanted in a partner.

But at least Meagan was trying to protect her kid. My ex was just cashing in. There's more to it, I know—and maybe the rage came from how I'd stolen her life. I had promised my wife everything and then wasted our future hustling low-hanging fruit on a car lot and surfing Swami's while she obsessed over Marshall. My life was about paddling out with the local crew and happy hour with my sales guys, or sneaking off with some Betty who'd winked at me at the Seaside Market.

By our fifth anniversary, my wife and I had perfected the marital art of unavailability. We were mainlining monotony, and, I am now ashamed to say, I only occasionally tugged at our son, to break the boredom or piss off my wife. It's a wonder I didn't shoot myself. Would have saved us both a lot of trouble.

At least with Meagan and the boys I showed up, as if paying it backward could make up for abandoning my son and all the pain and suffering I was a part of.

"Are you ever afraid, living down here?"

Marshall had been looking out at the border town barrios as I drove south toward Hermosillo.

"Not too much," I said.

"It looks pretty scary," Marshall said.

We were driving through a particularly desolate roadside village about two hundred miles below the border.

"That's what poverty looks like," I said.

In SoCal, being poor meant that you were the only kid on the block with an aboveground swimming pool.

"But we'll be okay?" he asked.

I nodded.

"If a gringo is looking for trouble in Mexico, he'll probably find some. But if you make it like the drug wars and that stuff are none of your business, you probably won't run into it."

"Do you take drugs?"

Marshall was maybe getting a little curious about his old man. Too bad it was this kind of curiosity.

"I take Epilim for my seizures," I said, hiding behind

the truth-matters strategy. "It prevents me from having ones like I used to get, like when we hit that tree—when you broke your neck and we almost lost you."

"And you think that's why Mom wanted to shoot you?" Marshall said softly—like he didn't want to wake up that side of his heart.

"Your mom was devastated over what happened to you, Marshall," I said. "But by that time, I'd already been shot."

Marshall was struggling to put the parts of this nightmare into a straight line.

"Before your mom and *Uncle* Steve hired some guy to shoot me, I was a fuckup. I'll admit it. But I was a normal one," I explained. "Getting shot was how I lost my eye and when my brain was *traumatically* injured."

"And why you got those seizures."

"Yup," I said. "And a *seizure* is what caused the car accident."

"If that's what they find out at Mom's trial, I'll be fine with it," Marshall said. "But we don't really know for sure yet."

I couldn't blame my kid for trying to defuse the family bomb as slowly as possible.

"Well, we do, actually," I said. "If I hadn't been shot, there'd be no seizures—no meds *not* to take. We never would've hit that tree, and you wouldn't have spent a year in the hospital with a broken neck."

I looked over at Marshall to make sure I wasn't drowning him—but it looked like he was holding his breath okay. Maybe this was all starting to make a little sense to him, in that same way it had finally started making some sense to me.

"It's going to take a while for me to figure this out," he said.

"Take your time," I said.

"But do you take *real* drugs, is what I meant before," he said. "Like illegal ones."

"Not anymore," I said. "Do you?"

"No."

"Do you think you will?" I was trying to sound all open and honest and reasonable.

"I could see trying it when I'm old enough, probably."

"Will you tell me?"

"I doubt it," he said, tipping his seat back and closing his eyes.

I clicked on the high beams, marveling at how life can take you by surprise—and how the trick is not to let it take you hostage.

I've never believed in fate, but here was my son riding next to me again. I know things don't happen for a reason—they just happen—but somehow I was taking Marshall home to live with me in Mexico.

The universe wasn't out to teach me a lesson, but Jade and Obsidian absolutely prepared me for this second chance. I dreaded missing them in the way I had missed Marsh—but I knew I could survive it.

What doesn't kill you actually does make you stronger.

Holy shit, I thought, brilliantly grasping the obvious—*the clichés are true.*

* * *

WE MADE IT TO CULIACÁN AROUND LUNCH THE NEXT DAY AND BLEW through a McDonald's drive-thru for a couple of *cuartos de libras* and Mexican Coca-Cola in tall paper cups. Then, for reasons probably known only to teenage boys, for the rest of the afternoon Marshall harped about getting another tattoo. He had started this campaign above Mazatlán.

"My body is a road map, and I want to keep marking the journey."

"Oh, yeah? Where'd you get that one?"

"From Johnny Depp," Marshall said. "It's what he does."

"Johnny Depp's journey is chauffer-driven," I said. "Don't listen to him."

"I've already lost my tattoo virginity, Dad," Marshall said, like a big shot.

"Which is another thing your uncle Steve should be in jail for," I said. "No."

"You have a tattoo."

"I do," I said. "And it marks the part of my journey that was a wrong turn."

"Who's Meagan, anyway?"

"It's Spanish," I said. "For *mistake*."

"Then let me make my own mistakes," he said.

"There'll be plenty of time for that," I said.

I could tell that Marshall was used to doing what he wanted to do—probably because nobody paid much attention to him. I should probably work on changing that.

"How do you do in school?"

"Pretty okay," Marshall said. "Except I got suspended for falling asleep in yoga class."

I just looked at him.

"You get to take it instead of gym," he continued.

"Only in California," I said.

"Yeah, but it's *yoga*, right? You're supposed to be relaxed. I should've gotten an A."

"Makes sense."

"And they say I have ADD."

"That's hereditary," I said. "I had it so bad, I thought it was called AD."

Marshall got the joke and laughed. He was quicker than I'd been at his age.

"We're alike," he said, a little prouder than he probably should have been.

"I hope too much hasn't rubbed off."

"Not since I was seven."

That hurt. I looked away. "I'm sorry," I said. "I missed a lot, I know."

"Me, too," he said. "But what did you do? I mean, you've been gone a long time."

He was getting curious again.

"Not that long."

"Just half my life," he said.

He wasn't going to make this easy, and I couldn't really blame him.

"Well, mostly I just kept trying to feel better. I fucked around and surfed and tried not to think about you."

"Not thinking about me is what made you feel better?"

Marshall knew what I had meant, but he wanted to gouge me a little.

"Well, I'll never know that. Because I could never do it."

"But you still left."

"Yup."

"Why?"

"Because it was the best thing for you, Marshall."

"No, it wasn't," he said.

I nodded. "And I've never been able to forget that. But at the time, it was the last lifeboat left."

"The ship didn't sink, Dad."

"I know," I said.

Marsh slowly unraveled the rim of his paper cup. "Sometimes there's a secret code written under these."

"I could use one," I said.

Then he pointed to my tattoo. "Tell me about the mistake."

"It's a long story," I said.

"It's a long trip," he said.

"But with less baggage," I said. "She's gone."

"Did she have kids?"

Jesus.

"Cut to the chase, why don't you?"

Marshall shrugged. He was waiting for an answer.

"Two," I said.

"What kind?"

"Boys. Your age."

"Twins?"

"Unrelated Irish twins," I said, ad-libbing an entirely new category of sibling. "But they aren't skaters."

"Let me guess." He was maybe a little jealous. "They're surfers?"

I nodded.

"Any good?"

Definitely jealous.

"About like you are at skating. One of them even wants to be a pro."

I meant it as a backward compliment, but Marshall laughed at me. "Every grom in SoCal wants to be a pro something. Like being great is *that* close and we're entitled to it."

It looked as if I'd hit a sore spot, but Marshall was making a great point. He lived in a world where only fame seemed to matter—Instagram likes and Kardashian click-bait.

"Just get as good as you can get at whatever you love," Marshall continued. "That's what matters. Nothing else."

It was a pretty smart way to look at life. I was impressed.

"Who told you that?" I asked.

"You did, Dad. When I said I wanted to play pro ball after we won that big game."

I turned away so Marsh couldn't see that I was about to cry.

"Do you still play ball?" I asked.

"Nah," he said. "That was the last time I ever played."

We filled up for the last time and headed south. I was planning to drive straight through to Tepic and maybe even Sabanita before sunrise.

Marshall was dozing on and off and listening to his iPod. I had tuned the Suburban's AM radio to a *local* double-header. I missed a lot of the details, but I could tell that the

Culiacán Tomateros had beaten the Venados de Mazatlán by a couple of runs in the first game. It was tied up in the second one.

I reached over and took Marshall's hand in mine. He opened his eyes and looked over at me, and I was hoping he wasn't too big to hold hands with his old man.

"I think I can feel your heartbeat," he said.

"I think I can, too," I said.

56

The last hundred-mile chunk of the trip was safe but slow. I had no choice but to follow a dozen semis down the switchbacks out of Tepic. We didn't make it to my casita until noon. Marshall was on his second siesta, and I squeezed his knee to wake him as we pulled into the dirt driveway.

Tilly sat straight up, her tail wagging like a jackhammer. The casa's garden had been weeded; someone had raked the lawn and bagged the leaves. The place looked storybook.

"You live *here*?" Marshall asked.

"I do," I said.

"Who's that?"

Meagan was standing in the doorway. She was wearing an apron, and her hair was up. She looked like the all-American mom on a Mother's Day card. It felt like a hallucination.

I grabbed Marshall's hand to make sure he was still there and counted back to the last time I'd taken my meds. My son was staring at me. I pointed to my tattoo.

"That's who," I said.

"The mistake?"

"Yeah, maybe," I said.

"But you said she was long gone."

"Yes, I did," I said. "Gimme a minute."

I got out of the Suburban and moved to Tilly. She was vibrating with joy. I gently lifted her chin and stroked the back of her neck.

"*Hey, good girl,*" I whispered. I couldn't look at Meagan. But then it occurred to me that something might have happened to Jade and Obsidian, and I turned to her.

"Are the boys okay?" I asked.

I slowly walked to the casa's front steps. Meagan and I were face-to-face now. I was a step down, so we were the same height. It looked like she had what was left of a black eye. It was still a little bloodshot.

"The boys are fine," Meagan said.

"Are they here?"

"Of course," she said. "They're surfing."

"What's with the eye?" I asked.

"I fell."

Meagan touched the little bit of makeup she had on and tried to smear it over the bruise.

"What's going on, Meagan?"

"Danny's the same asshole he was in college," she said. "All he cared about was cutting the boys' hair and changing their names. I didn't want it to rub off."

"So you came back down here?"

Meagan shook her head.

"That's why I left him," she said. "You're the reason I came back."

"Yeah, right."

I reached out and put my hand on the side of Meagan's face. The bruise felt warm.

"Does that hurt?"

"It feels good," she said.

"You have shitty taste in men, Meagan."

"Not always."

I shook my head and took my hand away.

"You were always nice to me, Nick," she said. "You didn't have to be, but you were."

"I had my reasons," I said.

"And so good to my boys—always, no matter what, without asking."

"Don't make it sound like a song," I said. "Like this is suddenly all okay."

"My kids love you, Nick."

Meagan took my hands and pulled me to her. Then she kissed me, but I didn't kiss her back too much. I have to admit that I felt like it—but I didn't want to start making out in front of my son with someone he hadn't even met yet.

"And I love you," she said.

"Hey, Dad?" Marshall interrupted. He was standing

outside the Suburban and keeping an eye on Meagan. "Is it okay to pet this dog?"

"Sure," I nodded. "Her name's Tilly."

"What kind is it?" Marshall asked, cautiously stepping to the dog.

"A Mexican Rescue," I said. "Which is a very popular breed down here."

Marshall let Tilly lick the back of his hand.

"That's my son, Marshall," I said.

"He's shy," Meagan said.

"No," I said. "Just stunned. Like his dad."

Meagan smiled. "*Totally* stunned?"

"Don't confuse it with hope," I said. "Where's José?"

"He moved out. The day after you left, the kids and I came back to town."

"And people say there's no order in the universe," I said.

"There isn't," Meagan said. "But sometimes the right thing just happens."

"I owe José some money."

"Not anymore," she said.

I didn't want to ask Meagan the details—but I think she knew that, based on the way she was grinning at me. "I gave him Winsor's computer," Meagan said. "I think he was happy with that."

I was relieved. I had been obsessing about what might be on its hard drive, in some secret perv file, which was why I hadn't taken the MacBook with me across the border.

"I'm Meagan," Meagan called out and then hopped down the steps to Marshall. "I'm your dad's girlfriend."

"I didn't know he had a girlfriend," Marshall said.

"Well, he does, and I'm it."

"Does he even know?"

"Dude, c'mon. I mean, he tattooed my name on his arm."

She was beaming and charming, and it was hard not to beam and smile back. The Marshman was trying his best to resist, but he was about as successful as I was.

"And I have two boys just about your age, too," Meagan continued, and then took over stroking Tilly's ears.

"The surfers?"

"Yup," she said.

"Well, I'm not a surfer," Marshall said.

"They weren't surfers, either, until they moved down here."

"I skate," he continued.

"That is so cool," Meagan said. "My kids suck at skating."

57

We took Tilly for a walk on the beach. I let the Marshman lead the way and hold the leash. He had to be feeling like he was in an elevator full of strangers, and we were all being careful not to stand too close to each other.

"I saw your dad knock a guy out once," Obsidian suddenly said, reaching out to the new kid. And I loved him for it.

"Why did he do that?" the Marshman asked.

"Because the kook was snaking my waves," Jade said.

"That sucks," my son said.

"Totally," Obsidian said.

"Is that a real tat?" Jade asked and pointed to the gothic skateboard tattoo above Marshall's bicep.

"What do you think?" Marshall said.

"I think it must've hurt a lot," Jade said.

I'd hardly recognized the boys when they'd first run up to Marshall and me. I thought we were being mugged—by a couple of student-council presidents. About a foot of their dreads had been cut off, and they'd lost their tans. But they were still wet from the surf.

"Is *that* the kid Mom told us about?" Jade asked as he let me out of a bear hug. It wasn't the friendliest question I'd ever heard, and Obsidian was giving Marshall some serious stink eye.

I nodded. "This is my son, Marshall."

The Marshman and I had been standing under the *higuera*. I had been trying to explain why it's never called an higuera tree but just an *higuera*—something gringos can never quite get.

"It's okay with him, then?" Obsidian asked.

"Is what okay?" my son asked, staking out a little territory.

"That we get to have some of Nick, too."

"He's my dad."

"But we know him better," Obsidian said.

"You do not," Marshall said.

"Hey, look," I said. "It's still pretty low tide, so let's go easy."

"We're just asking," Jade said.

"Everybody can have as much of me as they need."

"If there's enough," Marshall said.

"I'll make sure," I said.

My son took a step away from my side and closer to the boys. I could tell he was digging that he was taller than both of them.

"That's Jade and Obsidian," I said. "Meagan's two precious stones."

"I'm the semiprecious one," Obsidian said.

I had wanted Chuy to meet Marshall, but before we headed over to Pirata's I'd needed to make sure it was cool with Jade to go back to where Winsor had molested him.

"It's okay if you don't want to go," I had said earlier.

"I'm good with it," Jade said.

Pirata's was packed, but the sign I had painted just last week had already been replaced with one that spelled out DON PELÍCANOS in drippy red letters.

We stepped through the door and worked our way toward the bar, where a wall of *locals* sat watching Mexico vs. the Netherlands in the World Cup elimination round. They were screaming and bitching about a bad call—two of them were crying.

Chuy was behind the counter, pouring shots and opening beers. He saw me and then pointed two thumbs up at the crowd.

"Pirata!" he said. "I'm glad you are coming back to save us."

I was stunned at how busy the place was.

"How did this happen?" I asked.

"Everybody wants to see *el pájaro de milagro*," he said.

Chuy pointed to an upside-down barstool that had been placed on a table in the corner of the tavern. The one-winged pelican was perched there, guzzling anchovies and hunks of cheese tossed by his devotees. Some of Señor Pelícano's feathers had grown back, and his wing stump had healed. The old bird looked oddly vibrant.

"The miracle bird," I said.

"For six thousand pesos, it's a miracle," Chuy said. "That animal doctor keeps calling here for money."

Chuy poured a half dozen shots of tequila into a circle of shot glasses.

"*Abrazos*," he said. "Welcome back."

Marshall reached for one, but I was able to stop him just before he tasted it.

"Dad," Marshall said. "This is Mexico."

"Doesn't matter," I said.

"Even for us?" Jade asked.

Obsidian tried to look taller.

"For everybody," I said. "These kids are barely fourteen, Chuy."

"When I was fourteen I was already almost a papa," Chuy bragged. "And I've seen these two groms out there ripping like men."

Meagan reached for a shot and toasted Chuy. "*Mi chicos*," she said.

"*¿Quién es el fugitivo?*" Chuy asked, winking at Marshall.

"This is Marshall," I said. "My son."

Chuy tipped his head back very slowly. He squinted at Marshall and then looked at me.

"*¿Su hijo?*" Chuy asked. He was solemn.

One time, during an over-the-top binge that I had talked Chuy into joining me on, I had confessed to crashing my car into a tree with my seven-year-old son in the front seat. But I had become so grief-stricken, with a grotesque and sobbing kind of agony, that I was unable to finish the story.

I was sure Chuy had assumed the worst, but having seen my extreme pain and suffering, he'd never mentioned it again. Over these past few years, I was grateful that he'd never grilled me for more of the details.

"Yes," I said.

"*Muy alto.* Like you," Chuy said.

Meagan reached for another tequila shot and downed it without a wince.

"It's good to be back," she said.

Obsidian picked up a piece of cheese that had fallen on the floor and flung it at the pelican—nothing but pouch. Marshall high-fived him.

"I thought you gave up on us, Meagan," Chuy said.

"Just on me," Meagan said. "But not for good."

"That's what counts," Chuy said as he salted the rim of a glass.

58

We enrolled the boys in the ninth grade at Sabanita's Pública Secundaria, which is the final year of schooling available for *locals* in this part of Mexico—and they were already dinging me about graduation gimme bags.

"I want a surf trip to Tavarua," Obsidian said. He was obsessed with a WSL clip of Gabriel Medina killing it at Cloudbreak.

"Or a Harley," Jade said.

"I already got what I wanted," Marshall said as his two new stepbrothers groaned.

"You are such a kiss-ass," Obsidian said.

Marshall bent over. "Give it a try," he said.

"Dudes, first you have to graduate," I said. The SEP curriculum in Mexico is taught entirely in Spanish. "Which is going to be like learning how to change tires on a moving car."

"*No hay pedo,*" Jade said.

Jade and Obsidian usually banged around Sabanita's beach break with Marshall after school, and after a few weeks he was ready for a real wave. The three of them didn't talk much, mostly just punchlines and zingers. They kept their spaces, as if they'd somehow ended up inside the same paper dragon at their very first Chinese parade. There was a job to do, each of them had to hold up a piece of the monster, but it was cool that they were willing to do it.

"Surfing is a gravity sport," Obsidian said. "Just like skateboarding."

"Your mom said you suck at skating," Marshman said.

"Doesn't matter," Obsidian said. "It's the same gravity management."

Marshall was straddling the TC Pang while Obsidian was treading water next to him. We were at Gagger's on an overhead day. I was standing on the beach. Jade was cruising out the back on my Red Fin. He had decided to become a longboarder.

"I appreciate the esoteric nature of it," he said, smarter by the minute.

A single pelican swooped low into a glide, and I could see a set coming in. Obsidian turned Marshall's board slightly and then pushed it hard as a wave raised the two of them up.

"Paddle!" Obsidian shouted.

And in three strokes the Marshman was down the face and made a pretty good get-up. He stood too tall at first but adjusted, crouching lower and guiding the TC Pang down the line. It was clean and sweet, the lip of the wave two feet overhead and curling just behind him—and then it closed out and took him to the bottom. I held my breath until he popped to the surface.

"That was so rad," Obsidian called out.

Jade whistled, paddling into an outside roller as Marshall threw Obsidian a shaka.

"Dude, thanks," he said.

I felt as if I had somehow survived myself—and I was more than a little surprised that such a thing could actually be done. It made me smile. I was happy to feel like a man with a lot to lose.

59

Buoyweather.com was forecasting a bomber day. I was heading over for dawn patrol at Surprises, with the Red Fin stashed inside the Suburban. The boys were in school. Meagan was the volunteer cafeteria mom today, Chuy was running the bar, and I was stoked for *reasonably* big and ready to celebrate a dad's day off.

As I passed by Gaviotas, a new golf resort and hotel under construction about halfway to Punta de Mirador, I noticed that a dark sedan had made a U-turn. The car dimmed its lights and then began to follow me closely, barely a car length off my bumper.

I started to get a little nervous. I was a legitimate family man now. I didn't want to get carjacked or kidnapped. I was hoping that this tailgater was just some nutter who didn't know how to drive.

But then one of those little portable police lights, the kind that undercover cop cars sometimes have on the dashboard, began to flash. The dark sedan pulled up alongside me, corralled me to the shoulder, and parked in front of me. It had white license plates—official plates from the US government. I put the Suburban in park and shut off the motor.

The sedan's door opened, and Agent Lloyd Jeffries got out. I was relieved. Jeffries covered his eyes. I turned off my headlights and rolled down the window.

"Agent Jeffries," I said. "Hey, great to see you."

Jeffries nodded but didn't smile. "Would you step out of your vehicle, please, Mr. Lutz."

At first I thought he was just being funny with this formality. But when I got a closer look at his face, I could see that this wasn't a social call.

I got out of the Suburban.

"What's the problem?" I said. "I'm just heading out for a morning surf. Like always."

"Turn around, please, Mr. Lutz."

"Dude, you know me, right? I own the bar—Pirata's with two *a*'s? You helped me get my son back."

"Winsor Baumgarten owned that bar," Jeffries said, leaning heavily on *owned*.

I let that slide and plowed ahead. "When did you get back down? I thought you didn't like Mexico."

But Agent Jeffries just unhooked a pair of handcuffs from the back of his belt.

"I'm going to put you in handcuffs, okay," he said.

It wasn't a question.

"I thought you had to arrest me first." I faked a chuckle, pretending that there wasn't a reason in the world to arrest me. "You know, read me my rights and stuff."

"Not in Mexico," he said.

Jeffries put the cuffs on me in about two seconds and then led me to a rear door of his sedan. He opened it, placed his hand on my head, and guided me into the back seat. There was a bulletproof partition separating the sedan's front and rear seats, and the inside back-door handles had been removed. Jeffries started up and drove off.

"Do you think it's okay to leave my Red Fin in my car like that?" I asked.

But Agent Jeffries just shrugged slightly. It didn't appear that it mattered to him much.

It looked like we were heading to the airport up in PV, and I was stressing over the idea that I was being taken up to jail in the US—that I wouldn't be able to tell Marshall what happened and why I had disappeared again. But Jeffries drove straight through Vallarta, and then finally turned off Highway 200 at Mezcales and started driving east.

I immediately knew that we were heading to Valle de Banderas, which is where the Federales and the military honchos hang out. If the FBI had a liaison office or if an agent needed to borrow a fax machine, this is the little city where they'd do it.

And if an American citizen was in some kind of deep Mexican shit, Valle de Banderas would be one of the first stops, if not the final one.

We drove to the front gate of the Delegación Municipio. Two soldiers were hunkered between stacks of sandbags and tank traps, and Jeffries honked at them to open the gate. One of them raised the heavy counterbalanced barrier by hand, and we entered the compound.

Agent Jeffries parked the sedan near a steel door at the rear of a gray-brick building. He helped me out of the back seat and then through the door, up two flights of stairs, and into a windowless interrogation room. He did all this without saying a word.

The room was dark and very hot.

When my eyes adjusted to the lack of light, I could see that José López was tied to a chair. His nose was bloody, one eye was swollen shut, and he was shirtless. His back was black and blue and bleeding neon red.

El Jefe was standing next to José. He was holding that four-foot bamboo whip I was so intimately familiar with. My legs went weak at the sight of it, and I nearly stumbled. Agent Jeffries grabbed my elbow and steadied me. "You know Comandante Venegas?"

El Jefe looked pleased that simply the sight of him could rock me so obviously.

"I do," I said.

What used to be Winsor's MacBook was open and sitting on a long hardwood table. José caught my eye and stared at me. He'd been beaten up, but he was acutely aware.

"So, Pirata, the new family is good?" El Jefe asked. "Your kid's a tough guy like you?"

"He'll be a tougher kid after foster care." Jeffries glared at me. "Nice job, Dad."

I glared back. Marshall's story had apparently been a topic of conversation between these two. It made me hate them both.

Agent Jeffries moved to the table and closed the Mac-Book.

"When I came down to Sabanita to tell you about your wife and kid, Winsor Baumgarten wasn't on my radar," he said, mostly to me—but he was keeping an eye on El Jefe. "But when you mentioned his name, it made you nervous. So when I got back to San Diego, I checked him out—and Baumgarten is on the Bureau's watch list of child pornographers. Seems he'd been trying to exploit the sexting marketplace that's blowing up with our kids. I figured you were involved."

I was staring at Agent Jeffries, breathing deeply and slowly. José was watching me closely, and I started to sweat about how much information El Jefe's bamboo had made him cough up.

"I'm not," I said.

Agent Jeffries looked to José and then back at El Jefe. It was obvious that he was repulsed by José's beating. But I wasn't repulsed—I was crystal clear. I'd do whatever it took to avoid another one.

"The pornography business uses all the latest Internet and computer gear, so it's routine for the Bureau to run down warranties and new purchase lists," Jeffries continued. "The guys who produce the really bad stuff use the best brands because they're the most reliable. So it wasn't a big job to find Baumgarten's name and his new MacBook's ID number. Then we got an IP address that led us back to Sabanita." Jeffries shrugged. "Except Winsor wasn't there—just this José López hombre who was using Winsor's brand-new laptop. And where does a humble Mexican fisherman get such a fancy computer? So I call my friends, the Federales, and I ask them about Señor López from Sabanita. But the only José López they know is this *local* who'd reported a body on the beach about a month and a half ago."

"Ringo Starr wasn't this lucky," El Jefe said.

"This isn't what luck looks like," Jeffries said as El Jefe glared at him. "Anyway, I send Winsor Baumgarten's dental records to the coroner's office in Guadalajara, where they're keeping the stiff that washed up on the beach. And what do you know—his bicuspids line up, and we get a positive ID."

I felt ice-cold. Two seconds ago, I'd been sweating.

60

hat does this have to do with me?" I said, as laid-back as possible.

El Jefe laughed out loud and cracked the bamboo whip across his boot.

"You are fucking *good*, Pirata," El Jefe howled.

"It has to do with the fact that your name was forged on Winsor's liquor license," Jeffries said. He wasn't smiling. "And his lease."

"I didn't do that," I said.

Which was true, of course. Meagan did. But I probably shouldn't bring that up.

"Wow, now there's an alibi," Jeffries said. "Did you go to law school?"

"It is what it is," I said.

But it felt like everything was about to tip over. As

if getting my son back and Meagan and the boys coming home was some kind of trick—a suckhole filled with a relentless and cancerous kind of karma.

"Motive, means, opportunity," Jeffries said. "It's all there—which is why I'm going to take you back to the States."

"Not yet," El Jefe said. "He's a Mexican resident, and these are Mexican crimes."

"The victim was an American," Jeffries said.

"That's the fucking problem with gringos," El Jefe said. "You confuse the criminals with the victims."

"I have an FM3."

"Expired," Jeffries said.

"Down here, they are all expired."

"So, when in Mexico, señor," El Jefe said, "do as a Mexican."

"He's very fond of clichés."

"And bullshit," Jeffries said.

"The truth hurts," El Jefe said.

"I could spend the rest of my life down here looking for the truth," Jeffries said.

"That can be arranged."

"Fuck you."

"You need to show some respect."

"Give me something worth respecting, and I will be the first guy in line," Jeffries spit back.

El Jefe was seething. I didn't want to get caught in the middle of this pissing contest. I could drown.

"That line forms here, *pendejo*." El Jefe took a black pistol from the brown leather holster on his hip. He let the gun hang by his side. Jeffries looked at it and shook his head.

"I can't imagine that anyone has ever taken you seriously, *comandante*," Jeffries said. "So you're just going to have to forgive me for not being the first."

Jeffries moved to Winsor's MacBook as El Jefe cocked his head slightly and tried to pick his way through what the agent had just said. I could see that he wasn't quite sure just how insulted he should be.

Jeffries jerked his thumb at me and then to the door. "Let's go."

But El Jefe finally figured it out and pointed his pistol at the FBI agent's chest—and in an instant, Jeffries knew exactly how seriously he should take the *comandante*.

"The American stays in Mexico," El Jefe said.

"Okay," Jeffries said softly.

El Jefe nodded to my handcuffs. "*Llaves.*"

Jeffries put a hand up and then deliberately took out his handcuff key. I turned around, and he uncuffed me.

"I'm going to file an official letter of protest with our State Department," said Jeffries.

"Too late," El Jefe said. "Put the cuffs on him, Pirata."

"Look, guys," I said, "we need to back away from the cliff a little."

"Do it," El Jefe commanded.

I turned Agent Jeffries around and slipped his wrists into the handcuffs.

"Tighter," El Jefe whispered.

I ratcheted the steel rings, and Jeffries winced. José was watching El Jefe intensely, as if he was trying to choose which side offered the best chance of staying alive. I was considering the very same thing—and the odds were stacked heavily against Agent Jeffries's side.

61

El Jefe handed me the thin length of bamboo.

"You know what to do with this," he said.

He had viciously pistol-whipped Jeffries across the back of the neck and then propped the agent against the long hardwood table. Jeffries was conscious but in pain. José sat motionless. I was terrified.

"Shouldn't we take off his shirt?" I asked, and then gagged on the phlegm of cowardice backing up in my throat.

"Up to you, maestro," El Jefe said. "Just make sure it's a lesson."

"In what?"

"Respect."

The bamboo felt lighter in my hand than I thought it would—but still full of a hard ugliness. I flexed my wrist.

"How many?" I asked.

"Start with one hundred," El Jefe said. "Then we'll see how your arm is holding up."

"That might kill him," I said.

"It could." El Jefe shrugged.

"I won't do this," I said.

"Yes, you will."

The butt of the bamboo cane felt slippery in my hand. My palm was wet. I felt dizzy.

"*Uno*," El Jefe called out.

I reached back with the bamboo and then measured the distance to Agent Jeffries. He was bent across the hardwood table with his eyes wide open, staring at the cinder-block wall in front of him. I slashed my arm down and forward as hard and fast as I could, pirouetting in one smooth motion as if I was cross-stepping back from the nose of my longboard—and landing the full force of the bamboo's wickedness straight across El Jefe's face, just below his brow. His flesh opened, and an eye erupted on impact— now a red glob protruding onto his cheek. He began to bleed as I hit him again, hard against the side of his head with the thicker end of the bamboo reed. El Jefe tried to aim the pistol with his only working eye, but I ripped it out of his hand and pushed him to the floor. The gun felt heavy. I backed away.

El Jefe rolled onto his stomach and climbed to his feet, cupping his eye. His breathing steadied. I looked at Agent Jeffries. He was still staring at the wall. José smirked in disbelief. I didn't know what to do.

"You won't get out of here alive," El Jefe said, gulping for air.

"Probably not," I said.

"Give me the gun, Pirata—and I promise, you will see your son again."

"And that's the truth?"

"Of course," El Jefe said. "Nothing else matters now." He gritted his teeth into a smile and tried to steady his breathing—as if to show he was still in charge.

"Okay," I said.

I extended the gun toward El Jefe, and he reached for it. I pulled the trigger and shot him in the heart. He buckled and fell to the floor.

"Take these off me," Jeffries said.

I uncuffed the FBI agent, and he began to untie José.

"We're going to need that uniform," Jeffries said, nodding to El Jefe's body. "If anyone comes through that door, shoot them."

I was still holding the pistol. I handed it to Jeffries.

"No, thanks," I said.

62

We walked down the two flights of stairs from the interrogation room. I was in front of José with my hands behind me, pretending to be handcuffed. My fisherman friend was wearing El Jefe's bloody fatigues—it was the first time I'd ever seen him wearing long sleeves. Agent Jeffries marched behind us, the pistol in one hand and Winsor's MacBook in the other. He waved me into the back of the sedan. José jumped in shotgun, and Jeffries slid in behind the wheel.

We drove to the front gate. Jeffries honked his horn and woke the guard. El Jefe's gun was cocked and ready in his lap. Another guard raised the barrier without giving us a look, and we exited the compound.

"Lucky us," Jeffries said. "The only guy who knows we were here is dead."

He took a satellite phone out of the glove compartment and tapped a series of numbers into its keypad. We drove for about an hour, due south. I was afraid to even hope for the best, but it looked like I was heading home.

Until we turned east at Puerto Vallarta toward San Sebastián.

"Where are we going?" I asked.

Jeffries didn't say a word.

"Where are you taking me?" I asked again. All I could think of was Meagan and the kids, and I regretted giving Jeffries the gun. Then he skidded off the highway onto a dirt road. We drove another few hundred yards and entered a clearing. There was a large trailered fuel tank parked under a *huanacaxtle* tree. The FBI agent parked the sedan next to it.

"What's this?"

"*Rincón de urgencia*," Jeffries said, in surprisingly perfect Spanish. "The Bureau's got a bunch of these hidden around Mexico."

A large white *X* had been chalked out on the dry grass. It was hot, and probably around noon. I began to think that Meagan and the boys might be worried I was in trouble, or maybe they'd figure the waves at Surprises were big and righteous today and I was making it last.

Jeffries shut off the sedan. "Let's go."

José and I got out of the car, and Jeffries motioned us toward the trunk of the large tree. That he was still holding El Jefe's pistol in his hand wasn't lost on us.

"That was one hell of a hero move you pulled, Pirata," Jeffries said. "Some big-time kamikaze shit."

"*Ese bravo loco*," José said, under his breath but reverent.

This must have been the kind of talk tough guys tossed around with each other after a barroom brawl or a shoot-out. But I didn't have anything to add.

"No matter what happens from here on," the agent said, "I have to give you your props."

"Okay," I said. "Thanks."

"You probably saved my life," he said.

"I was trying to save mine—you just got in the way," I said, looking down at the gun at his side.

"But I am still an FBI agent. An American was killed down here. I have to do my job."

"What the fuck?" I was incredulous.

"I'm by the book," he said. "I have to find out what happened."

"Even if Winsor was such a bad guy?"

"Especially if he was," Jeffries said. "That's how we know we're the good ones."

I stared at Jeffries and shook my head at the absurdity—but I wasn't going to lie.

"I didn't kill him," I said.

"You got a witness?" Jeffries smiled a little bit—it was the first real one of his I had ever seen.

"Pirata is *my* witness," José finally said. "I killed that *pinche puto*—and I wish he was still alive so I could do it again."

Jeffries looked at me, and I nodded. "He did," I said.

Jeffries pointed a finger at José. "You are very lucky I don't have jurisdiction down here, amigo."

José shrugged like he couldn't give a shit. Agent Jeffries moved a little closer and stared me down. "And *you* are even luckier, Pirata."

"I know," I said.

And then we could hear a helicopter approaching.

"That's my ride," Jeffries said. "You guys need a lift?"

"We're good," I said.

The chopper banked in, its rotor wash rippling the dry grass and pounding up plumes of sand and dirt. Agent Jeffries covered his eyes and nearly disappeared.

"Let's go," I said, and nodded to José.

We turned our backs to the turbulence and headed home.

63

We took the rest of the day to wind our way back to Sabanita. It was smart to stay out of sight. There weren't a lot of gringos in paradise this time of year, and I was probably the only one who'd just shot and killed a proud member of the *policía secreta*.

"Nobody is going to give a shit," José said. "He was just another motherfucker—you had to do it."

"What if we get recognized?"

"By who? Unless you put that *estúpido* patch back on."

I was following José through knee-deep canals of muddy water that irrigated a dozen hectares of rotting mangoes. He kept telling me to watch for water snakes.

"What about you?" I asked.

"The big shots don't give a shit about me."

About an hour after sunset, we'd made it back to my

Suburban. I was surprised to see that my Red Fin was still locked inside, but then I remembered that today was just supposed to be another surf day in my new life as a family man.

"Just take me back to my boat," José said.

We climbed into the Suburban and rode back to Sabanita in silence. I kept wondering if we needed to make some kind of a promise—but it was clear that José didn't have anything he wanted to say. He jumped out at the edge of the beach, and I drove home.

Tilly was sprawled in my casita's doorway. She wagged her tail—just once—to make sure I wouldn't step on her, and then closed her eyes. Jade was asleep on the porch couch. Meagan was sitting in the dark at the kitchen table.

"Did something bad happen?" she asked.

I turned on the tap and let it run until the water cooled. Then I cupped my hands and took a mouthful, spitting out some mud and sand and then finally swallowing.

"Nope," I lied. "Just good waves."

I moved to Meagan and kissed her deeply. I was shivering, and she squeezed me in her arms.

"Are you lying?"

"Yes," I said.

"Are we okay?" she asked.

"We are now," I said.

I kissed her again and then stepped into the boys' bedroom. Marshall was on the top bunk. Obsidian was stretched out below. I put my hand on my son's chest to make sure he was breathing.

"You still do that?" he whispered.

"Sorry," I said. "I thought you were sleeping."

"I was worried," he said.

"I'm okay."

"Was it big?"

"Giant," I said, "but makeable."

"That's good," Obsidian said from the bunk below. "As long as you can make them and you have a chance, that's all you want, right?"

"It's all I want," I said.

THE PALE BOY WAS LYING UNDER THE *HIGUERA*. HE'D BEEN ASLEEP for hours. His dad crouched next to him, quietly drawing circles in the hard dirt with a shard of adobe. The dad had removed his bush hat, and what remained of the zinc sunblock had left his face streaked and ghostlike. It was hard to tell if he'd been sweating or crying. But I knew he had been listening.

"Jesus," he said finally, tossing the jagged *tejas* into a collage of similar bits scattered on the ground. The kitchen corner of my casa had been knocked off, and its brilliant *naranja* roof was now just a skeleton of wooden *vigas*. "Sounds like a hell of a monsoon season," he continued.

"That's why it's called *tormenta*," I said, half seriously.

The dad reached for my hand, and I yanked him to his feet. He whacked the dust off his hat on his thigh and then regarded the beer box next to a pile of empty bottles.

"Did I drink all those?"

"Most of them," I said.

"Jesus," he said again.

"It's Mexico."

He nodded as if he understood what I meant, but he probably hadn't been down here long enough to get the full meaning. I began to arrange the empties back into the box. I came across one that was half-full and handed it to him. He took a long drink and then flipped it back to me.

"What happened to the boys?" he asked.

I slipped the last empty into its cardboard slot.

"Jade's running a gallery up in Vallarta," I said. "Obsidian is on a hotshot crew in Oregon. When it's not fire season, he chases the winter swell."

"What about the Marshman?" He looked back at his own son for a second, and we could see that the boy was starting to wake up.

"He's in school up in Santa Barbara," I said, trying to balance relief with pride and hoping to avoid the next question.

"And Meagan?"

"She comes and goes," I said.

It looked like he thought that was a pretty good deal. "Dude, you're living the dream."

"Just pieces of it," I said, trying not to blow up his Monday-morning fantasy.

He picked up the TC Pang and held it out in a way that made me have to take it or let it fall to the ground.

"I can't let you give me this board," he said.

His boy was watching us.

"Your son will be disappointed."

"Probably. But it needs to be hanging on your wall."

He nodded at my casa as if he had more to say, but then figured he probably didn't know me well enough. The boy had moved closer to us, and then took his father's hand. It was pretty clear he knew what was going on, but he looked like he was okay with it. His dad probably wasn't the kook I'd first figured him to be.

"I'm going to get you exactly the board you need," the dad said as they navigated down the deep ruts of my dirt driveway, "I promise."

"I know you will, Dad," his son said, and then they disappeared around the corner at Calle Coral.

I squinted into the sunset, and its accompanying gold rush filled in the missing pieces of my casa and made it look whole again—like the past version of a future that was no longer just close but actually here, and one that I was somehow standing in the middle of.

I whistled for Tilly, and then imagined Meagan walking up barefoot on the path from Palmitos. But Tilly was long gone, and I hadn't heard from Meagan in months. This moment was mine, and I was alone in it. Acutely present, if not complete.

I looked down at the TC Pang and ran my hand up its slow curve, over the chips and dings and the once-brilliant white deck that was now sunburned brown from a lifetime on the beach. I walked the board over to the casa and delicately placed it inside what was left of my front door.

The gangbangers were trying to jump-start the back-

hoe with what was left of the juice in the Suburban's battery. The backhoe's *maestro* was sitting in its rear bucket,
alternately taking deep drags from a cigarette and futzing
with his watch. He was paid by the job, not the hour, and I
could see that he wanted to knock down the rest of my casa
before dark.

But it was too late.

"*Alto*, amigos," I said and jogged over to the Suburban.

I reached through the driver's-side window, turned off
the motor, and retrieved the key. One of the bangers made
one last attempt to turn over the backhoe's diesel, but it
wound down to a couple of tired clicks and then went quiet.
The three of them looked at me.

"*Lo siento*," I said. "*No más.*"

"*¿Qué?*" the *maestro* asked.

"*Estoy guardando mi casita*," I said. "*Vete a casa.*"

The LA cholos laughed at my accent.

"What does *that* mean?" one of them asked.

"I'm keeping my house," I said. "Go home."

ACKNOWLEDGMENTS

Many thanks to David Gernert for his wise guidance and steady support, and the same to Hannah Robinson for her light touch and tireless input. Annie Hodgson's contributions to *Pirata* are immeasurable, and without Jake Epstein cheering me on and holding my hand I wouldn't have made it past page 20. I also owe a great debt to David Greenblatt, and I would like to thank the following people for their early reads and candid feedback as *Pirata* evolved into the book it needed to be; Richard Christian Matheson, Nancy Dittmann, Sally Preyer LaVenture, Nick Sherman, Mike Nunn, John James, Sergio Gonzales, John Wilder, Detta Kissel, Gabriel Gallegos, Ted Mann, Bill Nuss, Russ Landau, Alma Nereida Lorenzo Enciso, Gena Hasburgh, Jo Swerling, Jr., Tom Szollosi, Will Terrell, Andy Cattermole, Susanne M. Van Cleave, Mark Allison, Amie Johnson, Rachel Martinez, Eira Carranza, Mark Sharp, Beau Clark, Kevin Murphy, Breene Murphy, Reyn Murphy, Nazario Carranza, Chuy Venegas, Kerry Kirkpatrick, Ron Pentz,

Kathy Nicoleti, Peter Trigg, EJ Foerster, Mark Shaw, Robert Treta, Rick VanDeWeghe, Meagen Svendsen, Ron Parsell, Bruce Johnson, Jose Lorenzo, Stacy Raviv, Barry Golson, Michael Part, Mike McDaniel, Mark Rubenstein, Cory McLernon, Evan Miranda, Jill Bianchini, Virginia Rankin, Andy Hanson, Georgia H. T. Hanson, Terry Meyer, Ian Ingram, Mari Rainer, Jason Smith, Margarito Castillon, Larry Hertzog, Steve Cannell, Bob Jensen, Jean Hasburgh, and Big Jim.

ABOUT THE AUTHOR

PATRICK HASBURGH was born in Buffalo, New York. He moved to Aspen as a young man to work as a ski instructor and then to Los Angeles, where he wrote and produced television for the next two decades. In 2000 Patrick married Cheri Jensen and moved to Mexico to surf and write fiction. The Hasburghs have two children. Patrick is best known for creating the television series *21 Jump Street* and writing and directing the feature film *Aspen Extreme*. *Pirata* is his second novel.